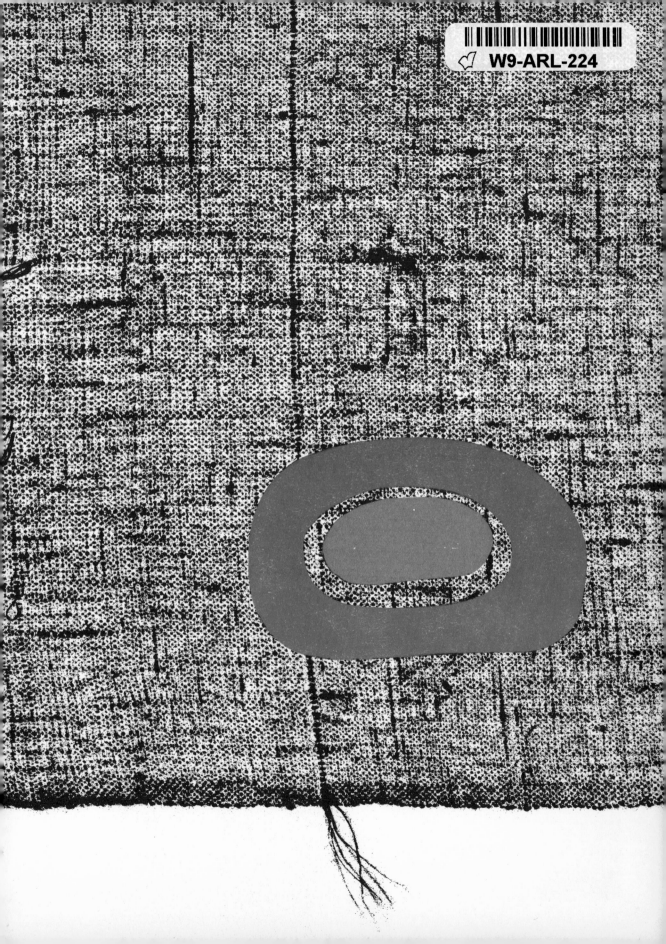

AMERICAN
FAIRY
TALES

Retold by

Vladimír Stuchl

Illustrated by

Luděk Maňásek

Translated by Vera Gissing
First published 1979 by
Octopus Books Limited
59 Grosvenor Street
London W1

ISBN 0 7064 0860 8

© 1979 Artia

Illustrations © 1979 Luděk Maňásek
Graphic design by Jiří Schmidt

Printed in Czechoslovakia 1/18/01/51 — 01

CONTENTS

THE GREEN PRAIRIE

Across the green prairie gallops the wild horse—a mustang.

He races like the wind through the country where once long ago Indian fires were crackling, galloping over land which at one time belonged to the Indians. They used to hunt bison in the prairie and near the lakes, while the Indian women tended the corn and during ceremonies the Indians sang a prayer to the Goddess Aurora:

> *Aurora! Morning Star!*
> *In the sky you appear high*
> *To shine and disappear far . . .*

The white settlers came in their ships across the ocean, took over the prairie piece by piece, felled the forests, ploughed the fields, prepared the soil for grain.

On the cotton plantations Negroes had to work for their white masters. They were brought from far away Negro lands in chains. They toiled in the fields by day and in the evenings their children learned a rhyme from their mothers:

> *A black cat to a white one says:*
> *Have a walk with me today.*
> *I'll go with you the white cat says*
> *But first your black coat throw away.*

Across the prairie gallops the wild white stallion—a mustang.

He races like the wind through the green prairie.

In the old, old days bulky wagons with white awnings and pulled by oxen crossed this same prairie from east to west. The settlers rode in the wagons on their long journey in search of a new home.

This wondrous, but rather desolate country, which once belonged to the Indians, was gradually inhabited by people of white skin: The hunters hunted deer and bears in the forests, the woodcutters felled giant firs, pines and oaks; the farmers ploughed and cultivated the prairie, in which for long ages only tall grass brightened by flowers had grown; the prospectors searched for gold in streams and mountains; and large towns, spanned by roads and rail spread in the places where only bison and wild coyotes used to race.

The wild white horse gallops across the prairie.

And on the farm, as evening falls, the descendants of the white settlers are listening by the fireplace to their grandmother's rhyme:

I'll tell you a story
About Jack a' Nory;
And he had a calf,
And that's half;
And he threw it over the wall,
And that's all.

Across the prairie races the wild horse. Each time his hoof strikes a pebble, a spark flies. And each spark transforms into a fairy story. Into a story of Indians, Negroes, and of the white settlers . . .

COWBOY BILLY COYOTE

'There's no room even to breathe in Texas these days,' sighed Billy's father. 'It is packed with too many new people; just look across the river, there's yet another new settler building his homestead.'

The woman looked up, and true enough, a roof was rising in the distance in the tall grass, like an anthill.

Actually there were not too many people in Texas in those days, but the settlers who had moved to the West and had grown accustomed to solitude, did not take too kindly to newcomers who trampled the tall grass swaying from horizon to horizon.

'We must move away from here,' Billy's father decided without much hesitation.

They loaded their sacks and packs onto the canvas-covered wagon, harnessed their four oxen and set out on their journey through the prairie further to the West.

As they neared the far shore while crossing the Coyote river, the wagon rolled sharply and little Billy fell out of it.

He was too young even to talk, he just closed his eyes and rolled into the tall grass. Neither his father, nor his mother noticed that they had lost Billy. They had so many children that the baby was not even missed.

Not until a month later did the mother realize that Billy was not among her fourteen children. But, by then, they were far away and the father did not wish to turn back.

'Someone is sure to find him,' he said with a wave of the hand, 'and bring him to us.'

Little Billy rolled right into the bushes and there he was found by a prowling coyote. He sniffed at the baby, and because Billy was whining just as plaintively as a coyote pup, the old coyote picked him up carefully by his teeth, carried him into his lair and placed him among the coyote pups.

It did not take very long for Billy to feel perfectly at home in the den; he played with the coyote pups, fought them over a gnawed rabbit bone, ate with them whatever the coyote mother and father had caught in the prairie—in fact he lacked nothing. He crawled on all fours and ran on all fours and barked and yapped loudly or softly—just like all coyotes.

One day a cowboy's cow wandered off to the Coyote river and the cowboy went to look for her.

At that very moment Billy was sparring with two grey bears by the riverside. He knocked one of them to the ground, the other ran off. Billy started eating the bear's flesh with relish. After a hard fight he was really hungry.

The coyote pups caught sight of the cowboy and ran to hide in the lair. Only Billy remained by the river, picking the bear's bone and taking not the slightest notice of anything else.

The cowboy was surprised. 'What are you doing among the coyotes? Why are you running about all naked and on all fours? And how is it that you are eating raw bear meat?'

'I am a coyote,' Billy said crossly. 'Whoever heard of a coyote roasting meat?'

'You are no coyote,' laughed the cowboy. 'You are a man, the same as I.'

'But I have fleas,' Billy spoke in his own defence. 'I have to keep on scratching, they bite me so hard. And at night, when the moon is shining, I howl at the moon just like all the other coyotes.'

'So you have fleas?' the cowboy roared. 'Everybody who lives in Texas has fleas. It can't really be otherwise. And that you howl at the moon? That doesn't mean a thing. Just show me your coyote's tail.'

Billy glanced round and had a shock. Only then did he notice, that although all the coyotes had a fine, thick tail, his was lacking.

'It seems I really am a man then,' Billy sadly agreed and stood on his two feet for the very first time. He swayed a little—for after all, he was used to running about on all fours—but soon he grew a little daring and darted around like any other normal boy.

The cowboy lifted Billy on to his horse and took him to his camp.

The cook cooked Billy beans and bacon, the boy licked his lips and by the time he had downed a cup of sweet coffee, he did not give the coyote den another thought.

And because that cowboy had found him by the river among the coyotes, they all gave him the name of Billy Coyote.

When Billy Coyote had learned all about being a cowboy, he started to get itchy feet. He would sit on a little hill and gaze across the prairie to the west over the blades of the swaying green grass.

One evening, as he sat watching the sun fall into the grassy green sea, he rose quietly, bade no one goodbye and aimed to the west.

In the prairie he met a lone hunter of bison.

'Hi, old man, advise me, please,' he called to him. 'I am looking for work. Do you happen to know of a herd of the most mulish cows?'

'You mean such a herd that no one is capable of keeping in order?' asked the hunter of bison. 'If that is so, you are travelling in the right direction, stranger, for just such a herd of unruly cows is grazing beyong Rattlesnake river. Not a single cowboy has yet been able to drive the herd together once in a year.'

Billy Coyote thanked the hunter and hurried off into the prairie, with the tall grass falling in waves behind him, as if kissed by the wind.

In the mountains his horse trod on a stone, slipped and broke his leg. Dusk had fallen, so Billy unsaddled the horse, threw the saddle on his own back and continued on foot.

Suddenly a rattlesnake rose in front of him from the grass, rattling his tail and hissing. 'So you are that Billy Coyote, who fears no one and nothing? It will be interesting to see if you can beat me.'

With that he rattled his tail so mightily, it sounded as if peas were cascading into a pot.

Billy Coyote put the saddle in the grass, grasped the rattlesnake by his tail, twirled him round and round like a lasso and then tossed him high in the air.

The rattlesnake had such a fright that he opened his jaws wide in astonishment. As he was falling back to the ground he forgot to shut them—and that was his undoing. With one fast move of the hand Billy Coyote pulled out the snake's teeth with the poison.

'I have lost,' the rattlesnake whispered, trembling with fear. 'You are cleverer than I. But please don't kill me.'

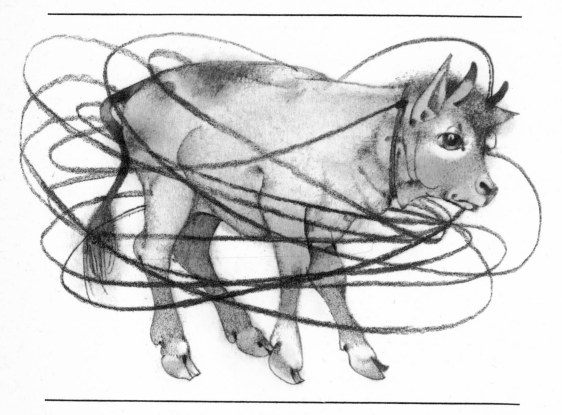

Once again Billy threw the saddle over his shoulder, picked the rattlesnake up and wound him round his neck like a scarf, and he was off again.

From behind a tall rock a cougar—a mountain lion—pounced upon Billy and roared. 'You have beaten the rattlesnake because you are faster and more clever than he. But you have me to reckon with now. I challenge you to a fight. We shall see who is the strongest.'

Billy Coyote put the saddle and the rattlesnake in the grass and cried out. 'I am ready, let's start!' The cougar crouched, then sprang at Billy like a shot. But Billy caught him firmly in his arms and spun him round so fast that the beast's eyes went dazed and dizzy. And Billy went round and round, faster and faster, till the air was thick with the flying fur of the animal.

In fact there was so much flying fur that it hid the evening sun.

'Let me go,' the cougar pleaded, full of shame. How embarrassed he was to be completely naked, without any fur at all. 'Didn't you know I was only teasing? As if I didn't know that you are stronger than I. Only please let me stay alive.'

Billy Coyote put the cougar down on the ground, picked up the saddle from the grass and saddled the beast. Then he mounted him, wound the rattlesnake round his neck again and rode on.

As they crossed Rattlesnake river, Billy saw canvas-covered wagons on the far shore, and a camp fire nearby. Cowboys sat round it, preparing to eat.

'Good evening, one and all,' Billy Coyote greeted the cowboys. 'Do you think you could spare me a bite to eat? I am really starving after all my travels.'

'Why, of course,' said the eldest cowboy. 'Help yourself.' All the others were suspiciously eyeing the saddled cougar and the toothless rattlesnake; they said not a word, but moved further away—just to be safe.

Billy picked the pan with beans and bacon from the fire, and before the cowboys knew what was happening, the beans and bacon were inside him. Then he took the second pot off the fire, filled with hot coffee, and downed the lot in one gulp.

As good manners commanded, he wiped his mouth and remarked, 'The beans were a little hard, the bacon slightly burnt and the coffee wasn't sweet enough. But at home one should eat as one demands, whereas when strangers are hosts—whatever they give him. So many thanks, gentlemen.'

The cowboys could only shake their heads.

'Who is in charge of this party?' Billy asked.

From the side of the fire rose a fellow, neither young nor old, dressed in patchy jeans and a leather jacket with tassels. He took a long look at Billy, then at the cougar and at the rattlesnake, and muttered between his teeth, 'I was in charge here. I am not any longer. From now on you are our leader, daring stranger.'

'If you insist,' Billy nodded, 'then I will be your leader. Now tell me, are your cows all properly branded?'

The cowboys sighed. 'That's just the trouble, Billy Coyote. That's just what is worrying us the most.'

'Well go on, tell me what is worrying you,' Billy remarked curtly.

'Never in my life have I heard of cowboys not being able to brand their cattle properly.'

'It's easy for you to say that,' the cowboys went on sighing. 'But it is our lot to look after the most mulish herd of cows that anyone has ever known.'

'That is the very reason I am here,' Billy Coyote said. 'For a long time now I have been looking for just such a mulish herd.'

He rose from the fire and started to unwind the lasso from his waist. He kept on unwinding it and unwinding it, yet the end of the lasso was not to be seen.

Not till daybreak did he unwind the whole length of the lasso.

Some of the cowboys were convinced, that when Billy Coyote's lasso was completely unwound, it was long enough to wind round the whole globe of the earth. But other cowboys laughed at them, saying, 'You exaggerate, friends. The lasso is all of two inches shorter than that.'

When Billy Coyote had all his lasso unwound, he twirled it round and just as a try he caught an eagle with it, who was circling above the mountains.

Then he spun the lasso more and more and threw the noose over the prairie.

The lasso swished like a gale, and when it hit the ground, Billy tightened the noose. He had caught and bound all the six thousand seven hundred and eighty-nine cows with the rope in one go and pulled them right to the camp.

Only one single high-spirited heifer had managed to slip through the noose.

'So that's your game,' Billy snarled and jumped on all fours. He had not grown up among coyotes for nothing. And on all fours he rushed after the heifer, and before that creature knew what was what, Billy had jumped on its back, pressing his knees hard into the sides—and the cow, as meekly as a little lamb, trotted with Billy on its back towards the camp.

Sometime later Billy acquired a new horse. He fed him with gun-fire and after half a year the horse was as fast as a pellet and as fiery as lightning. And he threw anyone who tried to mount him.

Only Billy Coyote was able to ride him.

Every cowboy who dared to come near the horse, paid for his boldness with his life and, then, the poor cowboy left a widow behind. So Billy named his fiery stallion Widowmaker.

'I am rather lonely,' Billy Coyote admitted to himself one day. 'I shall have to get married.'

For a long time now he had had his eyes on Susie. She was a girl like the wind, and sat on a horse as ably as Billy.

'It must be Susie or no one,' Billy decided. 'Within a month there will be a wedding.'

At first Susie played hard to get, but she was only pretending. As it happened she, too, rather liked Billy Coyote.

'Very well then,' she agreed, 'I will marry you. But I have one wish. If you fulfil it, I'll by your wife.'

'It's a bargain,' Billy said. 'And what is your wish?'

'That is a secret till our wedding day,' Susie laughed, then jumped on her horse and galloped away home.

On the wedding day Susie dressed in a silk dress which rustled. So that her wide skirt would keep nicely in shape, she stiffened it with a steel wire and decorated it with green and red ribbons.

When Billy Coyote saw his bride, he liked her even better than the first time.

'But don't forget, first you have to fulfil my wish, as you promised,' Susie reminded her bridegroom.

'Billy Coyote always keeps his promises,' Billy bragged. 'Go on then, tell me your wish, my dearest.'

'I want to ride to church on your horse Widowmaker,' said Susie.

'As you wish,' Billy nodded sadly. 'But I can't say I am particularly delighted by your wish. I should hate to have to call the horse *Widower*maker afterwards.'

Susie only laughed.

She walked over to Billy's fiery horse, and before Widowmaker had a chance to kick, Susie had jumped on his back.

The stallion snorted furiously, reared on his hind legs, danced around madly, pulled his muscles taut — and tossed the bride high into the air.

Susie flew upwards, higher and higher, then stopped under a white cloud and started to fall like a stone back to the ground. But as her skirt was stiffened with a steel band, as soon as she hit the ground, she bounced back up again.

And so she went, up and down, down and up, always falling and flying, flying and falling.

The sun was already high in the sky and Susie was still flying between the earth and the sky. Then it grew dusk, and night fell and morning was here again, and poor Susie was quite quite worn out from all this crazy flying.

Billy Coyote and all the wedding guests just looked on sadly, no one knew what to do.

'I must think of something,' Billy Coyote said in the end. 'If this goes on, all I'll have left of my bride by the end of the week will be a skirt.'

He pulled out his six-shot revolver and bang, bang, he fired all the six shots in one go.

It had an effect.

A strong gale whipped up and carried the flying bride all the way to Rattlesnake river. It dropped her right into the water and Billy Coyote jumped on Widowmaker's back, at full gallop unwound his lasso, threw the noose round Susie and pulled her out of the water.

But the gale just did not ease up.

It uprooted trees, tore rocks and carried furtile soil away from the prairie.

'So that's your game,' Billy Coyote shouted crossly. 'I'll tame you, just you wait.'

And he mounted the gale as if it was his horse.

The furious gale dragged Billy all over the place, and tried to throw him off.

It flew with him round the whole region from mountains to mountains, it squealed and snarled, screeched and spat, hissed and sighed, wailed and whined, whimpered and whispered and cried, but Billy Coyote held on firmly to its bristling mane.

The gale howled and carried Billy right up to the clouds, then tore down again plunging him into a lake; it dragged him through hedges and crashed into rocks, it cooled him on a mountain iceberg and fried him in the hot desert air.

But Billy Coyote stayed put, his knees firm round the gale's sides, his head protected by the mane, and he laughed, 'Just you wait, you naughty girl, I'll tame you.'

By the second day the gale was truly tired, it could hardly breathe after such a nightmare ride, it choked and rasped, croaked and gasped — it was really at the end of its strength.

In the end the gale felt so sorry for itself that tears streamed from its eyes, and there were so many tears that they turned into a wild river.

The gale turned into wind and the wind turned into a breeze and this breeze slowly and lightly slipped right up to the bride Susie and put Billy down right by her very feet.

Then there really was the most famous cowboy wedding and Billy spun his lasso, tossing the noose towards the sky, and as it was growing dark, he caught the brightest star in his lasso and gave it as a wedding gift to his bride Susie.

That star changed into a sunflower and ever since then wild sunflowers grow in abundance all over the prairie. They are bright yellow, just like the star which Susie had pinned to her blouse on her wedding day.

THE SPIRIT OF THE BISON SKULL

Bush, the Indian boy, grew into a youth. No longer could he play with other boys. Duties awaited him. Hunting and war.

First of all he had to find his very own Spirit, who would stand by him and protect him in peace and war.

Spirits bring the world to life, even a rock and a tree have their good Spirits and a cloud, jackal, man and a river have one too.

While a young Indian does not possess his very own Spirit, to whom he can pray, he cannot hunt, nor go to war. From a hunt he would return empty-handed, and no one would protect him in his fight.

'Pay attention to your dreams,' the old granny advised the youth. 'Maybe your good Spirit will appear in your sleep.'

But Bush dreamt of nothing at all.

So Bush set out to search for his good Spirit. Without anyone knowing, he left the village and aimed for the river, wishing hard all the way that the Spirit of a bison head would appear.

'The Spirit of the bison head will be my protector. Appear before me, Spirit of the bison head!' the Indian boy Bush whispered to himself, again and again.

But his pleading was in vain.

Perhaps the Spirit will show mercy and will notice me if I lure him to my side, Bush thought suddenly.

So he tied together four dried out bison skulls and pulled them behind him by the string through the parched prairie, over stones, through thornbushes, right up to the river.

The sun beat down unmercifully, the bison skulls were heavier with each step.

By the time Bush reached the river, he was so tired that he could hardly drag the skulls behind him.

He saw that the water in the river had risen.

'Perhaps the Spirit of the bison skull will have pity on me in water, since he took no notice of me on land,' Bill said to himself and stepped into the river.

The wave seized him and pulled him down into the deep.

And then he felt that all the tiredness and weight were leaving him. The bison skulls suddenly were as light as a feather, and kept him afloat.

Bush looked behind him. The four bison skulls, scorched white by the sun, had changed into four live bison heads.

The four bison heads were gazing at the youth with watery, kind eyes.

'Thank you, thank you, Spirit of the bison skull, for granting my wish!' whispered the Indian youth, feeling strong and unbeatable all of a sudden.

The Spirit of the bison skull would protect him in peace and war.

ANTS

In the beginning there was water. Water, nothing but water. Only water.

The sea was the world and the world was the sea.

Two Indian brothers lived in that sea. Chaypacomat and Cocomat. They saw nothing, for they were too afraid to open their eyes and let the salt hurt them.

Chaypacomat swam to the surface one day, stuck his head above the sea and opened his eyes. He could see nothing but water, a dark sea spilling round far and wide.

The younger brother Cocomat was too impatient to wait for Chaypacomat's return, and started swimming upwards towards him. But because he was so impatient, he opened his eyes before he surfaced, and the salty water blinded him.

'We must do something about this water,' said the elder brother.

He filled his palm with sea foam and tossed it upon the surface.

The foam immediately turned into red ants.

'Well, I never,' Chaypacomat laughed and filled his hand with the foam over and over again, scattering red ants upon the sea surface until there were so many of them, they pushed the water out.

That is how the earth was made.

Chaypacomat next filled his other hand with the foam, and a flock of pink flamingoes flew out of his palm. But above the sea was only darkness and the flamingoes were lost in it.

'We have to have a light to see where they are,' Chaypacomat said.

He filled his mouth with water and spat it out upwards.

And that was how the moon was made.

But it did not give enough light. There was still only semi-darkness over the sea. Chaypacomat filled his mouth with more water and spat it higher than before.

With that the sun started to shine brightly in the sky and all the world lit up.

THE GHOST RIDER

Merchant Peter Rug lived in Boston a long time ago.

He was a good man, with a heart of gold, but with a quick temper which was easily roused if something was not to his liking. He hated anyone to oppose him.

Once in December, when days are shortest, Peter Rug was preparing to visit friends on their ranch. He harnessed the horse while his wife lifted their little girl Jenny into the carriage, wrapping her well in a rug. The wife stayed behind, waving goodbye till the carriage disappeared from sight.

As they approached the ranch, it started to rain.

They had lunch, and in the afternoon little Jenny played with the children of their host, whilst he and Mr Rug sipped their drinks and talked of old times.

Outside the rain had worsened, low clouds hovered over the roofs, but in the hearth beech logs gave a warm, friendly glow, crackling merrily.

After supper Peter Rug rose, thanked his host for his hospitality and called little Jenny, saying they must be off home.

The rancher and his wife did their best to persuade Mr Rug to stay the night. 'It is raining harder all the time and there is a fierce gale blowing. Sleep here, it will be easier to travel back tomorrow in daylight. We have plenty of room.'

But Peter Rug refused to be convinced.

'I'll get back tonight or never,' he snapped sharply, bade his friends goodbye, harnessed the horse and drove off.

A curtain of rain cloaked the countryside, trees along the way bent their crowns and moaned, lashed by the wind. The carriage clattered on towards Boston through the unfriendly darkness.

In the meantime Mrs Rug kept peering worriedly through the window, gazing into the empty street, listening for sounds, waiting for her husband and daughter.

She waited in vain that evening and that night.

Her husband and little Jenny did not return even the next day.

Mrs Rug was so worried she could not sleep, and did not know what to do. In the early evening of the third day, she heard the clatter of hooves on the road. She jumped out of bed, looked out of the window, and sighed with relief. Her husband and Jenny were coming back. At last!

The carriage came right up to the house. Mrs Rug was just about to go down the stairs to meet them and to help Jenny alight, when her husband waved, looking up at her with despair in his eyes — and the horse drove off at full gallop.

By the time Mrs Rug had run down and into the street, all she saw was the carriage disappearing round a corner of a black tree-lined alley.

That was the last time Mrs Rug saw her husband and daughter.

Unhappy and heartbroken, she fell ill, and a few days later she died.

Since that day travellers often saw the carriage drive by in desolate places, with Peter Rug and Jenny inside. It usually flew by like the wind without stopping.

On rare occasions the horse slowed down as the carriage was passing the traveller, and the ghost rider called from his box, 'I have lost my way, how do I get to Boston? I must get home this evening!'

Travellers and vagrants were never too happy about meeting the strange carriage. Whenever it dashed past, it always started to rain and a storm blew up straightaway.

So they named the ghostly carriage 'the stormmaker'.

The innkeepers of the road taverns were also not keen on seeing Peter Rug. He never ordered anything to drink or eat, never stayed overnight, but only drawled from the door, 'Do you know how I can get to Boston? I must get there before dark today!'

And the moment the door slammed behind him, the wind rose, thunder roared and the first drops of rain hit against the windows.

Some years later when the days of carts and carriages were over, and highways were crowded with cars, drivers often noticed an old Ford. Behind the wheel sat Peter Rug and by his side was little Jenny.

The pump attendants advised drivers who stopped for gasoline, 'Try and avoid meeting Peter Rug the second time! If anyone sees him twice in one day, either his engine stops or he has a crash. Peter Rug brings bad luck!'

THE CAT IN THE BOX

'Well, what do you say, Simon,' planter Johnson asked his servant, 'will I be going into town tomorrow, or will I not?'

Simon thought for a while, then said, 'You won't be going, my Lord, for tomorrow my Lady's sister is coming here to visit.'

Planter Johnson nodded his head, duly impressed.

'You've guessed right again, Simon. I wish I had the same gift of foreseeing the future as you do.'

With that he gave Simon a sniff of tobacco from his porcelain snuff-box.

Simon sniffed, sneezed and blinked his impish eyes with contentment.

If only the planter was aware that Uncle Simon walked with a step of a cat, that he could creep unheard to a door and eavesdrop cleverly behind them.

If only he suspected that Simon did not let a single word escape him and that it was, therefore, quite simple for him to foretell the future, when he had first secretly heard the conversation of Mr Johnson and his wife, who—as all the servants well knew—made all the decisions in the household, while the master did as he was told.

One day many landowners and all sorts of gentlemen gathered at planter Johnson's house. They discussed all kinds of things, the weather, the harvest, horses.

Then the discussion turned to slaves.

Everyone complained how unreliable they were, how no one could fathom them out; how they would like most of all to revolt, to run away and to laugh at their master toiling alone on his cotton plantation.

'They look forward to such things in vain,' the district judge Dodge stated. 'Destiny has arranged it for Negroes to serve their white masters.'

The planters started to discuss the matter, to argue, to convince one another.

'I know of everything that happens and will happen on my plantation,' Mr Johnson said. 'I have a servant, who can foresee things so reliably, that I need not fear revolts or the rains. I know about everything in good time ahead.'

'How is that?' asked judge Dodge.

'It is very simple really. Every evening I talk things over with my cleverest servant Simon, who tells the future most reliably.'

'That sounds highly suspicious to me,' the judge remarked, shaking his head. 'You should not trust the Negroes, Mr Johnson, they are as artful as foxes. No one can ever tell what goes on in their heads.'

'I will let you see for yourselves,' Mr Johnson said, rather self-consciously. 'Then you can convince yourselves that all this is not my imagination.'

The following Sunday planters gathered from all the districts.

The Negroes, too, came to see how Uncle Simon was going to do his foretelling in front of the masters.

In the garden they stood up a soap-box, Uncle Simon climbed on to it as if he were a speaker, and all the planters sat in a circle round him. The Negroes stood behind, straining their necks with curiosity.

They blindfolded Uncle Simon's eyes.

The district judge Dodge then asked in his most impressive voice, 'Now, Uncle Simon, as you are so good at foretelling everything, tell us what is hidden in the box you are standing on?'

The Negro pressed his left hand against his covered eyes, thought hard and stayed silent.

He thought for a minute, he thought for two minutes, then three.

The planters started to smirk, the Negroes to roll their eyes, for sheer terror seemed to pour from Uncle Simon, who knew how to tell the future.

But this time he strained his brain in vain. He could not invent a thing. This time he could not eavesdrop behind the door, when the planters and the judge were in council. What was in the box? Who was to know?

He was sweating all over, thought after thought flew through his head just like sparrows over maize, but all was in vain. Today, Uncle Simon could not come up with any reasonable answer, or so it seemed.

I've lost, thought he, and so he would have all the suffering behind him, he cried, 'This poor black cat has been cornered at last and has lost everything.'

Mr Johnson walked over to Simon and untied the scarf.

Uncle Simon jumped down from the box, the judge took off the lid—and from inside jumped a large black cat.

The planters clapped, full of appreciation, the Negroes shouted, full of admiration, and Mr Johnson said, 'So you see, and now perhaps you will believe me at last that Uncle Simon is the best at foreseeing the future.'

WHY A RABBIT HIDES
IN A BURROW

'My children are dying of thirst,' lamented the bear.

'Do you know, brother wolf, where I could find a few drops of water for them?'

'Times are bad, brother bear, times are bad,' wailed the wolf. 'All the brooks have dried up, the wells have lost all their water and, for three days now, I have been roaming round the forest, my head spinning from my awful thirst.'

'What if we ask the wild ducks? They may know of some water,' the bear suggested.

But not even the wild ducks, nor the swans, nor the wise owl knew of any water.

The old jackal then asked all the animals to assemble in the forest clearing. They discussed the problem for a long time and wondered what to do, so all the animals would not die of thirst.

They decided they must dig out a deep well.

Only the rabbit laughed at all his animal brothers.

'Why should I toil? I shan't die of thirst!'

'If you won't help us, then we won't let you drink from our well!' the bear decided and then set to work, with all the animals from the prairie and the forest helping him.

They dug and dug, till they hit upon a strong water spring.

By morning the well was filled with cold water.

The whole day long animals from near and far trailed to the well to satisfy their thirst.

In the morning, when the bear went to the well to inspect it, what do you think he saw? The mud by the well was covered with rabbit tracks!

The bear called all the animals together.

'The rabbit did not want to help us and now he is stealing our water. Who is going to guard the well at night?'

'You are the strongest one of us all, brother bear,' said the owl, 'you stand on guard!'

That evening the bear kept guard at the well.

The rabbit crept near from the forest and began to sing.

He sang so sweetly, that he rocked the bear with his song to sleep.

The next morning the animals met at the well and were most surprised. Brother bear slept like a log and round the well there were rabbit tracks everywhere!

'What a fine guard you've proved to be,' the animals remarked crossly. 'That rabbit has stolen our water once again!'

That evening the wolf stood guard over the well.

He stayed in the grass right by the well and did not close an eye.

Then the rabbit crept near from the forest and began to sing.

He sang so melodiously, that the wolf just could not contain himself and he started to dance. He danced and he danced, and the rabbit darted to the well and had a good drink.

The next morning the animals met at the well and they did not know whether to laugh or cry. The wolf was dancing, as if under a spell, round and round the well, and the ground once again was covered with rabbit tracks.

'I shall advise you,' said the grey squirrel. 'We'll make a man from wood-tar pitch, and let him stand on guard!'

So they made a man from pine resin and when it grew dark, they stood him by the well.

Soon afterwards the rabbit crept from the forest and started to sing sweetly.

But the resin man did not move.

The rabbit was annoyed. He hopped right up to the man and spat at him.

'Why are you standing as if made of stone? If you don't leave this well immediately, I'll give you such a hard smack, it will make you see stars!'

The resin man still did not move.

The rabbit swung his right front paw with all his might. But dear me! The paw became glued to the man.

'So you still refuse to move from the well?' cried the now fuming rabbit, hitting the resin man hard with his left front paw.

But alas! The paw, too, was soon well and truly stuck.

'So that's your game!' the furious rabbit now hit out with his right back paw.

But the hind paw was also soon glued to the resin man.

The rabbit now lost his head completely. He struck the resin man with his one remaining free paw.

But the man still did not move.

Next morning, when the animals met at the well, they were most surprised.

The rabbit was glued by his paws to the resin man and his eyes had turned scarlet with fury.

All the animals laughed at the rabbit. 'He's been punished enough,' the bear said, and pulled the rabbit's paws away from the resin man.

The rabbit pelted away from the well as if his tail was on fire, and disappeared into a hollow.

Since that day a rabbit cannot sing and hides under the ground in a burrow, so that the other animals cannot laugh at him.

THE ENCHANTED FOREST

Deep in a redwood forest an old witch lived in a stone cave.

Some witches poison water in wells with their deadly breath. Others comb mist from their hair and throw it at passing travellers, making them lose their way.

The witch from the stone cave hung wooden cages on trees all over the forest. She turned maidens into birds and locked them inside the cages.

At noon, when lumberjacks were resting in the clearing, listening to the beautiful song of birds in the redwood forest, they had no notion that every one of those birds was in fact a maiden.

One day the lovely Melinda was walking past the forest with her bridegroom.

'I'd rather you did not go into the forest,' the youth advised Melinda. 'I have heard that it is the home of a wicked old witch.'

'Let me at least pick that beautiful yellow flower under the tall timber tree,' Melinda pleaded, stepping among the trees.

The youth feared for his girl, so he followed her.

'I must have that blue flower in my bouquet too,' Melinda added and went further.

Then she was tempted by a scarlet flower and an orange bloom, a white and a pink flower, and so she walked on and on, deeper and deeper into the redwood forest, the youth following.

The old witch knew well with what to lure the maidens. She scattered armfuls of beautiful flowers over the whole forest, decorated bushes with green ivy and spread soft silky moss over the ground.

And in the cages the birds sang on sweetly.

Melinda followed the colours of the flowers and the song of the birds as if bewitched.

'We really should turn back now,' urged the youth when they came to the black rock.

'Let me pick just one more flower, that blue one by the cave,' Melinda pleaded.

The moment she touched the bloom, the old witch hobbled out of the cave and caught Melinda's hand.

The girl turned into a bird immediately.

The witch opened an empty cage, pushed the bird inside and then hung the cage on an old oak tree. The young man was standing nearby and saw everything.

He seemed rooted to the ground with sheer terror.

By the time he ran forward, it was too late. The witch had crawled back into her cave, and the cage was hanging on the tree with a sad bird cowering inside.

The unhappy bridegroom set out into the world. He went on and on, he could not settle anywhere, and wherever he walked, wherever he was, he thought only of his Melinda. During his journey he asked everyone how he could set his bride free.

But no one could advise him.

'Witches, my dear boy, have a lot of power,' the old settlers and lumberjacks would say, nodding their heads. Such a witch has greater strength than all of us put together, so what can you do against her?'

Once the youth spent the night with an old miller.

The unhappy, lonely boy did not even dare to confide his suffering to his host.

But after supper the miller said, 'Listen, my lad, the way you look to me, you must have really gone through it one way or another. What is worrying you?'

'You won't be able to help me,' sighed the youth. 'The witch in the redwood forest turned my bride into a bird and imprisoned her in a cage. Nobody can tell me how I can set her free.'

'If that's the case,' the miller commented, 'then I know what can be done. You must go on searching, young man, until you find the bloom with the blue dew-drop. You must carry the bloom carefully back into the bewitched forest, making sure the dew-drop does not slip to the ground. And, when your bird has drunk the blue dew-drop, it will change back into your Melinda.'

For seven long years the youth wandered over the world and everywhere he went he searched for the bloom with the blue dew-drop.

On the banks of a pond he found flowers with green dew-drops.

They were there because at night little water-nymphs played and frolicked so heartily, that green water sprayed from their hair.

Along the path which circled the cemetery, the youth found in the grass blooms with red dew.

A little earlier a funeral procession had passed that way. A mother of three small children was being buried and the children's tears had turned to red dew.

But the flower with the blue dew-drop was just not to be found.

One summer night, the youth was sleeping under a bushy maple-tree.

'Wake up, my dearest, wake up!' Melinda beckoned him in his sleep, 'I am here, with you!'

The youth jumped up, groping round him in the dark.

His hand fell limply to his side.

He was alone, only the crown of the tree swayed in the fresh morning breeze.

The youth stood with downcast eyes.

At that moment he saw a white bloom at his feet.

And in its cup a blue dew-drop glittered.

He bent down to the flower, plucked it gently from the ground and hid it in his palm, so the blue drop of dew could not escape to the ground.

A whole year went by before the youth reached home.

He had to be extremely careful not to allow the sun to drink the drop of the blue dew.

So he slept through the day and travelled by night. At last, he came back to the aged redwood forest. It was a clear summer night, and all the birds in their cages were fast asleep.

The starry light led the youth to the stone cave and there he stood by his goal!

In front of him rose the well-remembered tree. In its branches, the cage with the sleeping bird.

The youth stood under the tree for all the remaining hours of the night, waiting patiently.

The dawn was breaking, and the sky grew red in the east. The birds in the forest started to wake up and to greet the new day with their song.

The youth stepped to the cage.

The bird inside opened its eyes.

The youth opened his hand and at the same time the sun came out over the horizon.

The blue dew-drop glimmered on the bloom like a transparent pearl.

The bird drank the drop of dew and turned back into the beautiful Melinda.

An icy wind howled, the rock tore in half and a snake slithered out of the cave. The old witch had turned into a black viper.

All the wooden cages fell from trees into the soft moss and broke apart and, all of a sudden, the forest became filled with lovely young maidens.

They sang and accompanied Melinda and her happy bridegroom to the village where they danced and sang at their wedding.

LIFE WITH THE WOLVES

The Sioux tribe lived on the banks of the Cheyenne river in South Dakota.

One day a young Indian woman quarrelled with her husband. He turned on her, shouting, 'If you don't like it at home, no one is holding you here.'

The Indian woman threw a blanket over her shoulder, ran out of the tent and waded across the snow-covered prairie towards steep rocks.

An icy wind was blowing over the plain, covering the whole region with a white veil, and soon there was not even the smoke from the camp fires to be seen.

The woman stumbled with difficulty through the deep snow, falling over and over again. Tiredness bound her feet and her breath.

He will think it over, the woman thought hopefully, for she well knew the character of her man. Anger will leave him, he will come after me and will easily follow my tracks.

But when she climbed a little hillock and glanced behind her, she realized with horror that the wind had cloaked her footprints with snow.

She was hopelessly lost. She did not know where she had come from, nor where she was going; her tired legs were refusing to go on, she was consumed with hunger and thirst and faint with fatigue. It took all her strength not to sink into the soft snow pillow and to fall asleep for ever.

Suddenly she came upon a tiny cave carved in the rocks.

How pleased she was! At last she could rest a while and hide from the wind and the frost.

She crawled through the opening. Inside there was darkness and warmth.

Wrapping herself in the blanket, she fell asleep.

When she awoke, she was horrified to discover four pairs of yellow eyes fixed intently upon her.

Four big grey wolves, their tongues hanging out, were squatting in a circle round the woman, gazing at her.

She sat up, her heart pounding with fear.

The wolves moved nearer, licking her hands, breathing warmth upon her, whimpering and barking gently, and it seemed to the young woman they were talking to her in the wolf language.

She, too, spoke to them, and the wolves swept the ground with their wagging tails, nodding their heads, as if they understood.

The next morning the wolves ran out of the cave, but returned soon with a rabbit they caught.

The woman was starving, so she ate the raw meat and went back to sleep again.

In just a few days time she had grown accustomed to the wolves. She swept the cave clean, collected young fir branches, laid skins upon them, and made herself a dress from deerskin, sewing with a thorn needle. She learned to eat uncooked meat, and soon became used to the cave's darkness.

The Indian woman of the Sioux tribe thus spent the whole winter in the wolves' den.

When the snow was gone and shoots of green young grass coloured the prairie, the wolves approached the woman. One by one they laid their heads in her lap, licking her hand lovingly.

Then they led her out of the cave and sat before its entrance, barring her return.

The Indian woman realized they were saying goodbye.

She looked round for the last time and saw in the yellow eyes of the wolves the warm light of friendship.

One spring day the Sioux men went hunting for wild horses, the mustangs.

Among a herd of stallions, mares and foals they found a strange creature.

It had long black hair and it ran about on all fours, like an animal. But its face was the face of a woman, though the body was thickly overgrown with fur.

Above the prairie the breeze played teasingly with the birds.

The mares and the foals and the young stallions were grazing peacefully by the river, guarded by a black stallion.

The hairy creature crawled to a bush, and picked young leaves and flower buds.

The grass was still not too high — if luck was with the hunters, they would be sure to trap at least two horses in their lasso.

They whistled piercingly and they were off.

They tried to separate the stallion from the mares, so he would be easier to catch.

But the black horse was well aware of what they had in mind.

The horses grouped together, the foals among them, and galloped over the prairie. They swam across the river and soon managed to disappear in the bush.

For a while the hairy creature ran persistently with them, and it would surely have saved itself by its fast gallop, if the Indians had not surrounded it.

They bound the human beast with rope, and it bit and gnawed wildly, scratching, clawing, screeching. It was all they could do to stop it from giving them the slip.

After examining the creature more thoroughly, they recognized it as the woman who, years ago, had run away from her husband into the rocks. Then they took her back to camp. From then on she used to sit in front of her tent, her sad distant eyes fixed on the prairie. She did not speak, but howled like a wolf now and then.

The women combed and washed her, and fed her in the human way. For a long time she was unable to sleep in a tent, for now she felt it suffocating.

But slowly she grew to accept human beings again, and slowly became aware again that she was a woman.

It took a long time for her to learn to think again like a human being, and to utter a few comprehensible sentences.

She would sit on a boulder and the Indians of the Sioux tribe would come and worship her as the sister of the wolves, for as long as she lived the wolves would not harm their tribe.

THE TOOTHPICK

Lumberjack Sol Shell lived in a cabin under the peaks of Pine Hills.

One morning he woke and thought it strange that the room was in darkness. He went to the door, tried to open it and couldn't.

The cabin was buried under snow, right to its chimney.

The snow had walled it in and Sol Shell was imprisoned.

The lumberjack investigated his supplies of wood and food. There was enough wood for two to three days, and enough food for a week.

He lit the stove and cooked some soup.

On the fourth day he had to chop up his chairs and shelves for firewood.

By the end of the week he didn't know what to do with himself with hunger and cold.

He had to do something.

He broke off the pipe which lead from the stove to the chimney, pushed an axe firmly under his belt and crawled through the chimney on to the roof. When he reached it, he pushed the smoke pipe right through the snow-drift, to enable him to breathe, and began to dig a vertical passage with his axe.

Somehow or other he managed to worm his way from the snowy mass.

He looked round him.

Everywhere nothing but snow, all signs of life gone, only the tips of the fir trees peeping over the white surface. On the hillside of the Pine Hills stood a lone fir, for the wind had blown away the snow-drifts round it.

The lumberjack aimed for the lone tree, to fell it.

On his way he gripped the tips of the firs to stop himself going under the snow, and at last managed to inch his way right to the tree.

He glanced upwards. The branches were crowded with half-frozen racoons. There must have been twenty of them for sure, maybe even more. When all the other trees started to disappear under snow, the racoons flocked to the fir as if it was an island in the ocean—but they were numb with cold and almost frozen to death.

So I have found myself some firewood and a roast for the oven, Sol Shell said to himself.

He shook the branches till the racoons fell to the ground, tied their tails together so they would not run away if they awoke and

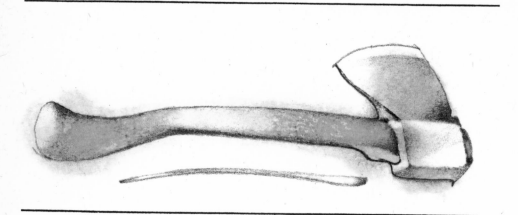

then started to work on the tree.

He felled the fir and cut off all its branches.

He happened to lean against the now bare trunk and all of a sudden the trunk started to roll down the hillside.

What an idiot I am, the lumberjack scolded himself, here I am left with a few branches and that great big log slips away.

He tied the branches together with a rope, threw the racoons on top and began to drag his supplies to the cabin. Suddenly he heard deep rumbling.

He looked round. The trunk had rolled right down into the valley, and rolled up again on the opposite hillside, stopped at the very top, then tumbled back down into the valley and up the side of the Pine Hills.

The lumberjack tried in vain to stop the great log. As it rolled past him, he swung his axe, bang!—but the log was travelling so fast, he missed it, and struck the snow instead of the wood. Before he managed to fish the axe from the snow again, the log was already on the opposite side.

After several vain attempts Sol Shell gave up, threw the rope back over his shoulder and dragged some fir branches and a substantial supply of meat down to the cabin. What would he do, though, when the wood once more came to an end?

For three days and three nights the rumbling in the valley continued. For three days and three nights the fir trunk rolled up and down the slopes, just as if some giant was playing with it, for want of better things to do.

Lumberjack Sol Shell roasted the racoons, the fire crackling in the stove inside his cabin.

On the fourth day, he was coming to the end of his wood supply.

He had to chop up the table, tear boards from his floor, so he could keep the fire going and keep himself from freezing to death. The following morning, when he had eaten the last piece of the racoon roast and was just about to cut up his bed, he heard faint sounds of hop, hop, hop . . . from behind the door.

Drops of water from the icycles were running down on to his doorstep.

It was thawing.

By lunchtime the lumberjack could squeeze through the door outside. He did not dilly dally, but pelted down into town to buy flour, meat, coffee and sugar.

Suddenly he realized that he no longer could hear or see the fir trunk rumbling and tumbling from slope to slope.

Only a faint rustling noise could be heard from the valley, as if the wind was whispering a secret to the trees.

He went to take a look.

How surprised he was!

Instead of the mighty log a splinter of wood, not more than five centimetres long, was rolling up and down.

The log had been rolling so long and so hard that all that was left was a smooth thin splinter.

And these days, when lumberjacks, hunters and farmers from the district gather to celebrate Sol Shell's birthday, the old lumberjack takes from his waistcoat pocket a fine smooth toothpick.

It is so hard and strong that it has outlasted all feasts and celebrations, dishes piled high with venison meat and bear paws.

And why not!

After all, it comes from a fir trunk, which had been worked to a fine toothpick by rolling up and down under the peaks of Pine Hills for three whole days and three whole nights.

ATAM AND IM

The desert stretched from horizon to horizon. No blade of grass to be seen anywhere; only stark rocks jutted out towards the sky.

The Spirit of the West Wind felt lonely. So he filled his lungs with air, and when he breathed out, his magic breath turned into a man and woman. He named them Atam and Im. Day after day he came to visit them and talked with them by the fire.

Deep down in the rocks hid Troublemaker, so the Spirit of the West Wind could not see him. That villain had no work to do and he was bored. So he wanted to amuse himself.

He created from river foam a white horse and sent him to Atam and Im. Then he hid behind a boulder and waited.

'Look, that must be the Great Chief, he is all white, he must be the Great Chief,' Im whispered excitedly, pointing to the white horse.

'Oh no, that is no great chief,' Atam said suspiciously.

The white stallion stood before them, his head erect, stars glittering in his eyes.

Atam gazed and gazed at the horse, and after some thought said: 'You are right, Im, it must be the Great Chief.'

The Spirit of the West Wind was descending from the sky on a wide rainbow and was shouting still from afar. 'Don't go near that horse. Troublemaker, that wicked-minded rascal has made him, so he can kick you.'

With that the Spirit of the West Wind walked to the white stallion, examined him well and eventually said with a wave of his hand, 'What can we do. Now the horse is here we can't very well send him away. Let him at least be useful to man.'

He gazed deep into the horse's eyes and pronounced ceremoniously, 'You shall serve man faithfully, and he will be your friend.'

Troublemaker grunted crossly. But he had no intention of giving up that easily. He sent a gad-fly to torment the horse.

'So that's your game,' the Spirit of the West Wind commented, his head nodding.

He waved his hand and sedge began to grow in the desert ground.

He picked a handful of the firm blades, made a tail with them for the stallion and advised him. 'Swish your tail hard to keep the gad-flies at bay.'

But the gad-fly moved further, and squatted on the horse's neck.

The Spirit of the West Wind plucked yet another bunch of the grass blades and made a mane for the horse.

'Graze to your heart's content,' he said to him, waving his hand once again. Soon the whole prairie was sparkling green from horizon to horizon. Grass, juicy and tall, flowered and scented the air.

The stallion bent his head and started to graze.

The Spirit of the West Wind smiled contentedly at his good deed and was about to leave. But suddenly he stopped, turned to Atam and Im, pointing his finger and warned, 'Do not eat any fruit till I advise you which ones are really delicious. Wait for me, I will soon return.'

Just then all the trees were heavy with ripe fruit. In those days even pine trees and willows yielded juicy fruit.

Atam and Im waited patiently for the Spirit of the West Wind to return and to tell them which fruit was the most delicious.

Troublemaker, deep down in the rock, was bored and was yawning with the boredom.

All of a sudden he patted his forehead and roared with laughter, so much that the mountain tops opened and spat fire.

He went to Atam and Im and picked a huge ripe fruit from a pine tree.

'Go and eat, good folk, for the Spirit of the West Wind is the most artful fellow. He is keeping the very best fruit for himself, that is why he did not allow you to pick any.' Im was rather hungry, so she took the big ripe fruit from Troublemaker and started to eat it. She put some into Atam's mouth and he ate it, too.

Troublemaker chuckled to himself, rubbed his hands contentedly and ran away.

In a trice all the fruit on the pine trees turned into small dry cones.

When at nightfall the Spirit of the West Wind returned and saw what had happened, he sent Im to Troublemaker. 'Go, you disobedient, impatient woman, as a punishment you shall live with that evil spirit.'

Then he tore a rib from Atam's chest and from it made him a new woman.

'MORNING, ALLIGATOR!'

It was a beautiful summer morning. Black Sam did not have to go to the plantation today — on Sundays even Negroes are allowed to rest — and so, he set off with his fishing rod to the river.

He sat on the bank, got the bait ready and was just about to throw the line into the water when he noticed a huge alligator lying in the shallows among the reeds. He was gazing at Sam most intently with his small, bright eyes.

Alligator opened a mouth full of teeth and said, 'Morning, Sam!'

The startled Negro tossed his rod into the grass and rushed back home. He ran into his master's bedroom without even knocking.

His master was still asleep. He woke up and scolded, 'What's going on? Why did you wake me?'

'Master, master,' stuttered Sam. 'By the bank of the river lies an alligator as large as a tree trunk. And, just imagine, boss, that alligator talks!'

'What are you blabbering about, you fool?'

Sam refused to be dismissed. 'If you don't believe me, master, then let yourself get up, dress yourself and come with me! With your very own eyes you will be convinced that in the river is an alligator that talks!'

The master rose, still yawning, dressed himself and muttered, 'Very well then, I'll go with you to the river to see this talking alligator of yours. But, if you are lying, I'll box your ears so hard that your neck will be tied in a knot!'

Sam went with his master to the river.

Among the reeds in the shallows was an alligator, his eyes blinking cunningly into the morning sun.

'So you see, boss, I did not lie,' Sam whispered excitedly.

'There are as many alligators in the river as logs in the wood,' the master remarked, 'but I have not heard a single one speak.'

'This one talks, master, just wait and see!'

But the alligator just carried on turning his back to the sun, his mouth not moving an inch.

Silence.

Only the water in the river splashed and the mosquitoes buzzed.

Alligator did nothing.

'Say something nice to him, boss!'

'Good morning, Alligator!' the master said in greeting.

Alligator just rolled his eyes at the sun.

The water splashed against the stones.

Alligator was silent.

The master's hand shot out and, smack!—it bounced off poor Sam's skull.

The master left, complaining crossly.

As soon as he had disappeared behind the willow bushes, the alligator raised his head out of the water and said, 'You really are an idiot, Sam! As if you didn't know that on principle I do not greet masters!'

THE TRAVELLER
AND THE INNKEEPER

It was growing dark and rain drizzled in little drops relentlessly from an overcast, heavy sky.

On a muddy path between the maize fields, a tired horse was stumbling along, on his back the huddled figure of a rider chilled to the bone.

He had travelled for two days now in this foul weather. He was hungry and thirsty, yet there was not a soul to be seen. In vain he looked for a farm or any dwelling where he could dry out, eat and sleep.

All at once he saw an inn behind some trees, with the innkeeper sitting on the verandah scraping on a fiddle.

The traveller dismounted and greeted the man.

The innkeeper simply nodded his head and carried on fiddling.

'Could I not spend the night here?'

'You're right, you could not,' barked the innkeeper, still fiddling.

'Do you think you could at least find me a drop of whisky? I am so thirsty I could drink the sea.'

'I could have found you a drop—but that was yesterday. I've finished the bottle.'

The traveller sighed. 'I am starving. I haven't had a bite since last night. Can you find some food for me in your larder?'

The innkeeper shook his head. 'In this inn you won't find even a crumb or a gnawed bone. We've eaten everything.'

'What about a handful of maize for my horse?'

The innkeeper, scraping on his fiddle without a pause, muttered from the corner of his mouth. 'We haven't even a grain of maize.'

'How far is it from here to the nearest cottage?' the traveller asked dejectedly.

The innkeeper looked up from his fiddle. 'Look here, stranger, how should I know? I've never been that far.'

'Do you know at least who lives in this tavern?' the traveller snapped angrily.

'Of course, of course,' nodded the innkeeper.

'If I may be so bold, what is your name?'

'My name? It could be Richard, or it could be David. But then it is not Richard, or David.'

The frustrated traveller sighed. 'Could you at least tell me, sir, where this track leads to?'

'This track leads to nowhere at all. It never did lead anywhere,' said the innkeeper. 'When I wake up in the morning and look outside, I see this track here still ends by my yard.'

'Where does this track fork off then?' demanded the now despairing traveller.

The innkeeper laughed. 'And why should it fork off anywhere, when nobody uses it?'

'It is obvious I shall not be able to find anywhere to stay tonight. Could I please at least sleep in your inn and tie my horse to the tree?'

The innkeeper scraped relentlessly on his fiddle and mumbled. 'Our house leaks. There's only one spot that is dry, and that's where I sleep with my missus, Sal. And you can't tie your horse to the tree. He'd shake the mulberries down and then Sal couldn't make mulberry jam. Sal loves her mulberry jam.'

'If your cottage leaks, why then don't you mend the roof?' wondered the traveller.

'Because it's been raining all day long.'

'In that case, why don't you have a go at the roof when it is fine?'

'Because when it is fine, the roof doesn't leak.'

'And how are you . . .'

'Not bad at all, thanks for asking,' muttered the innkeeper, cutting him short. 'And how are you?'

'That is not how I meant it,' explained the traveller. 'I wanted to ask how are you managing to get by.'

'By selling food and drink to passers-by. What else would an innkeeper do.'

'There you are, and yet you let me beg you for a whole half hour now for a slice of bread and meat and a dose of whisky.'

'Haven't I already told you there's not a crumb of bread or a drop of whisky to be had in this pub,' the innkeeper barked crossly, turning again to his fiddle.

'That is a great pity,' sighed the traveller adding, 'And why are you fiddling on that fiddle the same old tune all the time, without ever playing it all the way through?'

'Because I don't know how it ends. Do you play the fiddle?'

'A little.'

The innkeeper ceased to fiddle, his eyes examining the traveller distrustfully. Then he said with a sneer. 'You don't look like a chap who'd know how to play, but there's no harm, I suppose, to let you have a go.'

And the traveller, hungry, thirsty, soaked to the skin and exhausted by his long journey and the pointless frustrating conversation with the innkeeper, put the fiddle under his chin and played the song from beginning to end.

The innkeeper jumped off his chair. 'You're more than welcome here, stranger. Sal! Sal!' he shouted through the open door, suddenly all in a hurry. 'Don't sit there like a broody hen. Run down to the cellar and cut a joint off that billy-goat I slaughtered this morning, and mind you put that joint straight into the oven, so this gentleman here doesn't have to wait too long for his supper. And under our bed you'll find a barrel of whisky. Make sure you give our visitor a good measure. And you, Tilly, get that donkey out of our stable and tie him to the fence. Cover him with a sack to keep him warm. Then put this gentleman's horse into the stable and put plenty into the trough.'

The inn was suddenly all abuzz with activity, with the innkeeper firing orders. 'Dick, throw that tom cat out of the bread tin, he's always dozing in there, as if he couldn't sleep in the hay-loft. He's supposed to be a mouser. And that table-cloth, wrapped round the side of bacon, I want you to spread it over the table nicely, so this here mister will see how well we look after our guests.'

The innkeeper's wife peered from behind the door. 'I can't find a knife, husband. How will this gentleman cut his meat?'

'Take that knife I used to slaughter our billy-goat this morning. It will be somewhere in the shed. You sliced those over-ripe melons with it only this afternoon, remember now?'

When the innkeeper had given everyone jobs to do, he turned to the traveller.

'Excuse me, stranger, for ignoring you for so long. I'll make it up to you—you can stay with us as long as you wish and eat and drink to your heart's content. Would you, by the way, care for some coffee after dinner?'

The traveller nodded. 'I would like a cup very much.'

'We are out of coffee. But how about a cup of herbal tea? When it is sweetened, I'd say it beats the taste of bitter coffee any day. And why have you stopped playing? And don't worry about a bed, you can stay here with us, where would you go anyway at this time of the night.'

The traveller sipped his whisky, wedged the fiddle under his chin and played and played with the innkeeper listening in a trance.

Two hours later the traveller, fed and refreshed, rose from the table and asked. 'By the way, innkeeper, would you kindly explain to me, how to get out of here tomorrow?'

'Tomorrow,' smirked the innkeeper. 'You'll be lucky, my friend, to find your way out of this hole in a month. What an idea! But if you really insist on travelling further along this fiendish track, I'll tell you which way to go. Listen carefully.'

The traveller was all ears, while the innkeeper continued.

'Attention now. Do you see that puddle just past our yard? You cross that puddle and ride to those bushes yonder. You wade across that muddy stream and follow it till you come to a big maize field.

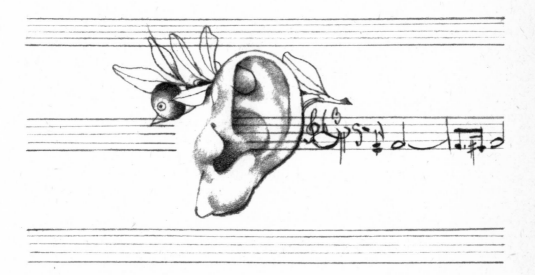

The maize is almost ripe, but don't let that muddle you. You've got to go right into that maize. It will take you a good quarter of an hour to get through it. Then you'll come to the most awful marsh you've ever seen. It can suck down a rider and his horse and no one will ever find them again. It would take a madman to look anyway. At the very bottom of that marsh is a path. And that is the shortest path from this inn here.'

The traveller sighed. 'How am I going to get across that marsh?'

'How! Now if it stops raining and the weather holds out, that marsh might dry out in a month or two. That's if it doesn't rain at all, mind you. Then you could ride across that bog and, after a kilometer or so, you'd come to a place where there isn't a path at all. There you can turn right, for instance.

'You go on an hour or so without getting anywhere, so you turn back to the spot from which no path leads, and turn to the left. When you travel about four kilometers without finding another path, then—I just don't know what you should do then. There's only one thing I know for certain, you'll be mighty relieved if you find the path which will bring you back to our inn . . .'

The traveller sighed and the innkeeper tried to pacify him.

'Why should you leave, anyway. Stay with us, eat, drink and fiddle, and be grateful that I've explained everything to you so well.'

THE GENERAL AND THE DEVIL

The retired general sat at the fireside one autumn evening. Outside it was growing dark, but by the hearth inside the room it was very pleasant; the beech logs glowed and crackled merrily.

The general though was not very much aware of the comfort of the fireside. He was pondering how he could grow rich quickly, and he could not think of a single idea.

Even if it costs me my soul, said the general to himself, I would gladly sell it to the devil for cash.

At that precise moment, the wind whipped through the chimney and there stood before him a dandy, dressed in a black jacket and clinging black breeches.

'At your service, general,' said the dandy. 'I await your command. But I beg you kindly to hurry. In a quarter of an hour I must be with the governor.'

Whilst talking, the black dandy picked a glowing cinder from the hearth to shine it on his watch.

'Come to think of it, there's not even a quarter of an hour left. So I would appreciate it, general, if we could get to our business straight away.'

The general was surprised. It was further than five sea miles to Portsmund from where they were, and that madman wanted to get there, to see the governor, in a quarter of an hour.

'You must be . . .' the general began to say, but the dandy did not let him finish.

'What does it matter who I am. The main thing is that we understand each other. We'll come to an agreement.'

The minute the general heard the word 'agreement', his ears pricked up. But he did not want to show that he was all agog with impatience to sign on the dotted line, so he pulled a penknife from his pocket and began to sharpen a piece of wood.

The devil, too, took out a fine black knife and began to clean his nails.

'How will you guarantee that you will keep your word?' asked the general. By now he was well aware that he was dealing with nobody else but the devil himself.

The devil raised his hand and straightaway gold coins were tumbling down the chimney on to the floor.

The general leapt out of his chair and rushed after one coin, that had rolled under the table. He caught it with his hand, but dropped it immediately. The gold coin was red-hot.

The devil laughed and egged the general on. 'Try it once more.'

The general picked up the gold piece with his fingers again very, very carefully — and the coin was cold.

'Satisfied?' asked the devil.

'Completely,' nodded the general.

'Now we must put together the agreement. But first I would like to have a drink of something.'

The general brought out of the cupboard a bottle of Jamaican rum and poured two glasses.

The devil sipped and the general asked, 'Do you like it?'

'Hm, not too bad, I suppose,' muttered the devil. 'I've had worse. I will show you how to make a real devilish drink.'

With that he took a burning cinder from the fire and threw it into a glass. The drink burned with a blue flame. Next he poured pepper and paprika into it and offered the concoction to his host. When the general took a drink, he trembled all over, his inners were on fire.

'Now let's get down to work,' the devil went on. 'Time is flying and I mustn't keep the governor waiting too long. I shall make you, general, sir, the richest man in the district. On the first day of every month I am going to fill your boots with gold coins. Only remember to hang them in the fireplace on a hook.'

The general listened, his ears burning with impatience.

'But if you try to cheat me in any way,' the devil threatened, his eyes gleaming, 'you'll see what I am capable of.'

He took a quill-pen from his pocket and passed it to the general. 'Sign.'

All of a sudden thoughts in the general's head started to spin, and he could not make up his mind.

'Why did you call me, then,' the devil remarked crossly, 'when now you dilly dally and delay me unnecessarily?'

And he started to stuff his pockets with the gold coins.

When the general saw that, he gripped the goose quill, dipped it in the soot in the fireplace and signed the agreement.

'Excellent,' cried the devil, picking up the piece of paper. Then he jumped into the fire and flew out by way of the chimney.

The general straightaway bought the highest pair of boots he could find. After all, it did not state in the agreement, what size the boots hanging in the fireplace should be. The boots he bought came up to his waist. And each month they were filled to the brim with gold coins.

The devil did not lie.

The general soon became the richest man in the district. But people soon started whispering and saying that he had made a deal with the devil.

The general was so ashamed that he hardly dared leave his house. He thought and thought how he could get the better of the devil. He did not eat. He did not sleep. Wherever he went he pondered how to cheat the devil.

He wondered and pondered till he came up with an idea.

The next morning, the first day of the month, the general came to the hearth, rubbing his hands together with glee. Gold pieces were tumbling through the boots; the floor was already covered right up to the general's knees. The devil was on the roof pouring and pouring without an end.

Then the devil flew down the chimney to see what was up. He examined the boots and hissed with fury. The boots were without soles. The general had cut them right off. The devil fumed, gave the general a threatening glance and disappeared up the chimney.

That night a fire started in the house. Firemen and neighbours vainly tried to put it out. The more water they poured on the flames, the faster the house burned.

The general paced up and down the garden, tearing out his hair. All his gold was still in the house.

Then he remembered, that gold melted by fire was of the same value as gold in pieces. So he calmed down and went to sleep in a neighbour's house.

In the morning, as soon as dawn broke, the general jumped out of bed and sped to the scene of the fire. He dug and fumbled in the rubble, trying to reach the cellar where the gold coins were hidden in a metal chest. When, at last, he managed to dig an opening into the cellar, he went stiff with horror. The cellar had fallen into chasm.

From that day, the general could be seen in a white nightshirt, walking round the ruins at night, searching for his lost treasure. But he never found it, for he who makes a pact with the devil must keep it.

ONE FOR YOU, ONE FOR ME

Two Negroes on the Miller plantation were hungry.

So, one dark autumn evening they stole a sack of potatoes from the field, then they wanted to divide it. They discussed where they could do this undisturbed.

In the end they agreed that the cemetery would be the best place. They dragged the sack all the way there, slung it across the low wall and jumped over it, too. Surrounded by graves, they proceeded to share the potatoes.

That evening black Bob was returning late from town, where he had been to sell chickens at the local market. He was driving the cart past the graveyard; it was pitch dark and low clouds were slithering across the sky.

It was then he heard voices from the cemetery.

'One for you, one for me, one for you, one for me . . .'

Horror of horrors!

Making the sign of the cross, Bob whipped into the mules and drove helter-skelter home.

He ran to find his master.

'Is something on fire?' Mr Miller grunted crossly, opening the door. 'What do you want at this time of night?'

'Boss, sir,' Bob stammered. 'Forgive me, boss, but there in the grave-yard a pair of devils are splitting souls between them!'

'What nonsense are you jibbering about!' laughed Mr Miller.

'I heard them with my own ears!' Bob assured him.

'Breathe on me, will you,' said Mr Miller. 'I bet you had one glass too many in town!'

'I swear, boss, I never touched a single drop! If you don't believe me, come back with me to the cemetery, then you'll see I'm no liar!'

Mr Miller said, 'Very well.' And off they went.

When they reached the cemetery wall, they crouched close to the ground, and listened hard. And indeed, from the graveyard the muffled words rose into the silence of the night.

'One for you, one for me, one for you, one for me . . .'

'So you see, boss, I am no liar.' Bob whispered, his teeth chattering with fear.

Mr Miller shook his head. He decided to climb over the low cemetery wall to find out for himself what was happening on the other side. But at that precise moment, the two thieves had just finished dividing the potatoes. Then they remembered that behind the cemetery wall were two large, beautiful potatoes that had fallen out of the sack as they were throwing it over.

One thief said, 'I tell you what. You take these two, and I'll go and get the two behind that wall.'

Who shot off home first and who was the fastest?

Mr Miller, or black Bob?

I doubt if anyone will ever find out but they both ran from that place as fast as their legs could carry them!

THE FAITHFUL TRIO

In the old, ancient days the world belonged to the animals.

Bison grazed in the prairie without a care in the world; wild ducks and swans bathed undisturbed in the lakes. There was no one to shatter the peace.

When work was done, the animals would sing, each in his own way.

Evening after evening they met in a large log cabin.

Right in the centre stood an oak column supporting the roof, so it would not tumble down during windy nights.

> *I like to dance, I dance in swamps*
> *The moss under my paws rocks and jumps,*

sang the bear, twirling round so fast, that the walls of the cabin rattled.

The reindeer, too, was singing away:

> *I dance in the hills on slopes snowy and steep*
> *All night till first light, then I fall asleep.*

The stag was next to be heard:

> *I love to dance in the woodland thicket*
> *And look out for the wolf who is wicked.*

The hare stamped his feet and gave a tune:

> *Dance, oak column, move, don't stand still,*
> *I'll complain to the fire, that I will.*

And that naughty hare shot an arrow from his bow right into the oak column, till the shot echoed.

The column shook and wavered.

The roof trembled and sighed and all the animals ran for their lives into the prairie, afraid of being buried under the roof.

Only the little mouse, the rat and the fly were not afraid and went on singing.

Ever since then in a man's dwelling they choose to stay. No one invites them in—man chases them away. But the house wants to repay them for not running away when it was in trouble, and so to this day, the house protects the fly, the rat and the little mouse.

THE SKUNK AND THE FROGS

The skunk by the muddy brook had grown old and frail, and he waited on the banks of the brook for frogs in vain. They always ran away from him and laughed at him from the water.

> 'Gunk, gunk, gunk,
> You can't catch us, you silly old skunk!'

A hare was running by and he enquired, 'Why are you so sad, brother skunk?'

'How can I be anything else but sad,' sighed the skunk, 'I have grown so weak with hunger that I can't even catch a frog for my supper!'

'Do you know, I'll give you some good advice,' the hare offered. 'Scrape out a hollow near the brook and lie down in it. You'll dine like a king!'

The skunk couldn't believe that he could have a good supper so easily, but as he was desperate, he dug a hollow and lay in it.

'Come and have a look, that ugly skunk is lying in a hole, and he isn't even moving!' croaked a young frog. 'I think he is dead!'

All the frogs jumped into the hollow to see the skunk and were overjoyed that he had breathed his very last breath.

'Try to jump out of the hollow again,' advised the hare.

The frogs jumped out, one after the other, so the hare said to them. 'That hole is too shallow. It is possible the skunk isn't quite dead. He could crawl from the hollow and gobble you all up. You should dig up more soil from underneath him.'

The frogs were full of praise how well the hare had advised them. They jumped back into the hollow and started to scoop out the earth.

'Try to jump out of the hole again to see if it is deep enough!' said the hare.

The frogs jumped out once more and the hare advised, 'You have to dig deeper still under the skunk, to make quite sure he couldn't jump out, if he did happen to come to life!'

The frogs jumped back into the hollow once again and set to work.

'Try to jump out now,' called the hare.

The frogs tried to jump out of the hollow in vain. It was now quite deep.

'Brother skunk,' hooted the hare, 'your supper is right under your nose!'

Then the skunk opened his eyes and gobbled up all the frogs.

THE GOLDEN RAIN

The farmer's wife gave birth to twin girls.

You could no more tell them apart than a pair of daisies.

But as they grew, a few people noticed that one little girl's cheeks were fresh and pink, whereas the other was always grubby and sticky, like a dirty old frying pan.

The little girl with the silky cheeks helped her mother with the cooking and the housework and, while she worked, she sang all day.

Her grubby little sister, however, dozed the days through on a bench by the stove. She did not know how to do anything and she got no pleasure out of anything, and she could not sing.

But what was the use of the nice little girl working so hard and always pleasing others, when her mother loved only that ragamuffin! She spoiled her lazy daughter awfully. She sewed one new dress after another and bought her oranges and goodies in town.

The good daughter was never given anything by her mother, except perhaps a kick in the back. If, for instance, she could rise at midnight and turn the whole farm into a crystal palace by morning, it would still mean nothing to her mother.

One day, the mother chased her daughter out of the farm.

'Here is a spinning-wheel. By this evening you must spin all this flax! And don't dare return home till you've finished.'

The girl settled down under an apple tree and set to work. A pile of flax lay before her.

The spinning-wheel span and the girl sang:

> *I spin silky flax on my loom*
> *Scented and soft like spring bloom.*
> *I weave linen as white as a lily*
> *For shirts and skirts, plain and frilly.*

The girl worked in such haste that she suddenly pricked her finger and it bled.

She leant over the well to cleanse her wound.

But the earth round the well was soggy with water and the girl slipped and toppled over the side.

She fell deep down into the well, her eyes closed in terror.

When, at last, she dared open them, the maiden saw that she was standing on a wide green meadow strewn with colourful flowers. A skylark fluttered above, singing away merrily; bumble-bees buzzed round flower petals; grass-hoppers creaked persistently in the grass.

The girl picked some of the flowers and sat down by a brook under a bent willow tree to weave a garland.

With the colourful crown adorning her head she walked on across the meadow like a young queen.

Soon, she came to a blackened stove in which a fire roared and a loaf of bread was smoking in the oven.

'Dear maiden,' begged the loaf, 'please be kind enough to take me out of this oven, otherwise my skin will burn to a cinder for ever with this terrible heat!'

The girl found a wooden spade and shovelled the well-baked loaf out of the oven, placing it on a burdock leaf in the grass to cool.

'Thank you, dear maiden,' said the loaf. 'Break off a lump of me and put it in your pocket. When you are hungry, then I will give you strength!'

With the lump of bread in her pocket, the girl thanked the loaf and walked on till she came to an old nut tree. It was laden with so many nuts that its branches were bent right down to the ground with the weight.

The nut tree rustled its leaves and spoke.

'My dear maiden, could you please shake me a little? I just don't know how much longer I can bear this weight. If a strong wind sprang up, my branches would surely break!'

The girl shook the tree till nuts were rolling in all directions.

'Thank you for your help!' the nut tree sighed with relief, 'and now please take as many nuts as you want for your journey.'

The girl picked a handful and walked on through the scented meadow.

She came to a cottage and, inside, an old shrivelled woman sat by a cold stove.

'Dear maiden, could you perhaps light me a fire and cook me a cup of hot soup?'

Straightaway the girl chopped some wood in the shed, made a fire and placed a pan of water for the soup on the stove.

When they had eaten, the girl washed the dishes and put the old woman to bed.

'I shall stay with you, old lady, for you have no one to look after you. I will cook and clean for you,' the girl offered and the old woman was happy that she would no longer be alone in her cottage.

The girl cooked and washed, wove flax and sewed, grew vegetables and cared for the trees.

The cottage suddenly came to life.

But a year passed and the girl started to be homesick. Though she never heard a kind word from her mother or her sister, she still was pining to go back home.

She confided in the old lady, who nodded her head.

'Home is home, and even if they fed you there only with buns made of ash, everyone still hurries home. I shall be unhappy to lose

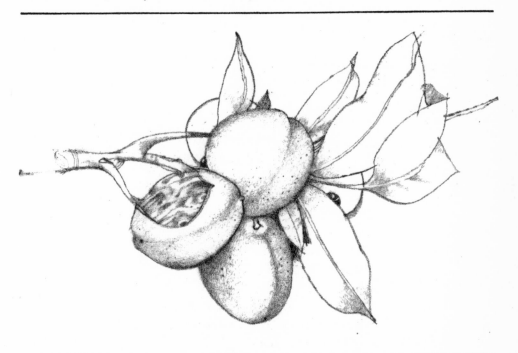

you, for I know you, too, liked it here. Tell me though, before you go, how I can reward you for your faithful service.'

'What an idea, dear lady,' exclaimed the girl with a wave of the hand. 'You don't owe me anything. I want no reward from you!'

'In that case,' said the old woman with a smile, 'I will show my thanks in a different way.'

She waved her hand, and immediately gold rain began to fall from the ceiling. And it rained till the maiden was covered in gold all over.

Thanking the old lady, she bade her goodbye and walked back

through the green meadow towards home. When she arrived, her mother and sister were eager to know where she had acquired so much gold.

When she had told them everything, the mother ordered the grubby daughter, 'Now, you are going to take the spinning-wheel to the well and spin some flax. When you prick your finger, you must lean over the well and fall in like your sister did.'

After much yawning, the grubby daughter rose from her bed, took the spinning-wheel and carried it to the well.

The spinning-wheel started to sing:

> *I spin flax on my loom*
> *Hard and black like dark day's gloom.*
> *Dirt and mud only you will hold,*
> *In the well you will never find gold.*

The grubby girl had never worked the spinning-wheel before. She had no idea how to spin, so she did not even know how to prick her finger.

But she wanted the gold so badly that she jumped into the well and fell and fell into the great depth. At last she hit the wide green meadow filled with flowers and bird song.

The grubby girl started to walk across the huge meadow, on and on, till she came to the red-hot stove.

'Please take me out of the oven, please,' begged the loaf of bread, 'or surely I will be burnt to a cinder with the heat!'

'No one will miss you,' laughed the grubby girl, 'and, anyway, I only eat cakes and buns, I don't care for bread. Burn to a cinder, by all means!'

Turning her back on the bread she carried on through the green meadow, until she came to the old nut tree.

The branches with the weight of the fruit were bent right down to the ground.

'Shake me please!' begged the nut tree, 'otherwise all my branches will snap.'

'Who wants your nuts,' sneered the girl. 'My mother peels all the nuts for me herself, and I don't intend to dirty my fingers for you.

With that she turned her back on the tree and walked on.

When she had crossed the meadow, she came to the cottage.

The old lady was sitting inside by the cold stove and begged the girl, 'Could you possibly light the stove and cook me a pan of soup? I feel so weak from my illness.'

'Cook your own soup!' snapped the girl. 'I only eat meat and

besides, I am not cold. So I don't know why I should light your stove!
But if you pay me well, I will put you to bed, where you would soon
get warm, fall asleep and forget your hunger.'

'For such good service I should like to pay you in advance,' said
the old lady.

She waved her hand and dirty rain started to fall from the ceiling in a steady downpour.

Thick, muddy drops settled on the girl's cheeks, neck and hands,
and before long she was completely encased in a shell made of mud.

When the dirty girl returned home, her mother could not even
recognize her.

She heated a kettle of water on the fire and scrubbed and
scrubbed her daughter all night long. But she scrubbed in vain.

The muddy shell stuck to the girl's skin so firmly, that she could
never ever wash it off.

WHEN THEY GAVE OUT WISDOM, HARRY QUEUED UP TWICE

Harry Thompson was looking around for some well-paid, but easy job, but could find nothing suitable.

Either the pay was too low, or the work was too hard.

As he wandered from east to west with a slow vagrant step, he entered the state of Colorado. That is where they mine for silver and many other precious metals.

Harry found a flooded mine and went to its owner with the offer to pump the water out of it. When they both signed a written agreement, Harry took a pump and started to work.

He pumped for an hour, he pumped for two, then three, but the level of the water did not move.

Harry sat on a large stone and thought hard how to ease the hard work. At this rate he would still be at it in three months' time! The flooded mine contained far more water than he had thought. The owner had outsmarted him for sure!

Harry went on sitting in the shade of a tree, thinking hard.

Then he noticed a dead dog lying under a bush.

That is when he had an idea.

He jumped up and set to work.

First he attached a big stone to the dog's neck with a wire, and threw the dog and the stone down into the flooded mine. Next he pulled his old hat from his bag and down it went, too, after the dog. Lastly, he tossed a tatty coat given to him by a farmer on his travels, in the grass.

The hat was floating on the surface, as Harry Thompson rushed to the town to see the sheriff.

'I want to bring something to your notice,' he announced in the sheriff's office. 'I was sauntering past a flooded mine up yonder out of town. I happened to glance at that deep pool and there, down below . . .'

He stopped, his teeth started to chatter, and he began to sigh and to stutter, unable to utter a single word.

The sheriff rose from his chair and tried to pacify Harry.

'Now, my friend, keep calm, we'll get to the bottom of whatever it is. Just tell me everything from the beginning!'

Harry Thompson wiped his eyes, blew his nose and explained.

'Forgive me, sheriff, but it was such an awful sight, I haven't quite come to.'

'Now keep cool, have a drink, and tell me what you saw in the water!'

Harry took a drink from the sheriff and stammered, 'I have a feeling ... sheriff, that down there ... in that pool ... you'll find ... a corpse!'

At once the sheriff was on his feet, dashing into the next room, firing instructions.

'Mark, you're to go to that flooded mine and have a good scout round. It seems likely someone has fallen in and drowned.'

Deputy Mark was soon back, announcing that everything in the flooded mine certainly did not seem in order. A hat was floating on the water, and an old coat lay in the grass.

Sheriff sent his men to the mine, equipped with hoses borrowed from the Fire Department.

This was Harry's cue to disappear, and he did just that.

What use would he be anyway!

Let the experts get on with the job!

The men pumped and pumped till sweat poured off their brows. Four fire-fighting hoses are something to be reckoned with, and the sheriff's men were strong—all muscle and bone. When they had drained the water, they came upon the dog tied to the stone.

They cursed and swore and glared and got sore, and were itching to lay their hands on Harry.

Harry Thompson, hidden by a bush, was observing the commotion from a distance, hardly daring to breathe.

As if he would come out at that precise moment!

When the sheriff's men with the hoses were gone at last, Harry came out of hiding, brushed the dust off his trousers and headed for the owner of the mine.

He whistled as he walked, happy with the completed task.

He knocked on the door, entered and said. 'Finished, boss! I've done the job two months in advance. I am, therefore, entitled to extra pay.'

He got it too! He stuffed the dollars inside his pocket and went to have a hair-cut.

PISTOLEER MIKE FINK

Mike Fink, famous as a mariner and even more as a crack-shot, was sailing down the river with a cargo of salt.

'Captain,' his deck-hand announced one day, 'we've come to the end of our meat. What shall I cook for dinner?'

'Wait a moment,' Fink retorted, 'I'll think of something.'

In a pasture by the river a large herd of sheep were grazing, guarded only by a sheep dog. Mike steered the boat towards the shore.

He opened a wooden crate, took out a snuff-box and put it in his pocket. Then he climbed ashore, tossed a slice of bread to the dog to stop him barking and turned towards the sheep.

Mike caught five and rubbed their noses with the snuff.

He called out to the deck-hand to run to the nearby farm and to tell the farmer to hurry to the river.

'Tell him,' he shouted after the deck-hand, 'that if he doesn't come immediately, all his sheep are likely to snuff it.'

A moment later the deck-hand was back, the chubby farmer puffing behind him.

'Fine kettle of fish this is,' remarked Mike, pointing to the herd. The five sheep were all sniffing and sneezing, their eyes all streaming, wiping their noses on the grass and staggering about like drunks.

'Well I never,' muttered the dumb-founded farmer, 'there was nothing wrong with them this morning. What's happened to them?'

'D'you mean to say you don't know? And you call yourself a farmer?' asked the horrified Mike. 'Haven't you ever heard of cattle plague?'

The farmer was terrified.

'You really think my sheep have got this cattle plague?'

'I don't think it, I know it. You can, after all, recognize this disease at first glance. Pastures high up by the river have all been cursed with this ghastly plague; whole herds of sheep and cows are flat on their backs, feet up in the prairie. Two farmers have gone quite mad from it all.'

The farmer stuttered.

'Is there any medicine for this disease?'

Mike Fink sighed deeply.

'There's only one cure for cattle plague. Shoot the infected sheep, so the rest of the herd won't catch it, too.'

'But how can one man separate the few sick sheep from a herd of this size and then shoot them?'

'There's only one man in the district capable of such a thing and that is I, Mike Fink.'

The farmer breathed a sigh of relief.

'Now that's a different story. I'll say no more. Mike Fink is here, so I am afraid of nothing. Will you be good enough then to help me shoot and bury these infected sheep?'

Mike Fink now dilly dallied. He well knew why.

'I really don't know, farmer sir ... Wouldn't it be better to talk it over with other farmers from round abouts? I may be wrong. And then, what if a jackal digs out the sheep after we bury them? The infection would wipe out the whole herd.'

So the farmer tried to persuade Fink to throw the sheep after shooting them into the river.

'Oh no, not that!' Fink protested. 'To me, water is holy. And the river doubly so. And anyway, water would carry this disease and by the end of the week you'd have the whole area full of the plague.'

'What if you were to take those sheep on your boat and bury them somewhere in the wilderness, where there are no other sheep?' the farmer suggested to Fink.

'That might be possible ... I am saying might,' Fink pondered aloud, 'but well, you know, you can't expect me to do it for nothing.'

'I wouldn't expect you to,' said the delighted farmer. 'I'll give you a barrel of peach brandy if you help me out of this mess.'

Mike Fink nodded graciously and took his six-shot pistol from its case.

That same evening the deck-hand was cooking lamb chops and pouring the potent peach brandy into glasses.

And the moon was winking impishly on Mike Fink — the renowned mariner and even more renowned crack-shot from up the river.

THE UNWELCOME NEIGHBOUR

Two brothers lived on the banks of a deep wide river. They hunted animals and caught fish and deep forests sparkled green far and wide round the river — forests in which no human foot had ever trod.

The brothers loved peace and solitude.

Whenever they heard the squeak of a wagon pass by their cabin and the passers-by asked how life was treating the two brothers, they would sigh craftily,

'A terrible region this is! One year it does nothing but rain, the next year there's an awful drought, the mosquitoes torment us day and night, the bears devour all the food we've stored — what a frightful life we lead! You'd better go on further to the west, they say it's real paradise there!'

The immigrants whipped their oxen and drove on, thanking the brothers for their impartial advice.

One evening at dusk a stranger stopped by the cabin, on a dappled horse. He dismounted and went straight inside. He made himself comfortable by the hearth, as if it was his home.

'I want to settle right next door. Then at least you won't be lonely. The soil is excellent here, perfect for farming.'

The brothers tried to talk him out of it, telling him, in vain, all the unfavourable weather conditions and the difficulties of living by the river.

'I have made my decision, this is where I'll settle,' said the stranger firmly. 'We'll be neighbours, that is why I've come to make your acquaintance.'

When the two brothers saw they could not move that pig-headed fellow, they winked at one another and made a plan.

'I am sure you will not refuse if we invite you to supper,' the eldest asked the stranger in a honey-sweet voice.

'I'd be glad to sup with you, I'd hate to offend you!'

A moment later the younger brother was carrying dishes to the table.

He sprinkled a thick layer of yellow powder on a venison steak and beckoned his guest to eat.

The stranger cut off a sizeable chunk of the meat—for he was very hungry—placed it in his mouth and immediately spat it back on to the plate.

'Brr, how bitter this is! What on earth have you put on that steak?'

'It's a powder against fever,' the younger brother explained, while the elder one added, 'It is pretty bad with the food here. Strange illnesses rage round this river and we have to sprinkle this anti-fever

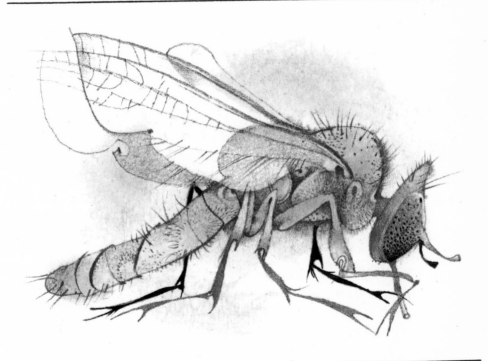

powder on all our food, otherwise we would have died long before now.'

So the stranger made do with dry bread, leaving the meat on the table, and then prepared to depart.

'Where would you go at this time of night!' the brothers protested. 'The alligator would pounce on you from the river and there'd be nought left of you by morning but bones! You see, we live in the wilds here, the river and the forest don't treat anyone too kindly.'

The stranger reluctantly had to agree.

The younger brother prepared a bed of fur skins right by the hearth. He put thick logs on the fire, and threw an armful of bearskins on the guest, then wound thick rope round the unfortunate man and tied the whole furry packet to a post.

'I'll surely choke to death,' wailed the guest. 'Why have you smothered me so? And why the rope?'

The eldest brother explained. 'Packs of bears roam all over the forests here. At night they crawl into our cabin through the chimney, so we have to defend ourselves. We wrap ourselves well in bearskins. If a bear crawls through the chimney into the cabin, he looks round, sniffs at everything thoroughly, looking for human flesh. He approaches the bearskin, and says to himself, ah, some faster relative of mine has been here before me, I'll have to look for human flesh in another cabin. And he wobbles away. But some of the furry creatures are real foxy and won't be tricked even with a real bearskin. So to be quite safe, we tie ourselves to the pole for the night. Just think, the bear grabs the sleeping man wrapped in bearskin and tries to carry him off into the forest. But the rope grows taut, the bear gets a fright and runs off empty-handed.'

'Oh, this is terrible!' moaned the guest, half fried with the heat. 'I like to sleep in a cool room under a light blanket. If I live to see daylight, I'll never be afraid of anything else again.'

'If you enjoy the cool of night, you're not likely to get much sleep here by the river,' said the brothers, nodding their heads. With that they bade their guest goodnight and slyly opened an outside window.

Straightaway a cloud of biting mosquitoes descended on the stranger.

Next morning, the stranger, tired from lack of sleep and swollen with mosquito bites, was preparing to move on.

'As you are here,' said the elder brother, 'we shall take you into the forest on a deer hunt, so you would see everything the river and the forest have to offer.'

The stranger agreed and rushed outside.

'Wait a moment!' cried the younger brother, 'we can't do things in such a hurry here!'

With that he brought the stove pipe outside.

'What's that for?' asked the bewildered guest. 'Do you mean to say you go hunting in a stove pipe? Why, in a thing like that you can't even bend your knees!'

'What else is there to do, stranger,' said the elder brother. 'Round this river there are rattlesnakes everywhere. Such a scoundrel lies in wait in the tall grass, then hop! he bites into your leg. An hour later you're out of this world. That is why we prefer to go hunting or fishing inside a stove pipe.'

The stranger tore the pipe from his legs, jumped on his horse and rode off at a gallop.

'Rather than live in this hell,' he shouted instead of saying goodbye, 'I prefer to look for another spot further up the river!'

The brothers smiled at one another.

They would stay alone in the wilderness, their only neighbour would be the peaceful, silent forest and the murmuring, lapping river.

FIRE

In ancient times the bear was the master of the world. Fire, too, was owned by the bear. Nobody else knew how to light a fire and how to keep it alive, so it would not go out. The bear was the only one.

In the forest thicket raspberries were ripening and the bear went to pick them. He zig-zagged through the bushes, picking whole handfuls, swallowing greedily the dark, scarlet fruit; he just could not satisfy his appetite.

He went further and further away from the fire, forgetting that he should add wood to it, so it would not die.

'Feed me, feed me,' the fire cried. 'I am hungry!'

But the bear was far away in the forest, picking raspberries and did not hear the call of the fire.

'Feed me. I have great hunger. I will die,' whispered the fire and life was slowly ebbing away from him. Only burning cinders were left now.

A man walked by and heard its moaning. 'Give me food, I am dying of hunger.' The man quickly tore a handful of dry grass from the earth and placed it upon the hot cinders. When the grass caught light, he broke off some dry pine twigs and on top of those he placed larger branches.

One of the branches faced the north, and the fire started to burn towards the northern side. The other branch faced the west, and the fire began to burn in the west. Soon it was crackling away in the east and south too.

The fire was now sparkling merrily and the man could warm himself, for he had saved the fire from death.

In the evening the bear returned from the forest, his belly like a drum, and he rushed to the fire.

But the fire turned away from the bear. 'I do not need you any more, no longer am I your friend. You left me to die of hunger. You thought only about yourself and your stomach.'

With that his flame shot out so high and so fiercely that the bear was afraid to come near the fire and had to run away into the thick forest. The bear never returned again to the fire. Since that time the bear fears the fire. Since that time the fire belongs to man.

THE SNAKE WITH AN EAR FOR MUSIC

There was an exceptional drought in Texas that summer. Springs dried up, rivers changed into little brooks, grass in the pastures turned yellow and, in the fields, shrivelled ears of corn hung limply.

A wealthy rancher by the name of Jess Bradford drove all through this region, buying up land from the ill-fated farmers like a greedy vulture. All he offered for a large field was a sack of flour. The farmers sighed, wriggled and objected, but sold in the end. They had to, for they were afraid that in a week's time that grabbing rogue would offer them no more than a bag of beans for their land.

Early one evening Jess Bradford called on farmer Jerry.

Old Jerry had a little farm, three cows in the cow-shed, a skinny mule and fifteen chickens.

And a mouth-organ.

Jerry was sitting on his verandah, his breath stroking the gleaming instrument, while song followed song like maidens walking in a row.

Jess Bradford jumped off his horse, touched his wide rimmed hat in greeting and drawled,

'Shall we strike a bargain, old chap?'

Jerry went on playing his mouth-organ, and said not a word.

Jess Bradford thought the old man must be hard of hearing, so he shouted. 'I'll buy that land of yours down by the river!'

Jerry shook his head and played on, saying not a word.

Jess shuffled right up to the verandah and, his voice low, started on the farmer, nagging, persuading, offering a higher price, then threatening.

But old Jerry did not say yes and did not say no, but said not a word and played on.

Jess Bradford, exhausted with all that hard persuading, dismissed the matter with a wave of the hand and jumped on his horse.

'Just you wait,' he sneered. 'Tomorrow you'll play quite a different tune! But when you beg me to buy your pastures, I shan't give you even a sack of maize in exchange!'

The next day, when the neighbours passed Jerry's farm, they shook their heads in disbelief.

'Have you gone quite mad, old chap? This drought will chase you out just as it did us, and you could have had a few solid dollars in your pocket. Now you'll leave here with one pocket empty and the other emptied!'

But Jerry only laughed.

'This drought can't last for ever. When it rains, it also has to stop. It won't be any different with a drought!'

The farmers left Jerry alone, and went to pack their few odds and ends.

So Jerry remained in the valley.

Mice and lizards moved into the empty farms.

One afternoon — one could hardly breathe with the heat — old Jerry sat on his verandah, concentrating on his mouth-organ.

He began with the waltz 'Beautiful Ohio', then followed it with the song 'Turkey in the Grass'. One after the other the songs poured out of the mouth-organ, one nicer than the other. He played the lot, everything he knew, ending the afternoon concert with the ever popular tune 'When the Saints Go Marching In'.

Old Jerry was so preoccupied with the music, that he forgot all about the heat, about hunger and his hardships. He played and played. While everything around was still, the trembling melody rose high to the burning Texas sun, slanting to the west.

Just then, Jerry's eyes slid to the toes of his shoes, as if something was drawing him towards them and, he very nearly swallowed his mouth-organ with fright. An enormous brown rattlesnake had settled comfortably on his knees!

Just one move, and the snake would pierce his body with its poisonous teeth, and that would be the end!

There was nothing else for it, he had to play on.

So the old chap puffed and blew with all his might into the mouth-organ, playing one song after the other and, when he played them all, he started at the beginning again, and again, and again.

The rattlesnake nodded his flattened head with pleasure, accompanying the mouth-organ with the light rattling of the tip of his tail, held completely spell-bound by the music.

It was quite obvious that the song 'When the Saints Go Marching In' was his favourite. When he heard it, he held his head real high, practically licking the mouth-organ with his tongue, smacking his lips with satisfaction, rocking from side to side, his eyes gleaming.

Old Jerry was gasping for breath, yet he did not dare to stop. His shirt was wringing wet with sweat, but he played on and on, while the rattlesnake listened in a trance.

All at once, Jerry had enough. Everyone knew him for the stubborn, obstinate fellow that he was. If something did not tickle his fancy, come what may, say what you will, he could be as immovable as a rock.

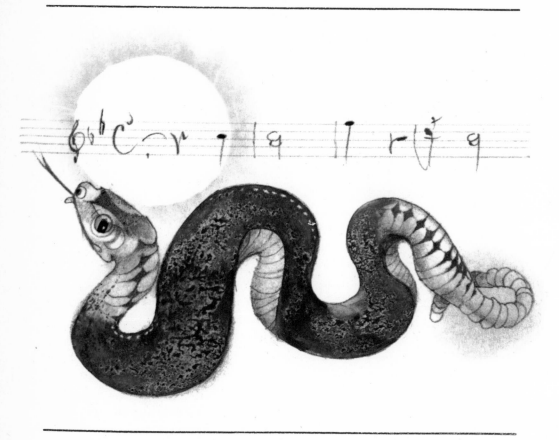

He stopped playing and said, 'I can't go on. If you want to bite me, you poisonous viper, then hurry up, so my suffering is behind me!'

But instead, the rattlesnake slithered slowly and peacefully from the man's lap on to the floor, where he rattled his tail, as if to say thanks for the entertainment. Then he slithered away into the bushes by the brook.

After that, Jerry held a concert each day on his verandah with the long brown rattlesnake as his audience.

84

Old Jerry grew used to the snake and called him Apostle, for the rattlesnake had been completely bowled over by the song 'When the Saints Go Marching In'.

The moment he heard it, Apostle's body would start to sway from side to side, as if he were dancing. He would hum to himself and rattle his tail, in fact he was in seventh heaven.

One afternoon, Apostle did not come.

Jerry waited and waited, telling himself that the rattlesnake must have been delayed somewhere.

But he waited in vain.

That day, and the next.

Jerry put his mouth-organ away and played it no more. It seemed to him he could not play without his faithful listener.

In the meantime, the scorching heat had worn itself out. One morning, little grey marks appeared in the sky, they climbed from the horizon and spread, forming thick dark clouds. By lunchtime rain was falling solidly, humming in the parched fields.

It poured non-stop, for two days and two nights. The river bed was filled with water, the brook by old Jerry's farm gurgled and sang merrily once more and the bright green returned to the pastures.

Jess Bradford reappeared, this time as meek as a lamb. No longer was he after Jerry's land. He knew he had lost.

He came with a request.

There was no fresh grass for his heifers on his ranch and, before driving them to the market in town, he needed to fatten them up a bit by letting them graze on good grass.

What if old Jerry were to lease him the pastures by the river, say for a week, or ten days!

'Now that's another matter,' nodded Jerry. 'Sell I would not but, if you want to rent the land, we can come to an agreement, so long as you don't strangle the dollars in your pocket!'

He pulled an old cart out of the shed, harnessed the mule and drove off with Jess Bradford to the river.

As the cart rattled over the field track, they passed a little hill and old Jerry suddenly heard strange sounds.

They seemed vaguely familiar.

They climbed off the cart and walked up the hill to see what was happening.

When they came to the very top, there on a flat rock sat thirty-three brown striped rattlesnakes.

They were nodding their heads, rattling their tails, unseeing, unhearing.

And over them, erect to his full glory, stood Apostle, just like an orchestra conductor.

There he was, conducting this large, rattlesnake band, humming quietly, but quite distinctly his favourite song 'When the Saints Go Marching In'.

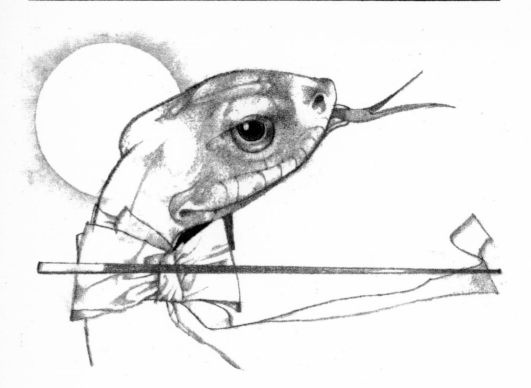

THE GOLDEN COMB

Once upon a time there was an old miller who was unlucky in everything. When there was a rich harvest and all his customers drove up with a full load of grain on their carts, there was so little water flowing in the brook, that the wheel of the mill stopped. So the miller's customers whipped their horses and rode on to the second mill further down the river. When the miller happened to have plenty of water in the brook, the harvest was poor and there was a shortage of grain. So there was no work again.

This went on and on and the poor miller had to come to terms with his humdrum, grim existence.

One early evening, he strolled to the dike in the brook, puffing away on his pipe and wondering where to find cash to repair his shingle roof.

Suddenly a golden-haired girl rose from the water and asked sweetly. 'Why are you so sad, miller? What is making you unhappy?'

'Sad or not,' said the miller, 'you can't help me with my worries.'

'Who is to know, miller,' answered the golden-haired girl, 'maybe I could help. If you promise me that I can have whatever is born in your mill first, everything in your home will change and, instead of bad luck, good fortune will move into your mill.'

The miller could not but smile at such a ridiculous offer. What could be born at the mill? Only some pups to his black and white bitch. The golden-haired maiden could have one by all means if that was what she wanted. At least the miller would not have to drown them all.

'Very well,' he said with a shrug, 'you can have the first thing which is born in our mill.'

'If you don't keep your word,' warned the golden-haired girl, 'things will go badly for you.'

With that she plunged into the deep pool and the miller slowly turned for home.

Under the linden tree in the yard an old man was sitting, drawing on his pipe.

'That bitch of yours was not meant to see her pups,' the old man said.

The miller was surprised. 'What are you talking about? What's happened to her?'

'Even I can't explain it to myself. She ran to the brook to have a drink and fell right under the wheel of the mill and did not surface again.'

The miller did not answer and went inside. His wife was watering the plants on the window and her face shone with happiness.

'How is it that you are all smiles today?' asked the miller.

'Why shouldn't I be all smiles,' explained the wife, turning to her husband from the window. 'For nine whole years we vainly hoped for a baby, and just imagine, now our hopes really will come true. The blacksmith's wife stopped by a while ago and she foretold that before a year is out, we shall have a son.'

From that day on everything went well for the miller. There was enough water in the brook all the year round, the fields were golden with wheat and rye, and, after the harvest, farmers from the whole area drove to the mill, their wagons creaking under the weight of sacks packed with good hard grain. The wheel turned from morn till night and cash flowed into the miller's pockets.

In the spring the miller's wife gave birth to a lovely boy.

But the miller walked about the mill looking very grim, nothing seemed to please him.

'Aren't you pleased at all?' asked his baffled wife. 'We've waited so long for our wishes to be answered, and now all you do is mope!'

'I have worries,' the miller would say snappily. But he did not tell his wife about the golden-haired girl, or about the promise he gave her. Why should she have to worry too.

The little boy grew into a handsome youth.

Wherever the miller went, he always saw in his mind the golden-haired maiden, how she appeared from the water, and he was very much afraid for his son.

'It is better if you don't go near the brook,' he warned the boy, telling him, 'In the forest the strawberries are already ripening, go and have a look in the clearing!'

The boy was perfectly at home in the forest. All day long he worked his way through the thicket between old pine trees, sunning himself in the clearing, picking raspberries and strawberries, not really wanting to return home even at night.

When he was fully grown, the miller gave him a gun for his birthday and the lad used to hunt the squirrels. He loved the forest; water did not tempt him at all.

'I've arranged it very well,' the miller rubbed his hands with satisfaction. 'The golden-haired maiden will wait in vain for my son!'

One day, when he was roaming in the forest, the miller's son met a pretty girl returning from the pasture with a basket filled with grass.

'Wait a minute, I'll help you with that heavy load,' the young man offered.

Before they reached the gamekeeper's cottage, the youth had fallen in love with the girl.

And before the miller had ground all the corn from the new harvest in his mill, his son and the daughter of the gamekeeper were married.

Autumn was coming to an end, the leaves on the trees started to turn colour, the deer were calling in the forests.

The miller's son was lying in wait in the pasture. Once he shot at a majestic stag but the stag reared and ran into the bushes. The hunter went in hot pursuit after him. He tore his way through the birch bushes, till he came to the forest brook.

On the bank lay the stag he shot at, the green moss round it turning blood-red. The hunter bent over his kill.

At that very moment, the golden-haired maiden rose out of the water, caught the youth's hand and dragged him into the deep.

His wife was waiting impatiently at home. Again and again she ran along the path, gazing towards the forest. The hunter was not to be seen. It was growing dark, but there was no sound or sight of her husband.

The young woman could hardly bear to wait till morning.

The moment dawn broke, she dressed and set out into the forest

to look for her husband.

She came to the shot stag and looked all round her, but there was no sign of him.

Under an old willow by the brook sat an aged woman.

'Are you looking for your husband, young woman? Are you looking for the miller's son?'

'That I am, old lady,' the wife nodded.

'I will help you then,' the old woman said. 'Take this golden comb. When it is full moon, sit in the dark by the mill's dike and comb the water with it.'

When the moon ripened to its full glory, the young woman walked to the dike, bent towards the water's surface and started to comb it.

The calm surface kissed by the silvery moonlight suddenly started to ripple and the head of the miller's son rose above the water.

He smiled at his wife and in silence disappeared back into the deep of the brook.

Not long afterwards the young woman met again the aged woman on her way through the forest.

'I know what is making you unhappy, dear girl,' the old lady said kindly. 'Take this golden harp. Sit by the brook when there will be a full moon and play on this harp.'

With these words the old woman disappeared into the thicket.

The young woman waited for a full moon.

That evening she took the golden harp and went to the brook.

She placed her fingers on the strings and the air was filled with gentle, beckoning sounds, just as if a bee was buzzing amid the flowers.

The miller's son rose from the pool, the water round him subsided further and further, till it came only up to his chest.

He smiled at his wife, beckoned her with his hand and, at that moment, the water closed over him again.

Only moonlight was trembling upon the water's surface.

The young wife met the old lady for the third time in a forest.

'I have been expecting you, dear girl,' the aged woman said. Here is a golden spinning-wheel. When the full moon is shining bright, sit with it by the brook and spin!'

With that the old woman disappeared, just as the shadow of a sparrow-hawk in flight flashes in the forest dusk.

The young wife waited till the moon was ripe.

Then she took the golden spinning-wheel and went to the pool's dike and there on the bank she started to spin.

When the little wheel had turned and purred once, the miller's son rose from the water.

The surface of the water surrounding him sank lower and lower, and soon the water reached only his ankles.

'Give me your hand,' his wife encouraged him, leaning towards him from the shore.

As soon as she touched his hand, the weir in the pasture above roared and the water cascaded over it like a herd of startled horses.

The water quickly rose again and a moment later the miller's son was completely submerged in the pool.

But the brook's surface rose higher and higher, the water burst over the banks and spilled over the meadows, strong winds twirled above the mill and by morning the whole valley was under water.

All the people in the district turned into fish and frogs.

And the golden-haired girl took on the guise of an old ugly witch.

THE WAGER

Black Buck had very itchy fingers. Thieving fingers. He could steal even a nose from a sleeping man.

Buck's master was quite fed up with all his thieving antics. Week after week he lost at least one chicken from the hen house; year after year he was robbed of a fatted pig and, that's without mentioning all the eggs, melons and peaches which disappeared in great numbers behind the doors of Buck's cottage.

One day, when he happened to be in good humour, the master stopped his slave and asked,

'Tell me, Buck, can you explain to me how you manage to steal everything you come upon, without being caught?'

Buck laughed.

'It is quite simple, sir, really quite simple. If you like, we'll have a bet for a pig and a sack of maize, that this evening I'll steal your suit, even though you'll guard it well.'

'Done,' answered his master, 'you'll have your pig and sack of maize. But if you loose, you must promise me never to steal again.'

'That's a bet, master, that's a bet.'

That evening the master returned home and said to his wife,

'Take my best suit and put it on the chair. I am going to stick to it like glue all evening, so that our crafty fox Buck doesn't steal it.'

With that he told his wife about the wager.

The man sat at one side of the table, his wife on the other, guarding the suit, their eyes never leaving it for a moment.

When darkness fell, they heard a scraping of hooves and clanking of chains coming from the stables. The horses were snorting, as if someone was untying them.

'I bet that is Buck, that light-fingered sneak,' said the master. 'I am going to have a look to see what he is up to in the stables. You stay where you are, and guard my suit well.'

He opened the door and went to the stables.

Buck was not in the stables. He was waiting in the jasmine bush by the house. But earlier that evening he pushed a hedgehog into the stables. The horses were afraid of him and shuffled about uneasily.

As soon as the master left the house, Buck came out of the bush and crept to the open window. In a whisper he called his mistress, he knew well how to imitate his master's voice, so that only she would hear.

'Darling, I am so worried that scoundrel Buck will outwit you somehow. Hand me my suit through the window, I will guard it myself.'

The mistress had no other thought in her head but that it was her husband who stood under the window, so she took the suit off the chair and passed it through.

When later on the master returned from the stable and saw what had happened, he shook his head in astonishment and remarked,

'As Buck is such a foxy fellow, I will give him besides the pig and the sack of maize also his freedom. Otherwise, by the end of the year he will eat us out of the house!'

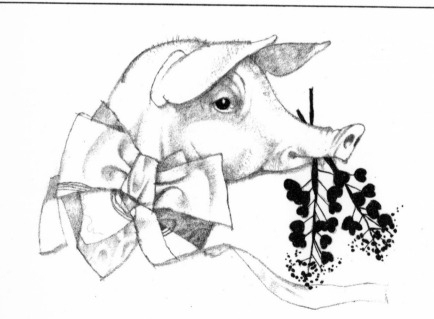

THE DEATH WALTZ

In those days the great plains belonged only to the Indians and to the bison. But from east to west immigrants were pushing in, taking over the soil, building cabins, burning out forests, sowing seed, planting fruit trees.

The Indians loathed to give up their native plains. The Apaches were one of the most warlike tribes. That is why the immigrants built a huge fort in a river basin. And in this fort, guarded by soldiers, the new settlers sought protection whenever the Indians with their painted faces raced over the prairie with their war cries.

In the fort, young officer Austin fell in love with beautiful Martha, the sister-in-law of the old captain, who was the commander of the fort.

He danced through many an evening with Martha, and often took her for a stroll behind the fort walls, where he picked bunches of yellow crocuses for her.

Martha was rather a frivolous girl. She loved to have a good time, and was mad about dancing. Austin watched her every step and was terribly jealous whenever she favoured another officer with a brighter smile than the one she had for him.

One day, a messenger galloped on horseback into the fort with the news that the Apaches had dug out the war axe and were attacking the settlers' dwellings.

The captain sounded the alarm. Lieutenant Austin was to lead the revenge attack against the Apaches.

While the soldiers were preparing for the strenuous march through the harsh land, the lieutenant went to bid Martha goodbye. He gave her a precious ring and asked for her hand. But Martha had no intention to marry soon, even so she promised Austin recklessly that she would marry him as early as possible.

'And if you were, by some misfortune, not to return from the expedition, I swear I will not marry anyone else.'

'I accept your promise,' said the lieutenant, bade her goodbye and drove off at the head of the column through the fort gates.

Martha followed outside and stood there, waving.

A fortnight later the regiment returned from the revengeful expedition. But lieutenant Austin was not riding at the head. The Apaches had captured him during the battle.

Martha did not mourn the young lieutenant for very long. Not even a month had passed before the word spread all over the fort, that the lovely fiancée of lieutenant Austin would wed another. She was to marry a merchant, who had stopped at the fort on his way to the west and had fallen in love with Martha.

The day of the wedding arrived.

The whole fort was abuzz with excitement since not often was a wedding held at a fort. The soldiers decorated the large officers' dining room with flowers for the evening ball.

When the wedding ceremony was over and the wedding guests had dined, dancing began.

Suddenly, just as the celebrations were at their height, the dining room door flew open and everyone felt a draft swirling round. The candles started to smoulder and die, one after the other. The spacious ballroom was now lit only by the moon.

Heart-rendering cries echoed through the building, but nobody could see who it was.

The wedding guests gazed in terror at the open door.

Framed by the door stood a man in a tattered uniform, his face deathly white, his right temple bloody from a fierce blow of an Indian axe, his eyes, under the scalped head, gaping wide and motionless.

The apparition looked over the ballroom and slowly made his way towards the newlyweds, who up till then had danced without a care in the world. Now they stood rooted to the ground with terror in the centre of the floor.

Then the dead man tore Martha from the bridegroom's arms and the musicians, as if under instructions, started to play an old waltz.

The strange pair began to dance in the ballroom, now filled with the blue moonlight from the night sky. Round, always round, round and round Martha danced with the apparition to the sound of the sad waltz, ceaselessly round and round. Blood was ebbing from her face, she grew pale and yellow, her chin sagged and her eyes ceased to move — life was slowly leaving her body.

The apparition stopped.

He lay the dead Martha on the floor, hesitated over her awhile, wringing his hands in his terrible bitter inconsolable sorrow, then like a shadow he slipped through the door.

Ghostly, ghastly cries filled the building once again, the doors closed of their own accord, the candles came to life.

All was as before, except for the dead bride who lay on the floor.

A few days later the soldiers brought back the corpse of lieutenant Austin. He had been found in a forest ravine. His temple had been cut open with an axe and his uniform was tattered and torn.

THE UGLY DOG

Miss Spring had an ugly dog. This dog was so very ugly, that Miss Spring could not even take him for a walk.

One fine spring day, however, she took him to the park where the children, other dogs and blackbirds, even a policeman, had such a fright at the sight of this monstrous creature, that soon there was not a soul to be seen. The chairman of the local Society for the Preservation of Beauty charged Miss Spring for disturbing the peace in the park.

Since that day Miss Spring loved her ugly dog all the more. She thought the world of him. 'My hideous darling,' she would say, fondling him, 'my divine ugly duckling, I wouldn't swop you for a curlless poodle, or for a six-legged greyhound!'

But what good was all that talk! The dog grew uglier day by day. He wasn't even allowed to stick his head out of the front door, for fear of frightening the postman to death!

One night, thieves broke into Miss Spring's house. They got in through the window in the hall, from where they wanted to steal an expensive fur coat. As they were about to climb out into the garden, coat and all, this monster of a dog tiptoed into the hall. The thieves were terrified.

'A gorilla!' their leader screamed. They threw the fur coat onto the floor and were off like a shot.

The dog did not even bark, but curled up happily on the precious fur coat and fell asleep.

In the morning Miss Spring praised her brave darling for saving the coat which once belonged to her grandmother, and she loved her pet even more fiercely.

'As you cannot go walkies with me in the day,' she consoled him, 'I will make up for it, my precious ugly love. From now on you shall sleep on my fur coat — the most expensive doggie-bed — and be the envy of every handsome hound!'

So the ugly dog lazed about on the expensive fur coat but Miss Spring never stopped wondering what she could do to make it possible for her ugly pet to reappear in the street.

One day, she noticed in a magazine the picture of a large ocean liner called the *Queen Mary*. Straightaway Miss Spring said, 'I will take my darling to England! They say that it is usually very foggy there. In thick fog no one will notice my pet in the park or in the street.

She bought a ticket for herself and for her ugly dog and soon they were sailing to England.

The moment Miss Spring and her ugly dog disembarked from the *Queen Mary*, one old man had such a shock when he saw the monstrous hound, that he passed right out with horror. Miss Spring wanted to help the man back to his feet and let go of the lead. Before the man came to, the dog was gone.

The man opened his eyes, but Miss Spring burst into tears.

She returned to America as sad as if she were going to a funeral.

When she was calmer, she placed an advertisement in all the newspapers:

'Lost, a large ugly dog. Large reward for finder.
All expenses paid!'

After that the door-bell on Miss Spring's front door never stopped ringing. People brought her all sorts of monsters, claiming they had found the lost dog, expecting a reward.

But Miss Spring only shook her head, wiping her red-rimmed eyes with her handkerchief at the same time.

Once some pupils brought their bearded teacher, bound with cord, and offered him to Miss Spring. 'We are sure Miss, that this is he. Everyone at school says that this is the most fearsome dog, who ever taught.'

But Miss Spring wouldn't accept the bearded teacher in place of her lost dog.

One day, a messenger brought her a telegram from England.

'Have found the ugliest dog in England — stop — send
fare for ticket — stop'

Miss Spring rushed to the bank at once and sent the finder money for the voyage. Next, she shook dust from the fur coat, so her little darling would lie in comfort at home and then, she cleaned out the whole house, so there would not be a speck of dust anywhere. And she baked an enormous chocolate cake, so she would honour her dearest pet with his favourite meal.

After that she waited impatiently, counting the days.

A fortnight later there was a ring at the door. 'That must be him,' Miss Spring cried out joyfully, running to open it.

She was so excited that she absentmindedly put her spectacles right in the chocolate cake.

She opened the door wide.

Outside stood a bearded gentleman. In one hand he held an English bowler hat, in the other a lead attached to a huge untidy dog with tangled fur.

Miss Spring looked at the dog but, as she did not have her glasses on, she had to turn her house upside down, before fishing them from the cake.

The gentleman was waiting impatiently by the door, the dog was defleaing himself and Miss Spring was putting on her spectacles.

She scrutinized the dog and sobbed in a broken voice.

'Oh, dear sir, my dog really was ugly. But even he was not as ugly as this!'

And she slammed the door.

But the bell was buzzing again.

Miss Spring's head reappeared. 'Haven't I made it clear, sir, that this is not my dog! What else are you waiting for?'

'For my reward, ma'am,' said the man with the bowler hat.

'What do you mean, your reward! For what? And incidentally, I am a miss, not a ma'am!'

The man with the bowler hat scratched his ear, sighed and said dejectedly, 'How am I supposed to get back to England, when I have no money for a ticket! But,' and at this point he looked shyly at Miss Spring, 'I have a suggestion to make. Would you take me as your husband?'

Miss Spring looked properly at the man with the bowler hat and she noted that he was exceptionally ugly. He was cross-eyed, with one eye pointing to the left, the other to the right, his nose was long and his ears even longer. And his beard was just as untidy as the coat of her ugly lost dog.

She did not think about it for long, but said with lowered eyes, 'I must point out, that with this ugly dog we shall only be able to go for walks at night. My poor lost darling! He dared not be seen even at the door in daytime!'

'That doesn't matter in the least,' laughed the gentleman with the bowler hat. 'I am used to sleeping in the daytime and being awake at night. You see I am a night watchman. Instead of keeping an eye on the factory, I'll be keeping an eye on our dog during our walks, my dearest!'

'In that case, come in,' nodded Miss Spring, the bride. And the gentleman with the untidy beard and the ugliest dog in the world went inside the house.

THE TURKEY WENCH

Once, long ago, an elderly Indian couple lived on the prairie. The wife was called Dried Corn, and her husband Magic Rob.

Dried Corn and Magic Rob had two daughters. The eldest bore the name of Yellow Corn and to the youngest they gave the name Turkey Wench, for she looked after a flock of turkeys.

There came a day of great Indian ceremonies and dances and the mother and father were setting out to reach the ceremonies in time.

'Come with us,' they suggested to the eldest daughter. 'Turkey Wench must stay at home and look after the turkeys.'

Father and mother and Yellow Corn left, and the turkeys were surprised to find Turkey Wench alone.

'Why are you not with them?'

'I should love to see the ceremonious dances,' sighed the girl. 'But how could I go anyway in this tattered dress? Besides, my mocassins are all worn out and what decoration could I wear, when I don't even own beads?'

'You'll have everything you need, so you can attend the ceremony,' the turkeys promised. No sooner had they said this when the eldest one jumped up on to a branch and fluttered his wings.

A beautiful scarf fell from them.

The second turkey fluttered his wings and out came a colourful sash.

The third turkey brought out mocassins as light as a feather, made of antelope hide. The fourth a silky cloth.

Then the very last turkey fluttered his wings and beads poured out everywhere, just as if handfuls of golden corn were strewn all over the yard.

'Nobody can say now that you are not prepared for the ceremonious dances,' remarked the eldest turkey. 'Dress quickly, Turkey Wench, and hurry, for you must not be late for the celebrations.'

When the girl reached the great meeting-place, the stars were already starting to fade and the dances were coming to an end.

The girl stood right at the back, so no one would recognize her and watched the eagle dance. But her elder sister, Yellow Corn, recognized her and immediately called to Dried Corn.

'Just look at that, mother. That scruffy girl of ours has dared to follow us. Who is looking after the turkeys? And from where did Turkey Wench get that lovely scarf, sash and mocassins? And do you see those glittering beads?'

The mother was furious and scolded Turkey Wench.

'Go home at once, you disobedient daughter. What if a fox were to attack the turkeys?'

The girl turned for home and cried all the way.

'Why is your face wet with tears, Turkey Wench?' asked the turkeys. 'Why do you return home so soon?'

'My mother scolded me, I had to come back,' sobbed the maiden. 'But I know what I shall do. I shall leave home,' she suddenly decided. 'You, my turkeys, will come with me.'

She took the path to the mountains and all the turkeys tiptoed behind. When they came to a lake, the girl bid them goodbye.

'Fly in all directions, my dears, in the mountains you will find a new home. I will live here in this lake. No one will harm me here.'

One after the other the turkeys came up to their mistress and one after the other they spread their wings and danced the goodbye dance.

Then they all flew upwards and aimed for the high mountains to the north, to the south, to the east and to the west.

'Farewell, my darlings,' Turkey Wench called after them.

Then Turkey Wench disappeared for ever in the depths of the blue lake.

THE DWARF WHO WANTED TO GROW

A herd of buffalo were grazing on the prairie.

The sun beat down, light breeze ruffled the high green grass scented by wormwood plants and a deep silence hung heavily over the prairie. Only crickets creaked monotonously and prairie dogs occasionally barked while playing near their lairs.

An old buffalo bull tore at a scented tuft of grass, then spat it out again crossly. A dwarf scrambled out of the tuft of grass, no bigger than a thumb.

'I really had a fright,' muttered the buffalo. 'What a close shave that was! You very nearly ended up in my stomach.'

The dwarf jumped clear and pelted away, without giving himself time to thank the buffalo.

He ran and ran till he came to a wild white horse.

'I am truly fed up with it all,' sighed the dwarf.

'With what, with what?' wondered the mare. 'Why are you complaining so?'

'A minute ago I nearly lost my life. The bull almost swallowed me. Couldn't you advise me how I could grow, so I could be as tall as you are?'

'That is easily done,' neighed the wild horse. 'You will have to eat in one sitting a whole sackful of corn, then run all the way to the river and drink from it. Immediately you will be as big as I am.'

The dwarf thanked the horse for his good advice, ate a sackful of corn and started running to the river.

He ran and ran, the corn like lead weight in his tummy. When he reached the river and drank its muddy water, he looked at his own reflection in the water and moaned.

'Why, I am even smaller than before. Of course I must be smaller after running all day! My legs have become shorter with all that running.'

A herd of cows were grazing by the river and the dwarf asked the oldest.

'Sister cow, could you tell me what I should do to grow to the same size as you?'

'That won't be difficult,' answered the eldest cow. 'First eat a basketful of grass and when you've eaten it, you must moo all day long — then you will be the same size as I.'

The dwarf was delighted. He picked a whole basket of prairie grass and chewed and ate mouthful after mouthful. When the whole lot was gone, he sat by the brook under a tall poplar tree and mooed all day long.

At dusk he looked down at his reflection in the brook's surface and lamented.

'Too much is too much. Instead of growing, I am smaller than ever. Why shouldn't I be. With all that mooing I've really shrunk.'

An old owl sat in the poplar tree and was just preparing to fly off to hunt in the night.

'Brother owl,' groaned the dwarf, 'please can you advise me how I can grow? I'd like to be at least as big as you are.'

The owl shook his head wonderingly.

'Why ever do you want to be taller? What good would it do you?'

'Why I want to be taller and bigger? So I could win all the fights, of course.'

The owl kept on shaking his head. 'Do you mean to say somebody wants to fight you?'

'To be honest, if I remember rightly, so far nobody has challenged me to a fight,' the dwarf remarked proudly. 'Most probably everybody is afraid that I would win.'

'Then who is there left for you to fight, if so many are afraid of you?'

'Even so, I would still like to grow,' sighed the dwarf. 'I am so tiny, I can hardly see over a molehill. And I'd like to see the distant snow-covered mountains at least once.'

'Nothing could be easier,' hooted the owl. 'Climb this tall poplar tree and the snow-covered mountains will be as clear as if they were in the palm of your hand.'

With that the owl spread his wings and soundlessly soared over the silent, sleepy prairie.

THE TREASURE

An old, limping man dragged himself along a rocky path which led from the sea to Lawrence's ranch. Every now and then he stopped, gasping for breath, coughing badly. Not till nightfall did he limp to the top of the hill.

Lawrence had been watching him for a long time. He was sitting on his verandah in the shade of a locust tree, waiting for the old man to grope his way along the path to the ranch.

Who could it be?

Lawrence saw the man for the first time in his life. He did not look like a house-to-house peddler, but what business would anyone else have on a lonely ranch such as this!

When the old man had dragged himself up to the house, he tried to speak, but the moment he opened his mouth, he gasped labouriously for breath and collapsed to the ground.

Lawrence rushed towards him, took him in his arms—the old fellow was as light as a sack of wool—and took him inside. He eased the collar of his shirt, washed his brow with cold water and opened all the windows, so fresh air would pour into the room.

Soon afterwards the old man woke up and wanted a drink. Refreshed, he went to sleep and slept peacefully till morning.

Lawrence and his wife Sally cared for the old man for a whole month, till at last he could stand again on his feet. But he was as weak as the first fly of spring.

One evening, when Sally had gone for water to the spring, the old man asked Lawrence to look outside, to ensure no strangers were about and to firmly shut the door.

It was an unpleasant winter day, but logs burned in the hearth and the whole ranch was scented with the smoke.

'Come and sit by the fire, Mr Lawrence,' the old fellow said to the rancher.

Lawrence looked at the old fellow inquiringly, filled his pipe and pushed a couple of chairs to the hearth.

'You have looked after me as if I were your own,' the old man spoke after a moment's silence.

'Don't mention it, old friend,' Lawrence grunted. 'It was, after all, our duty!'

The old man continued as if he had not heard.

'As yet I have not told you who I really am.'

'If you have a reason not to tell,' Lawrence assured him, 'you don't have to say anything. I shan't be annoyed.'

'I am a veteran Spanish sailor,' the old fellow continued. 'One of the crew of Laffit's dreaded pirate ship.'

Lawrence glanced at the old man in surprise, but the latter went on calmly in an unruffled voice.

'When our captain was taken a prisoner, we sailors fled to all corners of the world. But long before that our captain had let me, and two other members of the crew, into his secret. He told us where he had hidden the treasure. If anything were to happen to him, he told us that day, we three were to guard the treasure. I have hidden gold and silver in a couple of gun barrels. Then we had to swear to the captain that none of us three would take the treasure from its hiding place and that we would go to it only after we had met during our wandering through the world.'

Lawrence then asked, 'And have you ever met?'

'No, we have not,' the old man replied. 'We have not met and we will never meet again. Those two friends of mine are dead. I found that out only a short while ago, and that is why I am here.'

Lawrence eyed the old man questioningly.

'So you would understand, señor,' continued the old man, his voice a mere whisper, his head bent right to the flames, so that even an accidental passer-by would hear not a word, 'that treasure is hidden on Galveston Island.'

'Why, that is —' remarked Lawrence excitedly.

'Yes, it is quite near your ranch,' agreed the old man. 'And I have come to get that treasure. You have cared for me well. I would hardly have recovered without your help and so I am offering you half of the gold and silver, if you will help me to dig the treasure up.'

Lawrence's wife was returning with the water from the well, and the old man lapsed into silence.

A week later they set off to the island.

It was already dark, but the sky was shining, as if lit by an invisible hidden light beyond the horizon.

During such nights stars fall in Texas so thickly, as if golden rain was falling from the sky.

They camped under a bushy oak. The old man was breathing with difficulty. He grew pale, then ashen and he fell flat on the ground, with his eyes wide open staring rigidly into the sky. The breeze opened his shirt and the horrified Lawrence looked upon a man hanging on the gallows, tattooed on the old man's chest.

Just then, the skies opened and a golden flood of stars poured unceasingly to the ground. The heavens were aflame and the strange glow was mirrored in the old fellow's eyes.

Lawrence was terrified. Could this be the devil himself, thought he, who lured me into this wilderness and now wants to strangle me!

An owl hooted on the oak, right over Lawrence's head. Lawrence jumped to his feet and ran away. He did not look back, but jumped on his horse and galloped home.

About a month later, some fellow was looking for Lawrence. Sally called him through the window, for he was having a nap after dinner.

When Lawrence woke up, the stranger explained, that he had been sent by an aged sailor.

'What happened to him?' Lawrence enquired.

'He died a week ago,' said the stranger. 'But before his death he asked me to deliver this letter to you.'

With that he pulled a sealed envelope from his pocket. It contained the map of Galveston Island.

When the stranger had left, Lawrence examined the map thoroughly.

A walnut tree was sketched on the map. Seven hundred paces from that tree, in a marked direction, lay the gold and silver treasure buried inside two gun barrels. Lawrence called to his wife. 'Hide this document carefully!'

'Never fear,' Sally assured him, 'I will hide it so well, that not even a trained dog will find it.'

Lawrence saddled his horse and rode to his brother-in-law, to see if he could help to find the treasure. Three days later they were back and immediately prepared for their trip to Galveston Island.

They got together supplies of food, a pick-axe, a spade and a barrel of drinking water.

'Well, Sally, where is the map?' Lawrence called to his wife.

'D'you mean that piece of paper you asked me to hide the other day?'

'Of course! I sure hope you did not use it for lighting the fire!'

The woman searched and searched. She turned all the drawers inside out, looked into all the pots and pans, even tipped the scarlet geranium from its pot. She looked into all the shoes, swept out all the dark corners and secret hiding places.

But she could not find the map.

Lawrence climbed off his horse and searched with her. His brother-in-law helped too.

All in vain.

The wife had hidden the map so well, that they never found it.

So Lawrence set off with his brother-in-law to the island but without the map. They dug and dug but all in vain.

A few years later during a storm, two rusty gun barrels were seen drifting into the sea near Galveston Island. None who watched them then could know what fortune lay within their grasp—now only a treasure of the deep.

THE IDLER

Idle Mike was getting married and his neighbours gave him a wicker basket filled with coins as a wedding present.

'That will come in handy,' Mike remarked happily, 'at least I won't have to work.'

After the wedding he sprawled upon a bench and slept awhile. When he had dozed enough, he waited until he felt like sleeping again.

Days went by peacefully and, in the wicker basket, the pile of coins grew smaller and smaller.

One day, Mike's wife shook the very last five cent piece into her hand.

'Bad times are upon us,' sighed Mike. 'Tomorrow I shall have to find some work.'

'You should do that today,' suggested the wife.

'What day is it today?' asked Mike.

'Monday.'

Mike turned and preached.

'One shouldn't start anything on Monday. As our grannie used to tell us, Monday is a babe born to Mrs Sunday. And Sunday is a day of rest.'

The wife dismissed Mike's words with a wave of the hand and went to ask her neighbour for some food.

On Tuesday morning she woke her husband.

'Get up and go and look for work.'

'What day is it today?'

'Tuesday.'

'Then I am not going anywhere,' yawned Mike. 'Tuesday is such a peculiar day. Not the beginning of the week, nor the middle. I don't like Tuesdays.'

He turned to the wall and snored so loudly that the wall clock stopped.

The following day the wife woke her husband again.

'And what day is it today?' asked Mike.

'Wednesday. Its high time you found some work.'

'Wednesday? But that is the middle of the week. I wouldn't even be able to finish a job by Saturday.'

He wriggled under the blanket and slept blissfully.

On Thursday the wife shook her husband hard, saying crossly, 'Get up and go and find work, there's not a morsel of bread left in the cottage.'

'What day is it today?'

'Thursday.'

'Thursday?' wondered Mike. 'As I haven't found work by Wednesday, I'd hardly find some on Thursday,' Mike said convincingly to his wife and closed his eyes.

On Friday morning the wife tugged at her husband as hard as she could, shouting,

'Get up, you lazy lounger, and find some work!'

'What day is it today?'

'Friday.'

'Friday is the day of the hanged. On Fridays the condemned are hanged. I am not going anywhere on a Friday.'

On Saturday the wife neared despair as she woke her husband.

'If you don't get up today and don't look for work, you will never find any.'

'What day is it today?'

'Saturday.'

'Saturday?' said Mike wonderingly. 'Has the week already passed? On Saturday everyone is thinking about Sunday — who would have time to see me on a Saturday! Don't wake me up till Monday.'

On Monday Mike, after much yawning and stretching, got up and walked out of the cottage.

And as he was still half-asleep and somewhat dopey, he forgot that a river flowed right by the cottage.

He fell in and was drowned.

THE BARE MOUNTAINS

An Indian tribe lived under green mountains. Hunters frequented the bushy woods on the hillsides and down in the valley women tended corn and melons.

One day at noon, it suddenly grew dark, the sun was covered by the wings of an enormous bird. The terrified Indians ran to hide in their wigwams.

The brave warriors picked their stone axes, bows and arrows. But the huge bird's throat gave out such frightful, violent screams and his gigantic wings whipped up such a strong wind that even the bravest warriors hid their faces in the grass and slithered under bushes, so the bird would not see them.

Like a dark streak of lightning the bird flashed above the camp and then swiftly soared in a semi-circle on his gigantic wings towards the green mountains. He was gone and the sun once again shone brightly in the cloudless sky.

At that very moment, heart-rendering cries were heard from the wigwam of the Indian chief. His wife tore out her hair, rolled in agony on the floor, her mother's heart shedding tears of blood. For that monstrous bird had taken away the chief's year old son.

A year passed.

Once again the sky darkened with the wings of the gigantic bird and once again the monster left carrying yet another baby into the mountains.

Year after year the people waited with horror for the black day, waiting with fear to see which tiny child would be the dreaded bird's next victim.

They called for the help of the Great Spirit, but he remained silent, as if he was deaf and dumb to their pleadings.

The magicians asked at least for the Spirit's advice, but in vain. Perhaps the yearly human sacrifices, which the monstrous bird selected, had an unknown meaning, known only to the Great Spirit?

Perhaps it was necessary to wait, till time was ripe?

One year a new chief took over the ruling of the tribe, and he was clever and brave. He called together all the adult men.

'After discussions with our seniors,' he announced, 'I have decided not to wait for the bird to come from the mountains to seize his next victim. It is necessary for us to go after him into the mountains to kill him.'

The men welcomed the chief's decision with cries and immediately went to fetch their weapons.

The following day, they set off to the green mountains. They were among the white rocks and climbed ably higher and higher, circling frighteningly deep precipices with deafening waterfalls. It was tough going. But they decided it would be better to die in the mountains, than to wait helplessly down in the valley for the loathsome creature to come and claim another child.

When the men climbed over the highest range of the mountains and found themselves in a mountain valley, they were rooted to the ground with horror.

The valley was packed with monstrous birds, as huge and as ugly as the bird who, year after year, carried away one of the village babies.

The warriors were overcome by a feeling of awful helplessness and hopelessness and terror too; they hid their faces in the grass, waiting for the monstrous creatures to pounce upon them.

The chief, however, remained calm and resolute. He thought for a while, then gave out instructions. The men crept into the bushes and without a sound walked round the whole mountain clearing.

Now they were spread in a complete circle.

At the wave of the chief's axe, all the warriors set fire to the dry mountain grass and bracken on all sides.

The fire rose in a huge circle round the feathered monsters.

At that very moment the Great Spirit kindled a strong wind which prevented the giant birds from spreading their wings and flying away. The stormy wind rooted them to the ground.

The fire, inflamed by the windstorm, soared higher and higher and shrouded the birds with a veil of smoke and flame.

When at dusk the fire subsided, all that was left in the clearing of the fearsome creatures were burnt bones.

The wind died out and big and small stars lit up the sky.

Night covered the mountains and the prairie beneath them with its velvet cloak—a peaceful, silent night.

The men settled down under the rock and fell asleep.

114

They no longer had anything to fear.

The following morning they would descend the slopes into their village and life would once again be happy. Only the mountains which had, up to now, been green, would stay naked for ever after the terrible fire.

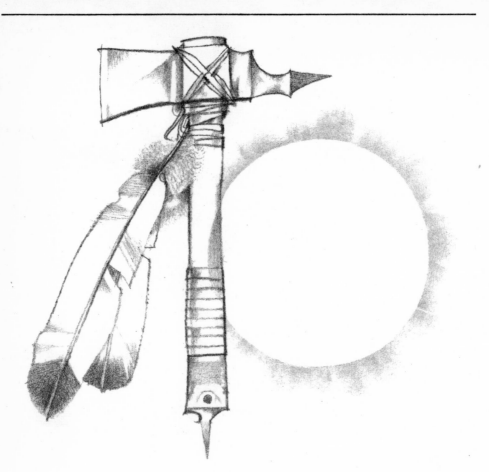

THE GOLDEN FINGER

Once there lived a lumberjack, whose wife was dead, so he lived alone with his daughter Virginia.

The lumberjack felled trees in the forests, while Virginia cooked, took care of the goat and looked after the household.

All the same, they were as poor as sparrows in winter. Their daily bread seemed to be always playing a game of hide and seek with them.

So one day, the lumberjack decided to get rid of his daughter.

The next morning he said, 'Virginia, I know a place in the forest where the raspberries are as large as nuts. Get a jug and I will take you there.'

Virginia did not suspect anything evil.

She took the jug and put bread and cheese in her bag and set forth with her father to the deep forest.

They walked on and on, tearing their way through the birch and blackberry thicket. Virginia now was so tired, she could hardly lift her feet, but her father did not even look round and just walked ahead.

'I hope we won't lose our way, father,' said the girl worriedly. 'I have never been round here before.'

'Stop worrying,' her father assured her, 'we'll be there soon.'

A little while later, they came to a dense forest.

The lumberjack said, 'Sit on this tree stump and rest. In the meantime I'll look for that raspberry patch.'

Virginia sank on to the beech stump and took her lunch out of her bag. After such a long walk she was very hungry. She drank from the brook and then fell into the soft moss to rest.

A moment later she was fast asleep.

When she woke up, darkness was already falling, like the sun. Virginia was afraid. She was all alone in the forest and her father had not returned.

'He must have got lost,' the girl said to herself and she started looking for him.

She called him, she ran hither and thither through the forest, but she did not find her father. In the end she completely lost her sense of direction and didn't know what to do or how to find her way home. She sank under a tree and began to cry.

A blue flame suddenly flared up before he.

Virginia blinked.

A woodland fairy rose from the old beech tree.

'I have been waiting for you here,' she said with a smile. 'Come, I will lead you to my kingdom.'

She took Virginia by the hand and they both started to run across the glade. Virginia felt as if her feet were not even touching the ground, so lightly they ran.

They ran over a bog and a pasture, passed an old forest, when suddenly in the misty evening twilight a velvety meadow filled with flowers glistened.

In the middle of the meadow a beautiful palace stood under three white birch trees.

'We are home,' the forest fairy said.

She rang the silver bell and the gates opened all on their own. They entered the palace and walked along a long marble passage with walls lined with flaming torches which lit their way. But they met no one. The palace was completely empty.

At the end of the passage tall doors opened before them and, Virginia with the fairy, entered a dining room with walls of larch wood.

The round table was already laid.

'Sit down and eat,' the fairy said to Virginia.

So the girl sat down by the round table laden with silver dishes filled with stuffed pigeons, duck legs and chicken livers. Scarlet strawberries perfumed the air and tempting fruit juices filled the crystal jugs.

When Virginia had had enough, the fairy led her to a bedroom.

'Sleep well, tomorrow morning I will show you my garden.'

In the morning the singing birds woke Virginia. She rose, washed herself and the doors opened before her of their own accord.

She walked again along the long passage into the dining room, where her breakfast was already waiting on the table.

The fairy was waiting and, after breakfast, she led Virginia into the large garden abundant with jasmine bushes and red and yellow roses.

'The only work you will have to do here, is to look after the rose bushes. Each morning you are to cut a bunch of the most beautiful roses,' said the fairy, giving Virginia a pair of scissors and a basket.

She smiled at Virginia and disappeared into the palace.

The girl strolled round the garden, watching the tom-tits feed their young. Then Virginia dug round the rose bushes and picked herself some raspberries.

From that day on she did not see the fairy again.

Each morning Virginia cut a basketful of rose buds and with

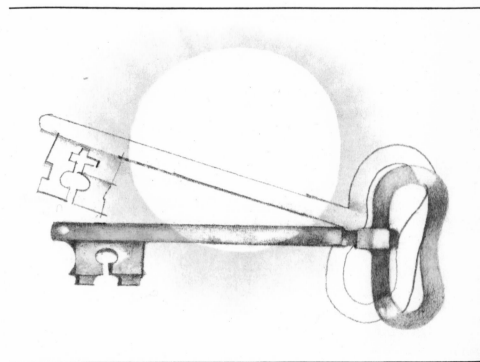

them filled the vases in the passage and dining room.

On her own she breakfasted, lunched and dined. But she was never lonely, for something new appeared in the garden every day to interest her and keep her occupied.

Day followed day, month followed month, year followed year.

When Virginia was fourteen years old, the fairy reappeared.

'You are a fully grown maiden now,' the fairy said, 'so you can tell good from evil. I am entrusting you with thirteen keys from thirteen chambers. You can enter twelve of them, but you must not go into, or glance into the thirteenth chamber. I am going on a far journey to my sister, the sea maiden. I am placing the whole palace in your care.'

The moment the palace gates shut behind the fairy, Virginia took the bunch of keys and ran up the stairs. Curiosity egged her on.

She unlocked the door of the first chamber and went inside.

The chamber was full of bird cages.

Yellow, blue and green birds were fluttering about in their cages and singing away. Virginia spent the whole day watching them.

The following morning Virginia unlocked the second chamber.

Round a black and white bitch six little pups were wobbling about, one more adorable than the other. Virginia played with them the whole day long.

On the third day she unlocked yet another chamber and spent the entire day playing with fluffy kittens.

For twelve days Virginia thus opened one chamber after another, and behind each door something nice was waiting for her.

In the end all that was left in her hand was the last, the thirteenth key.

Her heart hammered loudly as she reached the door of the thirteenth chamber. She fingered the key in her hand, it seemed to burn her palm and she was almost ready to push it into the lock. But hadn't the fairy instructed her not to unlock the thirteenth chamber?

For quite some time she shifted from foot to foot before the locked door.

Eventually Virginia thought, 'I'll open it just the weeniest bit and I'll peep inside. The fairy won't even know the door has been unlocked.'

She put the key in the lock and turned it, and then slowly and gently she prized the door slightly open. It creaked, as if it had not been opened for a long, long time.

Virginia now had the door open the tiniest, weeniest bit and was peeping through the narrow opening into the thirteenth chamber.

Her eyes were overcome by the intense, glaring glow.

In the chamber, on a throne strewn with yellow roses, sat the sun. The light it gave out was so intense that it made black circles dance before Virginia's eyes. She swiftly closed the door and locked the chamber.

Involuntarily she looked down at her right hand with which she had closed the door. Her little finger was completely golden. The fierce sunlight had turned her finger to gold.

In vain she washed it in water and scrubbed it with sand, in vain she cried.

The little finger remained golden.

The following day the fairy returned from her long journey.

'Give me back the keys, Virginia,' she said, 'I will put them away.'

Virginia handed her the bunch of thirteen keys with her left hand. Her right hand was hidden in her pocket, so the fairy would not notice the gold little finger.

'How many chambers did you unlock?' asked the fairy.

'Twelve,' the girl replied.

'Did you not enter the thirteenth one?'

'I didn't even look inside,' lied the girl, her eyes avoiding the fairy's face.

The fairy asked no further questions, but said instead, 'For seven years you've served me well in my palace, and tended my garden with care. Now I release you from service. So that you think well of me when you remember me, I will reward you.'

With that she stroked Virginia's head and all her hair turned to gold.

'Each morning a single gold hair will fall from your head,' said the fairy. When twelve hairs in all have fallen, they will turn into a golden harp and this harp will bring forth your happiness.'

The fairy then took Virginia's hand and led her out of the palace.

For the very last time Virginia looked round the rose garden and the green meadow, for the last time she turned to see the lovely castle shaded by the three white birch trees.

When they came to a wide pasture, they crossed a brook, and an impressive hollow oak rose before them.

'We have arrived,' said the fairy, pointing to the oak.

'You must hide in that hollow oak, Virginia. From here you will call your happiness. But you won't be able to hold on to your happiness for long. You won't be satisfied, until you own up that you have lied to me,' said the fairy.

With that she kissed Virginia's forehead and soon was lost in the evening mist.

The girl did not ponder for long, and hid in the hollow oak.

In the morning, the moment she awoke, she plucked the first golden hair from her head.

It sparkled in her palm, shining like the first ray of the early morning sun over the forest.

The second day she plucked the second golden hair from her head and so on until twelve days had passed and she had twelve golden hairs in her hand.

The hairs turned into a golden harp.

'Now at last I can call happiness to me,' Virginia said to herself and placed her fingers on the harp strings.

The harp echoed with sweet music. The bushy crown of the oak started to tremble, and so did the brook which flowed near, and the clearing strewn with bluebells and white daisies.

It was then Virginia heard a distant clatter of horse's hooves—someone was coming.

The clatter was coming nearer, it was growing stronger. On the path by the oak a white horse appeared from the thicket, on its back a rider in a green velvet jacket, with black hair falling on his shoulders.

'At last I have found you,' cried the rider, the moment Virginia stepped out of the oak. 'For seven years now I have vainly searched for you over all the land. Hurry and mount my horse. We shall ride to the royal castle, my father will give us a fine wedding and will make me reign over the whole kingdom.'

A year later, a little boy was born to the young queen Virginia.

The young king was so happy that he commanded that all the bells should ring throughout his land. Every beggar and vagabond could eat and drink to their heart's content in the courtyard of the castle for a whole week at the king's expense; music flowed from all the parks and gardens in the kingdom and white and red wine flowed from all the fountains.

That morning the young king came to the queen's bedroom.

'Where have you hidden our son?' he asked. 'I don't see him anywhere, and I should like to look at him.'

'I really don't know where he could have got to,' sighed the young queen. 'I dozed off for awhile, and when I opened my eyes, our son was gone.'

She did not tell the king that during the night the fairy entered through the window, took their son from the cot and carried him away.

The king had the whole kingdom searched for his son. But it was all in vain, he was not to be found.

A year later, a second son was born to the queen.

The king was delighted, but took no chances and had the bedroom watched.

A squad of musketeers was placed on guard along the entire passage in front of the queen's bedroom, with orders not to let anyone enter.

Once again all the little bells and the big bells tolled throughout the kingdom, music flowed in the gardens and parks and every pauper and beggar could feast in the courtyard of the royal palace.

The next morning the king entered the queen's bedroom.

'Show me my son,' he begged her. 'I should like to see him.'

The queen burst into tears. 'It would be better for you to throw me out, for I don't deserve to be your wife. Once again I did not watch over him enough and he is gone.'

The king was most angry and he very nearly did banish the queen from the palace. But when he looked at her and saw her tears, he sighed and in silence left the room.

Scouts on horseback rode all over the kingdom, searching everywhere for the king's son.

It was useless.

It was as if deep waters had closed over him and dense forests swallowed him.

A year later, yet another son was born to the queen.

The king ordered a whole regiment of hussars to surround the entire palace and not to let anyone enter.

In the morning the king went into the queen's bedroom to see his new-born son.

'I do not deserve your love any longer,' sobbed the queen, 'for the third time now I have failed to keep my son.'

The king was furious and he threw the queen out of the palace.

The unhappy queen Virginia wandered through the deep forests the whole day long, not seeing where she was going for the flood of tears.

At dusk she came to the old hollow oak.

But there was no sign of the golden harp, with which she was to recall her happiness.

She sank to the ground under the tree and fell asleep with fatigue.

A piercing glow awoke her.

Virginia opened her eyes and saw the fairy.

'I want to ask you only one question,' the fairy said. 'Did you open the door of the thirteenth chamber?'

Queen Virginia fell to her knees before the fairy and in tears she confessed.

'I opened the door ever so slightly—the door of the thirteenth chamber. I confess. I lied to you.'

The fairy smiled and said, 'I forgive you, Virginia.'

With that she walked over to the oak and from the hollow brought out the three royal sons, three golden-haired little boys.

When the king learned from his scouts that the queen was returning to the palace with the three sons, he ordered all the bells throughout the land to ring.

Music flowed and people danced and celebrated.

They covered the path to the palace with rosebuds and the queen walked along it, with the three sons in her arms, each as handsome as the other.

But the little finger of her right hand remained golden for ever. Until the end of her days it reminded her of her fateful lie.

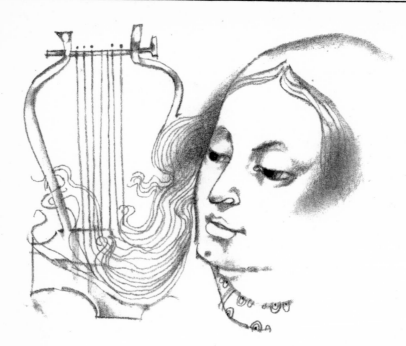

THE TIGHT-FISTED FARMER
AND THE CLEVER FARMHAND

There were three brothers, their father was dead, their cottage rickety, their stable empty and in their loft the mice were munching the last few grains of corn.

'There's nothing left for it,' said the eldest brother to their mother, 'I must try and find a job with some wealthy farmer.'

He put a slice of bread in his pocket and went wherever his legs carried him.

At dusk he came to a large farm. The farmer stood by the field, inspecting the harvest.

'Master farmer,' the lad called from the path, 'could you use some help on your farm?'

The farmer looked the lad over from head to toe and nodded.

'If you are as good at ploughing and reaping corn as I am at counting the money its sale brings me, then its worth a try.'

So the eldest brother started working at the farm. But a year later, he returned home with one pocket empty and the other emptied.

'Did thieves rob you on the way, that you return without any wages?' wondered the mother.

'Nobody robbed me,' explained the eldest son. 'Who'd pick on me, with two empty pockets! I worked the whole year for that farmer, he cheated me at the table as much as he could, and whenever I asked about my wage, he only laughed at me, saying I'd had it in food long before.'

'That's a fine state of affairs,' grumbled the middle brother, striking the table with his fist. 'I'll have a go at that sly farmer now. He won't swindle me.'

Taking a slice of bread for the journey, he started on his way.

The farmer stood in the orchard inspecting the apple harvest.

'Could you use a hard-working farm lad?' asked the youth.

'Maybe yes, maybe not, there's always plenty to do at a farm. If you can work as hard in the day as you sleep in the night, it's worth a try,' nodded the farmer.

The second brother worked, he worked very hard, sowing seed, gathering corn, milking cows.

After a year the farm lad said to the farmer.

'Master farmer, during this whole year I haven't had a single dollar from you. I'd like to bring something home to my mother to help her out. What about my wages?'

'What wages are you talking about, young man?' wondered the farmer. 'We've never agreed that you should be paid for your work. You've slept your wages away in bed.'

The second son therefore returned home just as poor as when he had left a year before.

'Do you mean to say you've spent all the money you earned?' asked the bewildered mother.

'How could I have spent the money,' sighed the second son, 'when the farmer did not give me any.'

'Just you wait, I'll collect the wages for myself and the pair of you from the foxy devil,' said the youngest brother.

He put a slice of bread in his pocket and was off.

He came to the farm and that miser of a farmer was walking round the yard counting his chickens.

The youngest brother greeted him and stopped by the gate.

'Why are you just standing and saying nothing?' asked the farmer. 'Are you perhaps looking for work?'

'T'is far more likely that work is looking for me,' laughed the youngest brother.

'Do you mean by that that you would like to work for me?'

'Maybe, maybe not,' said the lad, 'I didn't mention anything like that. But then if you didn't need help here, you wouldn't have asked me about work in the first place.'

'The way I see it,' remarked the farmer, 'you have a very glib tongue. If you can plough the field and cut the corn as ably as you can answer, it will be worth a try.'

'Who's talking about a try,' the young man said. 'I am more interested to know what my wages will be.'

The farmer scratched his ear.

'Surely you wouldn't suspect me of wanting to cheat you?'

'Maybe, maybe not,' the youth refused to budge. 'I can work just as well as you can put the money away. Therefore I am sure we will quickly agree. You give me some honest work, and at the end of a year you'll give me some honest one hundred dollars. Is it a deal?'

The farmer realized that this young man was no fool, so he scratched his other ear and grumbled.

'Very well, have it your way. One hundred dollars in your hand. They'll be yours.'

At the same time he was already wondering how to get the better of that young fellow.

'Before we shake hands on the deal,' said the new farmhand, 'we must agree on all points. Whilst in your service, if I hesitate to do all

I can, I will lose a month's pay. But, whenever you ask me to stop doing whatever you ordered me to do, you will pay me an extra month's wage. What about that?'

The farmer was overjoyed. 'Now you're caught in your own trap, you dope,' he thought. 'You're not as clever after all as you apear to be. I'll hoodwink you, just you wait.' He nodded and they sealed the deal with a handshake.

The next day the farmer woke his new farmhand early in the morning.

'Hurry with your breakfast, you're going to do the ploughing.'

The farmhand ate his breakfast and said,

'And what if I were to have my lunch at the same time, so I wouldn't have to return for it at noon?'

The farmer was all for such talk, for after all, the farmhand would be able to plough a bigger part of the field. So he asked the wife to bring the young fellow his lunch at once.

The youth ate his lunch, wiped his mouth, downed some cider and said,

'Now that I have lunched, what do you think, should I have my supper too? Then I could go on ploughing till dark, for I wouldn't have to come back for my supper at dusk.'

'That is sensible talk,' the farmer praised him, 'one can see you're no sloucher, my lad.'

The farmer's wife brought the farmhand his supper.

When he had eaten the supper and drunk a cup of buttermilk, the youth asked,

'What does a farmhand do here after supper?'

'You have to go to bed of course, straight after your supper, so you are fit and fresh in the morning.'

'Good night then,' said the farmhand and went to his room to sleep.

The farmer shook his head in disbelief.

Then he ran after the farmhand to his room and tried to pull him out of bed.

'Get up at once, who d'you think will plough instead of you?'

'I have no idea who will plough instead of me today. But I remember all too well that a minute ago you told me that after supper I must always go straight to bed. Now you're asking me to disobey the order and to go and plough after supper. You have not kept to our agreement, so you must give me an extra month's pay.'

The farmer swore till the windows rattled, but there was nothing he could do. A few days later he ordered the farmhand to keep an eye on his greedy-mouthed cow Melinda and to make sure she did not damage the maize.

The farmhand sat all day long at the field's edge, holding on to the string tied round Melinda, that greedy-mouthed cow.

The other cows were grazing near, and soon realized that no one was tending them and shouting at them, so they trotted into the maize and were soon munching away merrily.

'Are you blind?' screamed the farmer. 'Let Melinda be and drive all those other cows out of that maize field. On the double now!'

The farmhand let go of Melinda, that greedy guzzler, and drove the other cows out of the field.

'You ordered me, master, to guard Melinda. Now you told me to forget her and to drive the other cows out of the field. We have agreed, that I shall get an extra month's wages, if you ever ask me to stop doing what you had ordered me to do.'

This was not at all to the farmer's liking, but what could he do! An agreement is an agreement.

The next day the farmer said to the farmhand,

'When we drive to the field, we always have to go right round the bog. Go and make a proper track across the bog.'

'Master farmer,' asked the farmhand, 'tell me, who made that track across the hill over there?'

'What a stupid question,' muttered the farmer. 'It's a sheep track, of course, so it was made by sheep.'

The farmhand asked no more, but sharpened his knife and went to the hill, where he started to cut round all the sheep's tracks in the dried mud.

At noon the farmer turned up to see what he was doing on the hill. Already from afar he started to shout, 'Have you lost your wits? Why are you cutting out mud from a path?'

'I am not cutting out mud, but sheep tracks. If sheep can make a track across a hill, they can make one across a bog too. When I've cut out all these muddy tracks, I will lay them across the bog. To-morrow we'll be able to cross the bog by way of a proper track.'

'Leave it alone, for goodness sake leave it alone,' said the farmer, his cheeks purple with fury.

'Very well then,' agreed the farmhand, 'I'll stop doing what you ordered me to do this morning. You wanted me to make a track across the bog, but now you tell me to leave it alone and to stop. According to our agreement I am owed another extra month's wage.'

The farmer was beside himself, but there was nothing else for it, he had to keep his word. Day after day that miserly farmer was forced to pay out an extra month's wage to the clever farmhand.

He was so furious he was unable to sleep at night, he tossed about on his bed and pondered how he could get the better of that young fellow, but he did not come up with anything at all.

When at last he realized that the farmhand must have queued up to collect his brains three times when brains were given out, he called the youth to him and said,

'You've pulled enough cash out of my pockets. Take yourself and go wherever your legs will carry you. I don't need you any more.'

'I'll go,' said the farmhand with a smile, 'but only when you give me the wages which you refused to give to my two brothers.'

What could the farmer do! He put his hand into his pocket and counted out every dollar he owed his brothers.

'And now off with you, I don't ever want to see you again on my farm. Go on home, you could bamboozle a barren cow to give you a calf!'

'In that case I'll be off,' agreed the farmhand. 'But when I first came to you, you told me to work for you. I obeyed. But now you are ordering me to stop working. You have not kept your side of the agreement. Therefore you owe me another month's wage.'

The frenzied farmer tore the button off his jacket with anger, but that did not help him at all. Once more he had to put his hand into his pocket for more money. An agreement is an agreement.

He counted the dollars as he put them in the farmhand's hand, and the farmhand laughed, turned his back on the farm and started for home with a full purse.

As he passed through the gates, he sang to himself.

Cleverness is better than gold,
This I have always been told.
Goodbye, old miser, I don't wish to linger
Perhaps you're wiser, now you've burnt your finger.

THE BILLY-GOAT
AND THE HANDKERCHIEF

Once upon a time grandpa and grandma lived in a cottage near the railway track.

Grandpa spent all his days by the fireside reading books, in fact he was all shrivelled and yellow from all that reading.

'Come and have your dinner,' grandma tempted him, 'before it goes cold.'

'I'll just finish this page,' grandpa objected. 'Just listen to what they say. When fishing with a line, fish are best caught when there is a southernly wind blowing. It can be southwesterly, or even westerly. This book really is invaluable.'

As grandpa's dinner always got colder and colder and grandma was never able to knock any sense into him, she always ended up by eating his dinner too, rather than let it get completely cold.

So she was nicely rounded, whereas grandpa was all dried up and thin, like a reed in winter.

But grandpa did not mind, he read his books and was quite content.

In their stable they had an old spotted billy-goat.

That bearded rascal was the bane of grandma's life. He devoured everything in sight. Once he guzzled up grandpa's shirt, then he had a go at grandma's skirt, he gulped down salads and meat, towels—even a sheet. He did so much damage and was always on the rummage. Grandma did not think it at all funny, that so many things disappeared into his tummy.

But grandpa could not care less. He sat in the warmth by the fire in bliss, reading his books. It did not matter to him one bit if that spotted four-legged devil gulped down even a mattress!

Grandma, however, was furious with the billy-goat and whenever he swallowed something like her blouse or an apron, she would rush into the living room straight up to grandpa. 'You lazy, good for nothing sloucher, you bookwormy monk! Here you sit, all cosy and warm, your nose in that wretched book, oblivious of all that's going on. Grab that billy-goat and give him a good hiding! That thieving devil has just gobbled up two pairs of my stockings!'

Grandpa tried to defend himself. He tried to hide behind the door, he even hid his head right in the hearth, but in vain. His old nagging woman dragged him out and grandpa had to chase that greedy billy-goat round the yard.

One day after lunch, grandpa fell asleep by the fire and his book fell out of his hand. When he woke up, he picked it up and started reading again with relish. But just when the story reached a climax, something tickled the old man up his nose and he went 'a-tish-oo', sneezing so hard the whole cottage rattled. He quickly put his hand in his pocket for a handkerchief.

The pocket was empty.

He looked round. A corner of his red handkerchief was just disappearing in the billy-goat's ever greedy mouth.

Grandpa was most angry. He took a strong rope, tied one end to the billy-goat and led him to the railway line. There he tied him to the track so tightly, the animal could not pull the rope away or gnaw through it.

A train hooted in the distance.

'Now we'll have peace,' grandpa thought to himself.

But at the very last moment he felt sorry for the billy-goat, so he closed his eyes, so he would not see their greedy spotted billy-goat disappear under the wheels of the train.

Suddenly he heard the train grinding to a halt. He opened his eyes, and lo and behold! The billy-goat had in his mouth the scarlet handkerchief and was waving it from side to side.

The train did stop. The billy-goat had saved his own life with grandpa's scarlet handkerchief.

'Come on then, you gluttonous tormentor,' grandpa said, smacking the billy-goat's backside, and he led him back home.

And to this day grandpa still sits over his books, while grandma nags and the billy-goat rummages in all corners for something tasty to eat.

GOLDEN APPLE
AND HIS STEPMOTHER

Once there lived a governor who had an only son.

One day his wife fell ill. She knew her days were drawing to an end, so she called her husband to her bedside and begged,

'My dearest husband, before I die, I should like to ask something of you. Promise me that you will not marry again until our son, Golden Apple, is grown up. I feel a stepmother may harm him.'

With tears in his eyes the husband promised that he would not forget her request, and that same evening his sick wife closed her eyes forever.

Day followed day and the little boy grew into a fine youth. His father remained always alone and he would not hear of another marriage.

His people were complaining. 'What a strange state this is, a head without a wife. Who is there to look after the governor's household; who is there to puff up his pillow at night when he goes to bed; who is there to welcome guests and converse with them during festive dinners? Why doesn't our governor marry again, so the new wife could decorate the windows of his residence with flowers?'

The governor only dismissed such talk with a wave of the hand. 'I promised my departed wife that I would not marry again until our son grows up. It is my custom to keep my word.'

But his people kept on pestering.

In inns and in markets, in workshops and town squares, one and all blamed him for staying alone and letting his house go to waste.

'Until our governor weds again, there'll be no peace in this state,' cried all the farmers and bakers, ranchers, tailors and undertakers.

'Have it your own way then,' the governor cried in the end. 'I'll tell you what, I will marry the first woman I meet. This I promise. But first I will take my son, Golden Apple, to a distant state for schooling. Let him discover new customs, new foods, foreign languages and different entertainments.'

They set out on their journey in great style. Six pairs of horses were harnessed to the carriage, which carried the governor, his son and valet far away from the palacial house.

In the distant state the governor placed Golden Apple in the care of the state council, then headed for home.

The moment he crossed the boundary of his own state, as the devil would have it, he met on the forest path a woman as ugly as a dirty clay pan.

'I have been waiting here for you with great impatience,' the hideous hag croaked with the one and only crooked tooth in her mouth. 'When is the wedding to be, my beloved bridegroom? I should like to warm my frozen feet by the fireside in your spacious house, for the wind is starting to blow from the stubble fields.'

The governor dismissed the idea with a wave of the hand, just as if he was brushing a wasp off his nose.

'What an idea, you poor creature! Getting married! I haven't time for such things. Why, as soon as I return, I must spend a whole year studying and signing new laws and decrees, new regulations and injunctions. Here's ten silver dollars for your dowry, go and wed some able fellow, and after the wedding buy a greengrocer stall in the market for the pair of you.'

But the hideous woman screamed, hands on her hips, 'That would be a fine state of affairs, for a governor not to keep his word. Why should his people obey laws and pay taxes, when the governor himself doesn't want to fulfil his promise. Did you say you would marry the first woman you met, or didn't you! Did you think you could shut me up and buy me off with a measly ten silver dollars? I would have to be an awful fool to give up the governor's house for a market stall.'

What could the poor unhappy man do!

'Get into the carriage then and stop your yapping,' the governor sighed with resignation. 'You shall drive with me to the capital and I will marry you. I don't care about anything any more.'

After the governor's return, a hurried, noisy wedding was held. They made the bride a thick veil, so no one could catch even a glimpse of her ugly face. The moment the guests departed from the wedding feast, the governor took his new wife by the hand and led her to a dark room in the tower. He turned the lock of the door nine times and did not let anyone in. Once every month the governor opened the little room to see if his ugly wife wanted anything.

'I don't desire a thing, except for your son, our Golden Apple, to return home from the foreign state. It would please me so much to see him,' croaked the woman as ugly as sin. And she begged and whined so much that he relented in the end and sent a coach to bring Golden Apple back home.

When the wife found out that Golden Apple was back in the house, she pleaded with the governor to show her his son.

What could her husband do? He could not stand tears.

He took Golden Apple to the little dark room in the tower, unlocked the door and pushed him in.

The room was so dark that Golden Apple did not notice how hideous his stepmother was.

So there was nothing to stop the ugly woman from suggesting to Golden Apple,

'Come on son, come on, Golden Apple, lets play a game of chess. If you win, I will never ask you to play another game. But if you lose, you'll have to fulfil one wish of mine.'

'Why not,' Golden Apple agreed, and the stepmother prepared the chessboard.

They played long into the night and then Golden Apple lost.

'Now you must grant me my wish,' the ugly hag smiled poisonously and tossed the veil from her face.

When Golden Apple saw her face, he turned pale.

But it was too late.

'So that you know,' squawked the stepmother, 'already tomorrow you must leave here and must not return until you can bring me an eight-legged dog.'

Whilst in the distant state, Golden Apple had learned to drink a witty soup with a spoon. So he thought a moment, then said,

'Very well, I will bring you an eight-legged dog. But so that you will be the first to see me as I return, you must climb right up the tower and keep a look-out.'

The stepmother nodded in agreement.

She climbed right up the tower at once, and at once her stepson took the ladder away from beneath.

Then he set out into the world to look for the eight-legged dog.

He is still looking, here, there and everywhere, in deserts, pastures and forests.

And the ugly hag, that stupid stepmother, still sits on the top of the tower, watching for Golden Apple to return home with the eight-legged dog.

The tabby cat says, everything comes to the one who waits.

THE WOLF AND THE CUB

Early one morning, an Indian woman ran out of her tent, tearing out her hair.

'Misfortune! The grey wolf has just strangled my husband!'

The hunters gathered round him, but they could not revive the dead man.

'There he goes, can you see?' hunter Bear Claw cried out, pointing towards the forest.

The grey wolf, as large as a calf, was proudly disappearing into the bush.

The following night the grey wolf sneaked again into the village, killed two men and disappeared.

Three villagers did not live through the third night.

'We really must go into the forest and kill that wolf,' the chief decided and sent four hunters after that grey beast.

Not a single hunter returned from that hunt.

So the chief sent five men into the forest.

No one has seen them from that day.

So the chief spread the news of what had happened through the whole region, asking for help.

An Englishman was the first to come to the village.

He wore short trousers and had a long gun.

'I'll shoot that wolf,' he swanked, 'and bring you his skin this evening. But first I'll make a pot of tea, to strengthen myself for the hunt.'

He sat by the fire and put a pan of water to boil. Then when he was slowly sipping his tea, the grey wolf crept towards the Englishman from the bushes and throttled the Englishman in his short trousers with the long gun.

The next day a German on horseback entered the village.

'First I must study the books to see how wolves are caught,' said the German with his porcelain pipe. With that he sat under a bushy

oak, took three fat books from his rucksack and skimmed the pages.

The grey wolf crept from the forest and choked the German with his porcelain pipe.

On the third day two Frenchmen drove into the village in a magnificent carriage.

They sat near the bushes, from where the wolf always came out of the forest, drank wine and waited.

Suddenly in the forest twilight two yellow-green flames flashed—the wolf's eyes. The first Frenchman took his gun and aimed. Then he lowered the gun, passed it to the second Frenchman, and said politely, 'After you, sir.'

But before the second Frenchman had a chance to take aim, the grey wolf pounced out of the bushes and throttled the pair of them.

Next to come to the village were three Americans.

They had beautiful shining guns and haversacks filled with juicy steaks. They fried them on the fire, downed them with white coffee and proceeded to clean their guns and to oil them.

In the meantime the grey wolf slinked silently towards them from the bushes and choked all three Americans, before they could even load their guns.

On a plantation in a valley there were Mexican workers picking cotton. Among them was a young Mexican lad called Cub. Whilst they worked, the men talked about the grey wolf, and the boy Cub listened attentively.

He threw to the side the sack into which he was gathering cotton, and said, 'I am going to get that wolf.'

Everyone laughed at him. 'What nonsense, lad! Even the Englishman couldn't dispose of that killer-wolf, who throttled the Germans, Frenchmen and Americans alike. How could you kill such a monstrous creature? You don't even have a gun.'

But Cub would not listen and set off towards the village.

He took nothing with him but three mirrors. A large one, middle-sized one and a little one.

When he came to the village, he asked from which direction the grey wolf sneaked in. The hunters pointed to the forest and the bushes, and pitied the Mexican lad, thinking that he would so uselessly sacrifice his young life.

Cub took the largest mirror from his sack, placed it against a tree and hid behind a boulder.

Later, the grey wolf crept from the forest and saw the mirror.

'I had no idea,' he said to himself proudly, 'that I was so big. I don't have to fear even the strongest enemy.'

With that he ran into the village and killed two horses.

The chief was annoyed with Cub. 'A fat lot of help you've been. Before now that killer-wolf choked our men, now he has robbed us of two beautiful horses.'

Cub tried to calm him. 'Have patience, chief, you will see that I will get that wolf.'

The next day this little Mexican boy went again out of the village to the forest; he took the middle-sized mirror from his sack and placed it against the tree.

The grey wolf appeared out of the bushes and aimed straight for the mirror. He examined himself in it and growled, 'How strange. Yesterday I was big and I slew two horses. How come that I've grown smaller in the night? Perhaps I've tired myself out too much, two horses, that may be too much even for me.'

He slunk into the village and killed a colt.

The chief reproached Cub. 'I've really had enough. Now we are one colt poorer. Pack your sack and go, Cub, from where you've come.'

But the little Mexican boy tried to convince the chief. 'Just you wait, tomorrow you will be thanking me, instead of scolding me.'

The following day Cub went to the forest beyond the village for the third time. From his sack he took the very little mirror. He placed it against the tree and hid behind a boulder.

The wolf was already waiting in the bushes. He sprang out of the forest and aimed straight for the mirror.

The moment he looked at himself, he howled sorrowfully. 'Alas, alas, this must be the end of me. Why, I, the poor miserable creature, have turned during the night into a wolf cub. I must disappear from here immediately, before the hunters get me and skin me alive.'

With his tail limp between his legs he pelted into the forest.

The little Mexican lad returned to the village and everyone cheered him. They were most hospitable to him, gave him their most magnificent horse and three silver dollars as well.

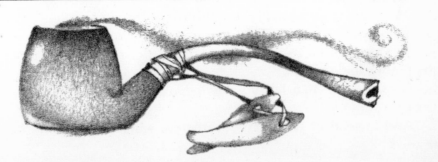

THE SCYTHE BITTEN BY A SNAKE

Farmer Buchanan was cutting down maize for fodder. Suddenly a large python rose from the ground, ready to strike. Luckily the farmer was not caught unawares, and he went for the python with the scythe. The furious serpent dug his poisonous fangs deep into the wooden handle of the scythe. But in the end the farmer managed to cut the python in half with the scythe.

As he was about to carry on cutting the maize, he noticed that the wood of the handle had swollen considerably. It was most suspicious! The farmer took a swing and swish! The scythe broke against a stone.

He took the head off, leaving the long handle propped up against the fence, and went home to replace it. Then he returned to the field, and by evening he had gathered all the maize.

About a week later, the farmer drove his cart by the very same field.

A fat log was propped against the fence. He examined it thoroughly, hardly believing his eyes. It was the broken scythe handle! When the python bit into it, injecting the wood with his venom, the stick began to swell, till it turned into a very fat log.

The farmer put the log on his cart and drove to the saw-mill.

There he had it cut into fine planks, from which he built a hen-house in his yard.

He painted the outside nicely with varnish, and his wife drove fifty chickens into their new home.

The next morning the wife shouted,

'Husband, come quickly! What a calamity!'

The farmer jumped out of bed and ran to the hen-house.

The varnish had sucked the python's poison from the wood and the planks had shrunk.

Instead of a hen-house, a wooden box of matches was in the yard.

And instead of hens, fifty feathered, winged flees were cackling in the box.

THE YELLOW RIBBON

Little Jane lived in the street in a green house.

Little John lived opposite in a white house.

They played hide-and-seek and blind man's buff; they played thieves and robbers and they played the rabbit game, where one sits all alone in a corner and does not know what to do.

But whether they played with a ball, or a chasing game, or a game about a soup, which boils over, or played statues, Jane always had a yellow ribbon round her neck.

'Why do you always wear a yellow ribbon round your neck?' asked little Jonny.

Jane always replied, 'I mustn't tell you.'

Then Jane and Jonny started school and, when they finished their first year, and before they both went away on their holiday, Jonny asked Jane again, 'Why do you always wear that yellow ribbon round your neck?'

'I mustn't tell you,' Jane dismissed him again.

After the holidays Jane and John went into the second year, then the third year. Time flew by, but always just before the holidays Jonny would ask Jane,

'Are you going to tell me at last why you always wear that yellow ribbon round your neck?'

But Jane always answered, 'Don't ask, I mustn't tell you.'

Then Jane and John started to study at college. They were bright pupils, and at week-ends they rode on their bicycles and had a picnic, they danced together at tea dances and they fell in love.

When they finished high school, John asked Jane once again.

'Perhaps now you will tell me at long last why you always wear that yellow ribbon round your neck.'

But Jane shook her head.

'It is useless to ask, I am not going to tell.'

John graduated and Jane, too, finished school, and soon afterwards they were married.

During the wedding feast John leaned over to Jane and whispered,

'Won't you tell me even today why you've always worn a yellow ribbon round your neck ever since you were a child?'

The bride Jane whispered back,

'We love each other, don't we, so why should it matter that I wear a yellow ribbon round my neck.'

The years came and passed, John's hair turned white, Jane, too, was going grey. When they were celebrating their golden wedding, grandfather John asked grandmother Jane,

'You are surely old enough now to have some sense and to tell me why you wear that terrible yellow ribbon constantly round your neck.'

But grandma Jane shook her head again.

'As you have waited for an answer for so long, I think you can wait a little while longer.'

Soon afterwards grandma Jane was taken ill and was about to part with life. Grandpa John bent over her bed and asked,

'I don't like to ask, but I should so like to know why you've worn that yellow ribbon round your neck all your life. To be quite honest, grandma, I can't even imagine you without it. It reminds me of the time when you were little, then when we started school together, even our wedding day I can see on that ribbon. It seems as if our whole life was tied up in it.'

Grandma Jane smiled sweetly at grandpa John and said quietly,

'Very well, the time is right, so untie my yellow ribbon.'

Grandpa untied the knot on the ribbon most carefully — and grandma's head fell away from the neck.

A RARE HORSE

The farmer was buying a horse from his neighbour.

'Take a close look at that horse,' the neighbour was saying, smacking his lips rapturously. 'Legs springy like wires, eyes like deep pools and a body—strong and firm like steel. You won't find such a horse anywhere around!'

The farmer liked the horse, so he did not haggle for long, and soon he was up in the saddle returning home with his new horse.

By the forest the horse suddenly stopped and refused to move. The farmer stroked him, patted him, argued with him, threatened him and in the end he even cut off a birch rod and whipped him. But to no avail. The horse stood still, as if rooted to the ground. When the sun went down, the horse came to life, stepped out without any prodding and trotted on towards the farm.

The farmer was furious. The very next morning he rode the horse back to his neighbour, intending to return him. 'Listen, neighbour,' he reproached him, 'why did you not tell me that this horse is obstinate? He stops all of a sudden and refuses to budge an inch, though I coax him with kind words, threats or a whip!'

The neighbour was surprised. 'Did a hare, or a rabbit happen to run by?'

'They did not. I didn't see a hare or a rabbit.'

'That is very strange,' muttered the neighbour. 'Or did you perhaps ride by a forest?'

'I have the feeling,' the farmer nodded, 'that there was a forest nearby.'

'That's it, then!' the neighbour's face shone happily. 'You see, this horse is no ordinary creature. He can catch rabbits and hares just like a hunting hound. He was waiting for a rabbit, that's why he stopped and refused to go on!'

The farmer did not quite know what remark to make after such an explanation, so he mounted his horse and rode towards home, shaking his head.

When the horse was wading through a brook, he stopped short suddenly and the farmer flew over his head and almost drowned in the water.

He turned the horse round and galloped back to the neighbour's farm.

Already from a distance he was shouting, 'Don't bother me with that stubborn devil! Why, he almost drowned me in the stream! I don't want to lay my eyes on that horse again! Give me back my money. You can have him all to yourself!'

The neighbour waited till the farmer calmed down a bit, then he explained. 'Forgive me, I am so forgetful! I forgot to tell you that this horse also loves to catch fish.'

'Now, that's different,' bubbled the farmer excitedly. 'Fish is my favourite food. If this horse knows how to fish, I'll keep him.'

Then he mounted the rare horse and rode off home.

HOLD ON, JIM!

It was dusk. Mist was creeping over the moorland and, in the reeds, a water bird raised his plaintive voice: ah, ah, ah.

Along the muddy track which led from the wood five goods wagons rattled, filled with merchandise.

The carriers were looking for somewhere to stay overnight. The nights were growing cool, they would have welcomed to sleep somewhere in warmth and comfort.

Round a bend of the road they came upon a spacious house, set amid maple trees. But it was in complete darkness, not a single window was lit.

The carriers halted and knocked on the door.

Nobody opened, nobody called.

An old shepherd was driving his herd of sheep by, and he called to the carriers,

'It is useless to knock, nobody will open up here. This house has been deserted for the past twelve years. They say it is haunted.'

He smacked his whip and was off with the sheep.

'If that is true, then I am not likely to sleep in a haunted house,' said carrier Jack and went back to his wagon, urged his horse to go on and the wagon rolled on along the coarse, dusty track. 'I'd rather sleep in the forest.'

The rest of the carriers stood for awhile undecided on the doorstep, then set off after Jack towards the forest.

Carrier Jim made fun of them.

'What a brave lot you are! Babies — all of you! Afraid of an empty house. Go on and sleep in the damp forest. Cover yourselves with mist and hide your feet in the brook, so you don't get frostbitten!'

Resolutely he opened the front door and went inside. An old lantern hung behind the door. He lit it and went further into the hall.

The spacious room was well furnished with old furniture, and clean.

A pile of logs stood ready by the hearth.

The table was laid, only the food was missing.

Jim therefore lit the fire and cooked himself beans and bacon.

When he had eaten, he fetched a bottle of wine from the cellar and sipped it in comfort by the warm fire, whilst outside the mist crept over the countryside and the night, heavy with rain-drops, sighed like a drenched dog.

When tiredness began to close Jim's eyes, he climbed into bed, covered himself with a soft featherfilled cover and fell asleep.

He slept the night through, no one disturbed him.

At day-break Jim woke up, rubbed his eyes, and remembered where he was. When he reminded himself how the shepherd had warned him and his fellow carriers the previous evening, he grinned and thought, 'Those silly fellows are now shivering with cold in the forest. If they had not been such chicken-hearted cowards and had stayed here with me overnight, they would have slept in comfort and warmth till morning, too.'

But all at once the door of the next room creaked open with a scratchy, grating sound; a floorboard squeaked, a window rattled, just as if high winds were blowing against it.

A spectre, dressed in a white robe, stood framed by the door.

Slowly he walked towards Jim's bed.

Before the carrier could jump out of bed, the ghost pounced upon him with the whole of his body, his bony, icy hands tight round Jim's throat.

Jim was choking, and for quite some time he was unable to free himself from the grip.

At last he managed to grip the spectre's hands and to leap out of bed.

They started to grapple with one another.

Each did his best to get at the other one's throat. The ghost began to whine in a most ghastly way. Jim shouted for help.

The carriers heard the frantic noise out in the forest, the shouts and the horrific squeals.

They ran to the haunted house and looked inside through the window.

The sight took their breath away. In the centre of the room, among upturned chairs and tables, Jim was wrestling with the white spectre. The fireplace was in shambles, the window broken.

Jack was encouraging his friend through the broken pane,

'Hold him down, Jim, hold him down!'

To that Jim replied, 'I've got him, I won't let him go.'

But then the ghost threw Jim straight out of the door and was about to slam it shut.

But the carriers were all behind Jim.

'Don't give up, get him, Jim!'

'Bet a new pair of shoes then, that I will win.'

Jim pressed hard against the now closed door, broke it down and the merciless fight continued again.

A little later the spectre managed to throw Jim out through the window.

'At him, Jim, at him!' cried his mates.

Jim managed to get back into the room and to grip the ghost's throat.

'I don't care if its curtains for me, I'll see him flat on his back yet,' cried Jim, battling on like a maddened dog.

Then, the white spectre clutched Jim in an icy embrace, rose with him to the ceiling and through the roof. Jim just had time to call down to his friends,

'I am holding on to him, but he doesn't want to let go off me either.'

With that the spectre and Jim turned into two old crows and, croaking loudly, they disappeared over the black forest.

THE SNOW STORM

Laura was getting ready to go to the ball. Mother was ironing her green silk dress, gazing worriedly now and then through the window.

'The snow keeps on falling more thickly than ever, it is a long time since I have seen such a storm. Don't you think you ought to stay at home?'

Laura shook her head.

'Paul is taking me on his sleigh into town, so what could happen to me!'

'Whatever you think,' mother sighed.

When Laura was dressed, her brother brought the sleigh padded with hay and rugs right up to the front door.

The snow storm was raging harder than ever.

'Put your fur coat on,' mother advised Laura.

But her daughter objected. 'My dress would get creased. I'll curl up in the hay, that will keep me warm.'

Mother sighed again. But she knew how stubborn Laura was.

Paul helped his sister on to the sleigh, wrapped her in hay and blankets, then put his own sheepskin on, and they were off.

Beyond their ranch the track was covered, and the horses sank into the soft fresh snow.

The snowy curtain, swept by the winds, tore over the countryside, whilst the icy gale stung.

'I am cold,' Laura complained.

'Get further into the hay,' her brother advised, urging the horses to a gallop.

But the horses kept sinking into the snow drifts, their eyes and ears glued with snow.

'I am terribly cold,' Laura sobbed.

'Take my coat,' her brother offered.

'No, my dress will get creased.'

They rode on, the snow storm cloaking everything in its thick, cold veil.

'I can't bear this cold any longer,' Laura whispered through blue lips.

'If you won't put on my fur coat, at least let me throw this double cover over your shoulder!'

'I would dirty my dress!'

They drove on, the storm raged, the horses were white from snow and frost, and Laura was silent.

'She's gone to sleep,' the brother said to himself.

When they arrived in town, Paul stopped the sleigh in front of the hotel in the square. Tempting sounds of violins poured from the bright hall, for the dancing had begun.

'Here we are, Laura, let me help you off the sleigh!'

Laura did not answer. Paul took her by the hand. It was as cold as a piece of ice. He felt her brow. Freezing like a frozen well.

Laura had frozen on the way.

The brother laid her upon the seat and rubbed her face with snow. But she did not move.

He rushed inside the hotel, calling for help.

People took lanterns and ran to the sleigh.

Then they saw it all. The snow whirlwinds suddenly lifted frozen Laura and the gale grasped her in its arms, twirling with her as in a wild dance above the square, rising with her higher, always higher—whilst the storm howled and wailed its song.

Before the people with the lanterns knew what was happening, the wind had carried the frozen Laura into the kingdom of winter.

THE THIEF

'Listen, my lads, you are not to give the cattle so much maize,' said farmer Parker sternly. 'If it goes on disappearing at this rate, it won't last out till Christmas!'

'But boss,' the boys protested, 'we are so careful with that maize, that the cows have almost stopped giving milk, the old mule is so weak he can hardly stand up and flesh is dropping of our pigs something awful!'

'Is that so?' remarked the farmer. 'In that case we'd better find that sneak of a thief.'

He brought a trap strong enough to catch a fox from his cellar, put it in a pile of maize in the barn, and attached it to a beam with a strong chain.

The next morning, neighbour Morris limped across Parker's back yard. One hand was wrapped in his cap, his face was blue with pain, and there was a long chain dragging behind him.

'Come in,' Parker said. 'I am just about to have breakfast. Come and have some too. You look somewhat hungry!'

'I can't,' neighbour Morris answered, hissing with pain, 'I have hurt my hand slightly.'

'Where did that happen? Were you bitten by a dog?'

'That's exactly so, a dog,' the neighbour nodded, 'his teeth were like iron.'

Parker took a key out of his pocket, and with it opened the trap, which gripped Morris's blue hand.

'Quite so,' agreed the farmer, 'that dog's teeth must have been made of steel! He bit into your hand with such a force, that he couldn't get them out again.'

Next he glanced at the long chain, which neighbour Morris was dragging behind him, and remarked, 'Perhaps you'd better go back home and hide. Just think, that dog might be still tied to the other end of that chain, and could go for you again!'

'You are quite right,' Morris agreed willingly, 'I should hide before that vicious mad-dog gets me again.'

With that he rose.

'Let us first pop into my barn,' said Parker, rising too, and neighbour Morris, blue till now, turned bright red.

When they entered the barn, farmer Parker picked up an empty sack, faced Morris and said sternly,

'Let's have one thing clear, neighbour! This is my farm! On this farm I am the sole master and the sole judge!'

Neighbour Morris shook with fear.

Parker pronounced judgement.

'Take this sack, neighbour, and fill it with maize!'

Morris, frightened out of his wits, filled the sack with trembling hands.

'Now put that sack over your shoulder,' Parker continued in a kinder voice, 'and take it home. The maize in it is yours!'

Since that day not a grain of maize has been missing from farmer Parker's barn.

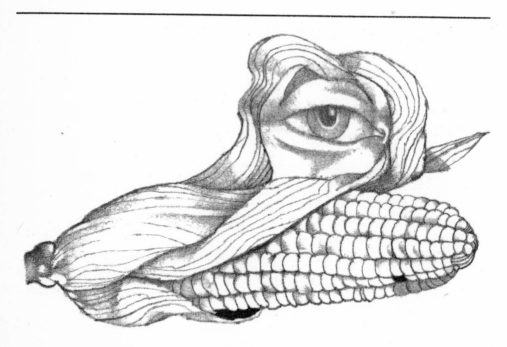

THE STONE MAIDEN

By the upper stream of a crystal-clear river lived the Indian tribe Arikara.

In one of the wigwams a beautiful maiden was growing up fast. Everyone who saw her looked upon her with pleasure.

The girl avoided people, she did not wish to play with other children. When she tidied up the wigwam, she called her little black and white dog and disappeared into the forest or over the prairie. There she talked to the birds and small creatures, to the flowers and trees. These she understood, and they understood her.

They were her very best friends.

When the girl was fully grown, prospective bridegrooms tried to woo her. Each one of them wanted this quiet, lovely and kind maiden for himself.

But she refused all suitors.

She felt in the depth of her heart that she could not truly love any man.

'I am at home in the forest and on the prairie,' she explained to the youths who wished to court her. 'I belong to the winged people and four-legged people, people who flower in the prairie grass and people who stretch their branches to the sky. These are my friends and only with them I have perfect understanding.'

The girl's grandmother observed worriedly how suitors crowded round her granddaughter, and it upset her to see the girl grow sadder from day to day.

The grandmother called her granddaughter and said,

'You can't go on like this, my girl. You must get married and bring up children like other young women do. Without children our tribe would die out.'

The grandmother did her best to convince her granddaughter for so long, that in the end the maiden lowered her head.

'Have it your own way, grandmother. If you say it must be so, then I will marry. It does not matter who the bridegroom is. But I already know that nothing good can come of the marriage. I am different from other girls, mother nature does not want me to marry.'

Three days after the wedding the young woman came to see her grandmother in the maternal tent.

Sad and unhappy she sat down in a corner in silence.

'What is the matter, my girl?' asked the grandmother. 'Isn't your husband kind to you?'

'He would bring me anything I desire. But I cannot love him.'

Then she rose and slowly walked off to the forest.

The grandmother, feeling most frightened, crept secretly behind her.

She found her sitting under an old maple tree.

It was the onset of autumn, leaves red and yellow fluttered to the ground and rustled in the grass, and chestnuts hit the earth with a bump.

'Tell me honestly,' asked the grandmother, sitting next to her granddaughter, 'what do you miss?'

The maiden sighed deeply.

'Do you recall, grandmother, how I said to you that nothing good could come of the marriage? I did not want to get married, my heart is pained and grieving. I do not love my husband and I do not wish to lie to him. He is an honest, kind man, he does not deserve to have me pretend to love him. We come from different worlds. I belong to nature and to nature I want to return. I long for silence and solitude.'

The grandmother rose and returned home, leaving her granddaughter in the forest. She did not want to intrude upon her thoughts.

The maiden did not return home at night.

The next morning the young men set out to find her.

She was on the hill over the prairie.

The lower part of her body had turned to stone.

The young men hurried back to the village.

The chief assembled all the men and women and they went out into the prairie.

When they reached the hill, the chief took a holy pipe, and tried to place it into the young woman's mouth, so the Great Spirit would enlighten her.

She shook her head.

'I am not refusing the smoke from the holy pipe because I want to ignore the laws of our tribe. I am not turning my face from the people with whom I've lived. But I belong to nature. Every blossom in the prairie, every green tree and every bird under the sky, every rushing brook is a part of my heart. I shall speak to you through the scent of flowers, through the freedom of bird's wings, through the trembling of tree leaves, through the song of bubbling waters, and I should so much like you to understand my language, when I am with you no longer.'

With these words the upper part of her body turned to stone, too.

And the little white and black dog also turned to stone.

The silent maiden made of rock now gazes across the prairie. Round her is the sweet-scented grass, the humming river, with the prairie wolves frolicking by their lairs.

The stone maiden stands here among her own kind—among sister and brother flowers and birds, rocks and passing clouds.

THE BLACK UMBRELLA

Elizabeth was a Negro woman who lived in a little house in a remote suburban corner. But for many years she had worked as a cook and a washer-woman for a rich merchant.

During the week, from morning till night she busied herself in her master's kitchen.

Only on Sunday afternoons, when she had washed the dishes and prepared cold supper for her master, she took off her white apron and cap and went home to the little house in the quiet suburb.

There she would sit by the window, looking at the sun slowly sliding down the darkening sky in the west, listening to the evening bird concert; their song always rocked her to sleep.

One evening, as she was thus dozing by the window, she was woken up by a strange song. This cannot be the singing of birds, the cook realized, still half asleep, and opened her eyes.

Dusk had fallen, but in the half-light she could just make out a group of dark stooping figures behind the low cemetery wall. And she heard them singing the ancient song, with which Negroes accompany the departed during the funeral procession.

> *Never again will rain soak your brow*
> *You are returning home forever now,*
> *Never again will you be drenched . . .*

Cook Elizabeth had sung that song many times, when she accompanied a deceased neighbour on his last journey.

She loved to sing songs, happy or sad; the sad ones best of all.

She closed the window, put on her shoes, put her old hat on her head and left her house.

In the cemetery she knelt by the singing crowd of Negroes and joined in singing the funeral song:

Never again will rain soak your brow,
You are returning home forever now,
Never again will you be drenched . . .

Now the night had darkened, cold rain began to fall from the low clouds, the wind started to howl over the graveyard.

Elizabeth pulled down the rim of her hat over her forehead and put her collar up; heavy rain was running down her back, but she sang on.

It was then that a long, skinny man rose from the ground and handed a large black umbrella to the cook.

'Such an excellent singer as you, sister, mustn't get soaked.'

With that he opened the umbrella over her head.

So the cook sheltered under the big umbrella and sang on with the others the funeral song of poor Negroes.

When the song ended, the long skinny man in his pointed black coat rose from the kneeling crowd and started to pray.

All the others joined him in prayer.

When at the end of the prayer the cook quietly said 'amen', the wind swished, rushed across the graveyard, sounding like the swish of wings of an immense black bird.

Elizabeth raised her head and was surprised. She was kneeling upon a deserted grave, overgrown with grass and weeds, and she was completely alone in the cemetery.

Only the rain murmured in the trees in the evening silence—and everywhere there was darkness, silence, emptiness.

She rose and hurried home.

When the cook closed the doors behind her, she realized that the large black umbrella was still in her hand.

She put it in a corner and trembled all night in her bed with fear. Would the spirits of deceased Negroes come for the umbrella?

But no one came, only the rain rustled monotonously and the branches bent by the wind knocked against the window pane.

For many years afterwards the large black umbrella stood in the corner of cook Elizabeth's little house. When it rained, she took it out of its corner, and when she returned home, she put it back again.

But never would she lend that umbrella to anyone else.

And no one ever laughed, when Elizabeth related how she had sung in the rain on a deserted grave the funeral song for the dead black neighbour, now forgotten by the living, in the company of spirits.

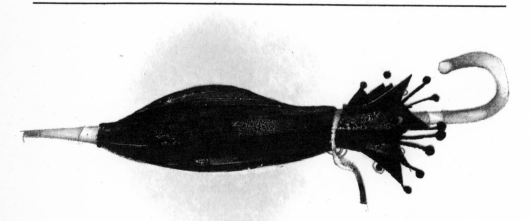

TISMILA WANDERS THROUGH THE FOREST

Whenever mother was cooking dinner in the hearth, little Tismila appeared by the pan, put his hand in as quick as lightning and fished out a piece of meat. He gulped it fast, but he was not satisfied with just one piece. When mother was adding logs to the fire, Tismila helped himself the second time. And by the time mother was ready to serve dinner to her husband and her other children, there was nothing left in the pan. Tismila had eaten all the meat.

Mother and father reasoned with him in vain. His older brother sneered at him, calling him a greedy-pig, but it was no use, Tismila did not improve.

One day, when mother was cooking supper and had just run to fetch some flour, Tismila's hand once again shot inside the pan to grab some meat before his mother's return.

But alas! The pan gripped his hand hard and Tismila tried to pull it out in vain. So he banged the saucepan against the floor, but it was no use; the pan refused to break. Tismila ran outside, his hand in the pan and pelted into the forest, banging the pan against the trees, trying to get rid of it.

It was all useless. The pan gripped his hand as hard as a snare holds a rabbit.

In Indian villages people often hear strange hollow sounds in the forest during dark nights.

The echoing steps come nearer, then go further and further away into the dense forest, till they cease altogether in the distant bushland.

That is that Indian greedy-pig wandering in the forests and hills, vainly trying to pull his hand from the pan.

THE GOLD TREASURE OF MISSISSIPPI

The countryside gleamed in the heat of the dying summer, and herds of long-horned cows grazed peacefully by the river. A bulky paddle-steamer slowly made its way along its surface, through the first fallen golden leaves.

From two long funnels towering over the two decks black smoke soared into the September sky.

The paddle wheel deliberately and tirelessly cut through the muddy water, and white foam hissed on the surface, as if on the boil.

A lengthy wave ran out from the aft of the steamer, spilling further across the wide dirty river, till with a gentle swish it hit the flat shore.

The steamer, *Drennan Whyte,* only recently built and launched, was sailing against the current from New Orleans to Memphis.

Under-deck it carried riches; a chest with one hundred thousand gold dollars.

Everything on the steamer was shining new.

Everything shone and glittered just like the gold dollars in the chest, just like an Indian summer gleams round the Mississippi river.

The ship was nearing the town of Natchez; the helmsman was puffing on his pipe whilst steering the steamer, the captain was joking with passengers. The river was peaceful and smiling.

It, too, glimmered in the sun just like the new steamer, which was sailing on her now, just like the gold dollars in the chest under-deck.

There was a deafening bang, the river arched its back, taking the full blast and carrying it in a long turbulent wave to the grassy shore.

Before the wave could hit the shore, yet another explosion rocked the steamer — an even mightier one. The steam boiler had split open, burning the stokers, and the pressure of steam tore the new boat as if it was a mere frail shell.

Five minutes later there was not a trace of the steamer.

The travellers swam towards the shore in confusion, grasping at floating pieces of wood.

The sun shone on without a care in the world in the clear sky, the river rolled on, as if nothing had happened, flowing over the wide river bed between green pastures and fields further towards New Orleans on that September day, golden like the gold of the autumn leaves.

When news of the disaster reached the owners of the sunken ship, they immediately sent the large boat *Evermonde* to the town of Natchez, so that the wrecked steamer could be recovered.

But the spirits of the great river Mississippi loathe to give up treasures which have come into their possession. Not far away from the tomb of the sunken steamer *Drennan Whyte,* the boat *Evermonde* went up in flames like a torch.

Sixteen members of its crew went down with it forever to the river bed.

The shippers left the river in peace for one year.

The following August, nearly a year after the explosion, they sent a third ship to the town of Natchez — *Ellen Adams.*

It was equipped with diving devices. The sailors were to find the position of the sunken steamer on the river bed, which still held the hundred thousand gold dollars.

But Mississippi is not a peaceful river.

Incessantly it throws mud and sand into the current, the banks grow in one place, and are torn away in another; and the face round the river changes, too—on its shores new towns, new roads and new ports keep on growing.

Since the fateful September day, Mississippi's waters had twice swelled with a terrible flood, and twice the river had moved its bed.

The divers from the *Ellen Adams* searched for the sunken steamer with the golden treasure in vain.

To top it all, in October the *Ellen Adams* ran aground in shallow water and sank half-way.

The spirits of the Mississippi river breathed easily again. The treasure had been saved for their watery kingdom.

Several times during the following years, fishermen and hunters noticed the shadow of the submerged steamer under the surface; several groups of divers tried to haul it out, but the vessel was firmly wedged in mud, and the river deposited on it further and further layers of fine soil and sand from the fields. The waters of Mississippi flowed on, the years passed and flowed over the mighty muddy river and the sunken steamer fell further and further into oblivion.

The spirits of the river were laughing.

Fortune means good luck, hope, a future.

Can good luck go hand in hand with the fate of a man, whose name happens to be Ancil Fortune?

He was the son of Caleb Fortune, the late captain of the *Ellen Adams,* which in vain tried to find the wreck of the sunken ship and to reclaim the golden treasure. He bought a small farm near the town of Jeffris, on the banks of Mississippi. He had many children and very little money.

That's how it is in the world of ours, poor or rich go after gold, if it is their wish.

In that spring farmer Fortune started digging a well on his land by the river.

When the hole was nearly three metres deep, his pick-axe struck something hard. He scraped away the soil and marvelled. He had dug to the very mouth of the ship's funnel.

He naturally wondered straightaway if it was the wrecked steamer with its treasure of gold! People still talked about the treasure on the bottom of the river bed, for the sunken ship had become a part of the past, which would never be forgotten.

But he curbed his hopes with doubts. How could the current carry the submerged steamer so far!

But hope still knocked on his door, though doubt kept chasing it away.

One hundred thousand gold dollars in those days was a fairylike fortune, even for the rich. For a poor farmer it was an unbelievable dream.

Farmer Fortune could not sleep. 'Is something wrong?' asked his wife worriedly, but the farmer only answered with a grunt.

Night after night he thought only about one thing now: how to get into the submerged steamer, choked with mud.

He well knew he must not let anyone into the secret. Otherwise a crowd of people would come, with power and law backing them firmly, and they would force the farmer to stop digging on his land and would themselves try to recover the treasure.

Ancil Fortune thought and thought, tossing about on his bed, sleeplessness had made his eyes sunken and his skin had a yellowish tinge. But, in the end, he did think up a suitable plan.

He cut off sticks from a willow tree, and planted them thickly side by side on the shore round the hole he had dug.

For five years he managed to keep away from that hole.

In the meantime, a dense willow copse grew in the meadow. Cattle could not graze there, and this was just what the farmer needed.

He cleared some of the growth round the hole, so he would not be handicapped in his work, and started to dig once more.

Soon he struck the upper deck of the wrecked vessel. Now he knew he was in for some real hard toil!

Alone, always alone he spent days and months removing the layers of mud and sand from the interior of the ship. The moment he finished his daily tasks in the fields, he'd rush to the hollow and slave into darkness day after day.

For weeks, for months, for years.

He did not know Sunday; he forgot the sweet taste of rest and the pleasure of reclining in the shade of a tree when the sun was burning. He forgot the cosy moments by his fireside, when outside it was spitting and the wind combed the untidy, sodden countryside with its sharp comb.

For three long years Ancil Fortune thus toiled in the pit surrounded by the willow copse.

And all this time he was consumed but with one thought: would this be the steamer with the treasure of gold? Or will all his work have been for nothing?

But one day he uncovered a part of the hull of the vessel, and beneath his pick-axe and spade he saw the glint of the much worn, but still clearly visible large letters:

DRENNAN WHYTE

He had found it after all.

He wanted to shout to the world that he had tracked down the treasure, that his three year toil had not been in vain.

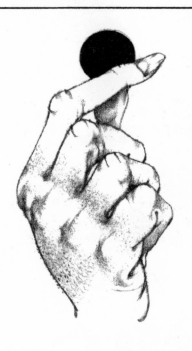

But he had to keep silent, always silent and never even hint to his wife or children what was hidden in the willow copse.

He dug out several tiny passages round the ship's frame, just wide enough for him to crawl through, and eventually he came to a small cabin filled with mud and sand.

He cleared it with his spade.

It took three months toil to find out that the cabin did not belong to the steamer's captain. For it was said that the chest with the gold dollars was placed in the captain's cabin!

Once again he thoroughly examined the lay-out of the ship's

area, and started to dig yet another passage in a different place.

Twice, during a heavy cloudburst, everything was flooded and he had to drain the hole. But he did not give up, hope supported him on his feet and sparkled in his heart.

After ten years, during the winter, he found at last the captain's cabin — he recognized it by the glass-covered map still framed on the wall.

The following May came his big day.

The spirits of the river Mississippi trembled.

His spade struck against the metal of the chest.

His heart was in his mouth, as his pick-axe worked at the rusty lock. He pushed aside the lid and — then he was drowning up to his elbows in a flood of gold dollars.

They shone as if newly minted yesterday.

A whole chest of gold!

'I must go home for some sacks', the farmer stuttered excitedly, not knowing whether to jump for joy or to cry with happiness.

He did not do one or the other.

As he was rushing to fetch the sacks, he tripped over a willow root and broke his right ankle.

He went to bed and waited for the doctor. Early tomorrow morning, as soon as the doctor puts my foot in plaster, I'll limp to the treasure, and by nightfall it will be safely under my roof.

No one will find it.

Why would anyone go there!

During the night he was awakened by rain.

A storm was raging over the Mississippi.

The spirits of the old river had been discussing how the treasure could be saved.

They called clouds, lightning and winds to help.

That night, the next day and the rest of that week torrential rain whipped the river and fields surrounding the Mississippi.

Brooks and streams overflowed, the river burst its banks flooding the countryside and the hollow in the willow copse, where the farmer with the name which means good luck, hope and a future had toiled for eleven long years with a pick-axe and a spade to recover the treasure of gold from the mud.

When the rain stopped, farmer Fortune gazed at the river.

It had flooded the land as far as the eye could see.

Only tips of trees were showing from the willow copse.

That was the end, the end of everything!

A light went out in the head of farmer Ancil Fortune.

He was not even aware that he was plunging into the deep, treacherous water.

As he was falling to the bottom, the gulls laughed mockingly above the swollen surface.

The spirits of the old Mississippi river were singing their celebration song.

The treasure was to remain in their power.

The sun came out again and the mighty river glimmered in its glow, a river ancient and wise, but impassive to human fate.

THE LAZIEST MAN IN AMERICA

Uncle Hubert in early childhood hit upon a fantastic idea. He was determined to find out how to survive without working.

That is easy, for those who have money, do not have to work in America.

But uncle Hubert, of course, had no money at all.

So right from his youth he wondered and pondered how to organize things, so he could live without work and without money.

Quite simply, uncle Hubert was so terribly lazy, that if he were, for instance, to sing all the year round the song 'My golden laziness, you make me sick, you I must lick', it would be no use at all, laziness would simply not part with him.

At work, his hands (even in the summer) always remained idle, whereas at the dinner table they worked overtime.

In other words, an idler to beat all idlers!

Best of all he liked to watch over the sun in the sky for days on end.

But laziness had bitten so hard into his hands and feet, that it was just too much for him to flick a mosquito away, or to stand up on his feet at night and go home to supper.

Uncle Hubert did not even get married.

He was by no means ugly, the girls liked him. Once some young miss from the next village convinced him he should marry her.

Hubert nodded, without even getting off the ground. He happened to be flat on his back in the garden, waiting for some pear to fall near enough for him not even to have to stretch his hand for it.

On the day of the wedding, Hubert did not show up.

He was asleep, and when his mother told him off, he murmured that he did not feel like going to the marriage office in the town, and for everyone to leave him alone.

He turned to his other side and went on sleeping.

Whilst his mother was alive, Hubert was fine. She spoiled him, she cooked for him and whenever the neighbours sneered that she had a loafer at home, she only mumbled, 'He'll work enough in his life later on, let him rest, I shan't let him die of hunger.'

So Hubert went on resting and pondering how to live without money and without work.

He did not come up with any decent idea, so he just went on eating and resting.

Those who like idleness best, have a Sunday every day—a day of rest.

Times were bad when Hubert's mother died. There was no one then to bring dishes with roast chicken and fried steaks, not even sweet corn hash, or white coffee and strawberry tarts.

Hubert pulled a side of ham and a loaf of bread to his bed, he cut off a bit here and there, munched at leisure and loafed on.

During the winter the wind tore its way through the shingles on the roof, and knocked them down one by one. The rafters tumbled down, the roof fell through, the ceiling was soaking wet and then it rained into the living room. A wall crumbled, and another, everything in the cottage was sodden, frogs jumped about by the kitchen stove, spiders wove such strong and thick nets that even a woodcutter's axe could not have cut through them and mice from all around held fancy dress balls in this semi-derelict house.

Yet uncle Hubert just covered himself with an old overcoat and slept, and when he was not asleep, he thought how he could survive without work and without money.

An idler gets wet even under his own roof.

In the end he fell ill from all the cold and all the damp, in fact his soul very nearly left his body for ever.

By then he was so lazy he was not even capable of coughing, his windpipe was almost blocked and he could have choked to death.

But he improved slightly, rolled out of his lair and staggered to his neighbour for advice.

'So you'd like to live without work,' muttered old Hutter, 'that's nothing unusual, there are many who would like to tie work to a chain, so it would not bite them and then go and graze in the meadow, that is if a man could feed on grass.'

Uncle Hubert sighed and neighbour Hutter pushed his cap further down his head.

'As it happens, I know the very place for you, but I don't know if it is still unoccupied.'

Uncle Hubert sharpened his ears.

'Now look,' old Hutter explained, 'you climb up against the river, till you come to a small island. In that place the river is shallow, you can easily wade over to the island. That is if no one has claimed it before you.'

As soon as uncle Hubert heard this, he did not even bother to say goodbye, but packed a shirt, a loaf and three chunks of bacon in a sack, called his dog and was off.

He waded across the shallow river to the little island and realized straightaway he was in paradise.

The soil on this island was as black as crow's feathers, the fruit on the apple trees were larger than marrows, melons resembled tubs of wine; in the shallows of the river trout larger than crocodiles were

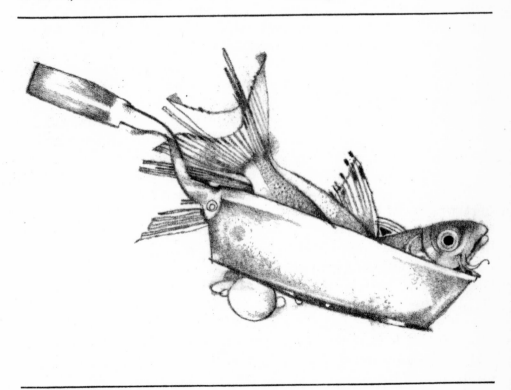

sunning themselves, while fat turkeys sat on tree branches and stags and rabbits played hide and seek amid the trees.

It was sufficient to plant a twig in the furtile soil and a week later it was in flower and a month later golden peaches weighed it down. The maple trees yielded thick sugar juices, butter flowed from the nuts.

Uncle Hubert just could not believe his luck, his head was spinning with delight. His old dream had come true after all. He was living in paradise on earth, where man could survive without work and money.

He found an old decayed oak, with grape vines growing over its crust, heavy with ripe fruit, and he made his home in the hollow.

All he had to do was to stretch out his hand and a juicy grape fell right into it, and when he was not utterly lazy and stretched his hand a little further, he would catch a pheasant.

Uncle Hubert lit a fire in front of the oak.

He did not have to gather wood; dry branches fell from the oak tree of their own accord onto the fire. Uncle stretched a wire across it and on this he roasted pheasants in the day and at night rabbits, deer, wild ducks, salmon and trout. When he wanted a drink, he did not have to think but raise himself the tiniest, weeniest bit, to break from the vine a grape or two, filled with the blackest, sweetest wine.

Uncle Hubert also liked to smoke a pipe.

But he could not think how to acquire tobacco with no funds at all. Luckily he had a bit left in his pouch. And as he filled his pipe, a few strands of the tobacco dropped to the ground.

While uncle Hubert was lolling about, green tobacco shoots started sprouting from the furtile soil; by the evening, the green leaves had dried and uncle's worries were over.

But uncle Hubert still thought he was doing too much.

So he wondered and pondered, till he invented some equipment for scraping fish scales off. Even a specialist would be surprised how simple, yet how effective uncle's equipment was. When the fish took the bait, all that was necessary was to lightly pull a string. This immediately loosened a stone placed on a branch in the tree crown; the stone fell down, hitting the end of the rod and tossing the fish up into the crown smack between two potato graters and a sharp knife. In a twinkling of an eye it came down straight into the frying pan, descaled and its head cut off. Five minutes later it was fried to a turn and all uncle had to do was to pick up this succulent delicacy with his hand.

The dog enjoyed the fish heads. He stood under the oak, his mouth wide open, waiting for the trout head or the salmon head to fall into it.

Uncle Hubert was now sprawled out by the oak, biting into the fried fish and thinking hard how he could acquire game without doing anything. He was growing sick of fish.

He puffed at his pipe and pondered, till he had an idea.

But he needed a trap.

It took him a month, before he made his lazy body rise off the ground and walk to the little town.

An hour later he was back with a mouse trap.

On his island he put it in the grass and covered it lightly with soil.

By morning the mouse trap had grown in the furtile soil, and uncle caught rabbits with it.

The trap went on growing and uncle managed to catch a stag.

But it took such an effort to release the trap and take out the catch that uncle had to put his thinking cap on again. Roughly two months later he had an inspiration. Why didn't I think of it before!

That tobacco, which uncle was growing in the very furtile soil, was, after all, terribly strong. Let the tobacco prove how strong it was!

Uncle stepped to the trap, puffed at his pipe, and lo and behold! The smoke from the strong tobacco opened the trap.

Uncle Hubert took out the stag and roasted it on the fire.

In the meantime the trap still grew bigger and bigger, till it was large enough to catch bears.

Now uncle Hubert lay under the oak, puffing at his pipe and pondering how to skin the animals without any effort.

If he has not come up with the answer yet, he is still under that oak today.

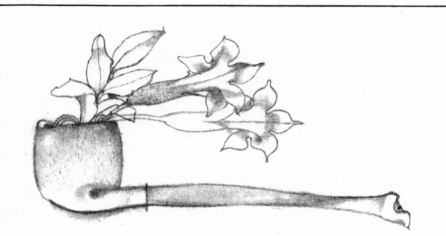

THE BIRD FROM THE GOLDEN LAND

Day after day the blue bird came from the Golden Land.

As dawn was breaking, he would fly down to the maple tree to sing most melodiously to Erin, the master of the great cotton plantation.

One morning Erin's three sons entered their father's bedroom.

'We should like to get married,' said the eldest son. 'Can you find us suitable brides?'

Erin thought hard and said, 'I will think about the matter.'

When his sons left him, he sat by the window, listened to the song of the blue bird and reasoned. 'I have a prosperous cotton plantation and I own other land. How can I divide my estate fairly between my three sons when they marry?'

He thought hard and harder still, but did not come up with the solution.

'What if I were to give my eldest son half of my land and the second son the other half?' he pondered. 'Then the plantation would come to the youngest.'

But straightaway he dismissed this idea.

He well knew that all three sons longed only to be the masters of the great cotton plantation and to live in the big house.

To which son then should he entrust the ownership?

The eldest?

Or the youngest?

Or would it be more sensible to give it to the middle son?

Erin was preoccupied with his thoughts the whole day long, and, by evening, he could not even enjoy his dinner.

Irritable and discontent that he had not solved the problem, he retired that night to his bed.

He had a very strange dream.

In the dream a white-haired, aged man came up to him and said, 'Send your sons to the Golden Land.'

The next morning Erin called his three sons to him and said,

'The best thing will be for you all to leave as soon as possible for the Golden Land to find the spot from which the blue bird flies each morning to my garden. It is quite possible that at the same time you will find brides for yourselves.'

'We shall set out immediately,' agreed the sons and the next morning they were on their way to the Golden Land.

By that evening they came to a high rock, and under it crouched a thatched cottage.

An aged woman-seer lived there.

'I am expecting you,' she said. 'Come in, your supper is ready.'

The youths were surprised that the old woman knew about them, but they did not question her, but sat at the table and ate.

After supper they went to bed.

In the morning, as the seer was bidding them goodbye, she advised them,

'I know you are journeying to the Golden Land. But you would search for it in vain on top of this earth. To find it you must descend down a deep well.'

Then the aged woman gave them all a gift.

The eldest was given an iron hammer.

The second a crib.

The youngest had what was left—a length of strong rope.

With that the seer showed the three brothers the way to the well.

They climbed to the top of a rocky mountain.

The eldest struck the rock with the iron hammer and hollowed out a deep well.

This was the way to the Golden Land.

They tied the crib to the rope.

And one after the other they went down the deep well in the crib.

When the youngest brother arrived at the bottom of the well, he looked for his elder brothers in vain.

He could not find them anywhere.

'So what,' he thought, 'what is there to be afraid of! I'll go on alone, I shall not get lost.'

He walked on and on, till he came to a huge mansion.

He opened the gate, crossed the courtyard and went inside a great hall, then passed from one chamber into another.

There was not a soul to be seen.

Not until he climbed into the highest turret did he find an old house-keeper in a tiny room.

'For a long time now I have been guarding this mansion,' said the old woman, 'and no human being has entered. As you were daring and were not afraid to pass through the deserted mansion, I will give you a present. Come with me to the stables.'

A dozen magnificent horses stood in the stable.

The house-keeper said to the youth, 'Choose one. You can have the one you like best.'

The youngest son looked round the stable. In a dark corner by a trough stood a dirty old mare with a drooping head. He felt sorry for her, so he said,

'I would like that mare.'

'You have chosen wisely,' the house-keeper remarked, 'for this mare will lead you to your destination.'

The youth scrubbed and brushed the mare, till her coat shone like silk, then he thanked the old woman and was on his way.

When they came to the sea, the mare halted, turned her head with the wise pair of eyes to the youth and spoke in a human voice.

'Do not fear, young man, for in the sea there are three islands. I will swim to the first, where we shall rest, then we'll make for the second island and for the third. When I have rested on the third island, I will transport you to the mainland on the other side of the sea and we shall be in the Golden Land.'

The sea was calm as they swam at last from the third island.

When they reached the opposite shore, the governor of the Golden Land was already waiting for the youth.

He said to him, 'I know why you have come. You want to take the blue bird. If you wish to get him, you must first discover me three times.'

That evening the disheartened youth was preparing to sleep in the stable. But the mare encouraged him,

'Don't worry, I will help you. In the morning, go in the garden and search for the nicest red apple. When you find it, cut it in half. The governor will be hiding in that apple and when he walks out, he will have a fresh cut on his head.'

The next morning the youth went into the garden to look for the nicest red apple.

When he found it and cut it in half, the governor stepped out of the apple, a red scar on his head just as the mare had foretold.

That evening the mare in the stable said to the youth,

'The second task awaits you tomorrow. But never fear, for I shall help you.' And she told him where to look for the governor.

The next morning the youth went straight to the kitchen. The cook gave him a bowl of soup and offered a silver spoon to eat it with. But the youth refused the spoon and dipped a knife into the soup instead. The governor crawled out of the bowl, and on his head he bore two red scars.

That evening, as the youth was preparing for sleep in the stable, the mare leaned over him and whispered,

'Sleep soundly, for tomorrow you must find the governor for the third time. I will tell you where.'

178

The next morning the youth picked a handful of wheat grain and went to the lake. He scattered the wheat in the grass on the shore. Just then a wild duck flew down from the sky and picked up all the grains. Next she made a nest in the reeds and laid an egg.

The youth took the egg out of the nest and cut it with his knife.

The governor stepped out of the egg, with three red scars on his head.

'You have discovered me three times and you have fulfilled all three tasks,' said the governor. 'But that is only half of what is required of you. The other half is still waiting for you. Now you must hide before me three times. And if I discover you just once, you will be shorter by a head.'

That night the youth went to bed heavy-hearted.

But the mare turned her head towards him. 'Don't worry, I will help.'

The first day she turned the youth into a flea. The flea crawled into the fur of the dog in the yard.

The governor searched through the mansion, he even looked into the dog's kennel.

But he did not find the youth.

The second time the mare turned the youth into honey.

The governor searched the bee-hives, but he did not notice the honey in the bottom honeycomb.

Again the youth was not discovered.

The third day the mare hid the youth in the hair of the governor's daughter. The governor searched all over her chamber, he examined her head hair by hair, he missed only the finest, shortest hair on her temple. He did not find the youth.

He was very tired after the three days of useless searching, so he went to bed.

'Your time has come,' said the mare, 'the governor of the Golden Land falls asleep only once every seven years. That happens to be today. Do not dilly dally, but take the cage with the blue bird. Do not stop on the way and return with it straight back to me.'

The youth went to the governor's chamber.

Very carefully he took the cage with the blue bird off the wall and hurried back to the mare in the stable.

'Sit on my back,' said the mare and she galloped away towards the sea shore.

On the return journey she rested on all three islands and so was able to swim safely across the sea, with the youth and the cage.

The old house-keeper was looking out for them impatiently from the turret of the deserted mansion. The moment the clatter of hooves echoed in the courtyard, she ran down the staircase to meet them.

After greeting the youth, the old woman said,

'You have saved three maidens. See the blue bird in the cage? It is the mistress of a great cotton plantation. And the old mare, who brought you across the sea to the Golden Land, is the mistress of a great tobacco plantation. I, too, am the owner of a large sugar cane plantation.

As soon as the house-keeper had finished speaking, the golden cage split open and a beautiful young woman, the mistress of the cotton plantation, stepped out.

She touched the mare and the old house-keeper and they, too, turned into lovely maidens.

All three thanked the youngest son for setting them free.

Then they all hastened to the well in the rock.

The elder brothers were already waiting for them.

First to step into the crib with the eldest brother, now her bridegroom, was the mistress of the tobacco plantation.

After the crib, tied to the rope, came down again, the second brother stepped into it with his bride, the mistress of the sugar cane plantation.

When it was the youngest son's turn to get in, the mistress of the great cotton plantation said, 'Now I shall show you how false your brothers are.'

She placed a large stone in the crib.

The brothers pulled the crib almost to the very top, then cut the rope.

The crib cascaded to the bottom with a clatter.

'So you see,' said the maiden, 'that would have been the end of us, if we had been sitting in that crib.'

In the meantime the eldest brother and the middle brother went with their brides to the thatched cottage under the rock.

The old seer was waiting for them.

'Where did you leave your youngest brother and his bride?' she asked.

'He stayed in the Golden Land, he did not want to come home.'

'You are lying,' said the seer and turned the brides into blue birds.

When the two elder brothers returned to the big house, Erin asked about his youngest son.

'We lost him as soon as we left here,' the sons lied, 'he didn't feel like going all that way to the Golden Land.'

Their father shook his head in disbelief but he said not a word and did not speak of his youngest son again.

The eldest son hung a cage with his blue bird in his bedroom. But the bird sat sadly in the cage, without singing a note.

'You wait till you hear the beautiful song of my blue bird,' bragged the second brother and hung his cage with the bird in his bedroom. But the bird hid its head and did not utter a single tweet. The father paced about the house in silence, thinking always of his youngest son.

In the meantime, the mistress of the great cotton plantation had also turned into a blue bird down in the well in the rock.

She flew upwards back to earth, where she turned back to a maiden.

She tied the severed rope together and pulled up her bridegroom, Erin's youngest son.

The moment the youth was back on firm ground, the maiden changed once again into a blue bird.

When the youngest son returned to the plantation with the blue bird in a cage, his father was overjoyed and ordered a great feast to be held and guests from all around gathered for it.

When the feasting was at its highest, the youngest son rose, pulled off the cover from the golden cage, and said,

'Would you like to hear the song of the blue bird from the Golden Land?'

The guests quietened down and the bird began to sing:

Back to the great house the brothers came to stay
Bringing dishonour, for they learned to betray.
The youngest brother they tried to slay
That is all this song has to say.

At that moment, all the three blue birds turned into three maidens. The guests could not help but point at the two elder sons of Erin. They fell to their knees and begged for their father's forgiveness.

'It is not me you should beg. You must ask your youngest brother for forgiveness, for you wished him harm,' said he, turning his back upon them.

Soon afterwards three noisy weddings were held, so that everyone knew then that the youngest brother did, in fact, forgive the other two.

ROAST DUCKLING

The blacksmith invited the town preacher for Sunday lunch. He called his daughter and said,

'Listen, Annie, I am off to the station to meet the preacher. While I am gone, I want you to put those two ducklings in the oven and to roast them to a turn. But no picking, mind!'

The daughter was all promises. 'Good gracious, father, why, I wouldn't dream of touching them, to tell the truth, I'm a bit sick of eating duck meat.'

The blacksmith went off to meet the preacher and Annie got on with the roast. Soon a succulent smell was oozing from the oven, but Annie resisted the temptation for quite some time. Then she mused, 'So what, I'll pinch just a small bit of the duck, and the preacher won't be any the wiser!'

She broke off a wing, ate it and reasoned, that as the duckling already had one wing missing, it would manage without the other one too. Next it was the turn of a leg and, before long, all that remained of the golden duckling were the bones.

That duck alone in the roasting tin looks awfully lonely, Annie said to herself, and gobbled up the second duckling.

Annie's father and the preacher arrived awhile later.

'Lay the table, my girl, while I sharpen the knife,' said the blacksmith, and went out into the yard where the grinding wheel stood.

Annie knew full well that she'd be in for a good hiding. But she usually managed to wriggle out of trouble and was determined to work her way out of this tight corner too! All at once she burst out crying and sobbing, wiping her tears with a handkerchief.

'What is the matter, dear girl?' asked the preacher.

'My father is really getting impossible. Every Sunday he invites someone from town for lunch, and then goes out to sharpen that awful long knife.'

'What does your father need the knife for?'

'He uses that sharpened, horrible long knife to stab the invited guest.'

The preacher's face turned ashen and he stuttered, 'My dear, please hand me my hat and my coat at once!'

He put on his overcoat, pushed his hat well down on to his face and pelted out of the cottage towards the station.

The blacksmith came back inside, his knife sharp for carving the duckling, only to be told by Annie, 'Just think, that preacher gobbled up both those ducks and nearly choked to death, because he ate with such speed. Then he got up from the table and left.'

The blacksmith ran into the yard and shouted after the guest, 'Wait, dear friend, why are you rushing off? Come back please!'

The preacher glanced back from the path and called out across the meadow, 'Don't count on me! You can't pull wool over my eyes, you barbarous brute!'

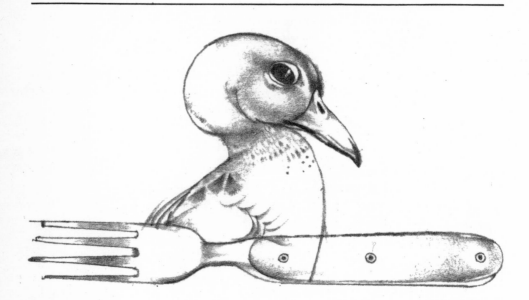

HOW HOOF LAKE GOT ITS NAME

The Indian tribe Chikaso lived on the banks of a wide, marshy river. The chief's son was born with a deformed right foot and dragged it behind him as he walked. The Indians, therefore, named him Hoof.

The boy had plenty of pluck. He knew other lads sneered at him when they were at play but he was determined to show them what he was made of.

Without anyone knowing, he learned to shoot from a bow, to stalk animals and catch fish. When he grew up, all the members of the Chikaso tribe admired him, praising him for his agility and courage.

Before very long Hoof became the tribe's chief. From that day there was always ample meat and corn in the village, no one had to go hungry.

But Hoof's wigwam was always silent and empty, for no girl from the Chikaso tribe wanted to marry him.

'Who wants a man with a club-foot for a husband,' the maidens would say, as one after the other they in turn refused the chief's offer of marriage.

The young chief sat forlornly in his tent. Solitude was really getting him down but what could he do? Wishes and desire alone could not bring him a wife.

One day the tribe's scout brought the chief some challenging tidings. Towards the midday sun lived the Chakto tribe, whose chief had the most beautiful daughter.

Hoof summoned his bravest and ablest warriors and left to find the bride immediately.

After a week's march through marshland and forests, Hoof and his men reached the Chakto tribe's territory. During the journey Hoof found out from the Indians that the chief's daughter was as sprightly as a sprig, with hands soft and smooth as if they were dipped in broken turtle eggs, and a voice as gentle as the rustle of leaves.

Hoof did not need to know any more. He sent a message to the chief that he came in peace. Soon afterwards the flap of the chief's tent was raised and he was admitted.

'We come to pay our respects to the brave and wise chief,' Hoof said, when face to face with chief Copiah. 'We have been told many good things about you. To prove we come in friendship, we bring you furs and strings of shells.'

Chief Copiah was pleased with the kind words. He accepted the gifts gladly and ordered a feast to be prepared in honour of the peace-loving guests from the Chikaso tribe.

When Hoof and his warriors had their fill and all the men from the Chakto tribe retired, Hoof asked the old chief,

'Who is the maiden sitting in the corner of your tent? She is the most beautiful girl I have ever seen.'

'She is my daughter,' was the chief's reply.

'If you add ten horses and ten rugs to your daughter, I will take her for my wife,' Hoof said graciously.

He was not concerned with the horses and rugs, he was simply testing the old chief.

The chief shook his head in silence.

'I could make do with five horses and five rugs then,' Hoof said.

The chief refused again with a shake of the head.

'In that case, I will take your daughter without a dowry.'

The chief fumed, 'Give my daughter to a hoof-footed cripple like you? Go away and let us be, find a wife from your own tribe.'

The insult hit Hoof's head like a red-hot arrow. He turned purple with anger and poured threats upon the old chief.

Copiah could see Hoof's warriors were well armed and he grew frightened.

He summoned the witch doctor and told him to make known to him the opinion of the Great Spirit. 'If the Great Spirit so wishes, I will gladly obey and will give my daughter to Hoof.'

The witch doctor came to the tent with rattles, snake skins and dog bones, and he called to the Great Spirit to speak.

On his knees and with his head lowered to the ground, the witch doctor listened to the voice of the Great Spirit. A few moments later he rose and passed on the words of the Great Spirit's message.

'Indian Hoof came out of the midnight forests and marshes and many unpleasant things lie before this man. Law forbids an Indian to carry off a maiden from another tribe by force. If Hoof breaks this law, he will bring disaster to his tribe.'

Hoof was utterly powerless. He and his warriors left the chief's tent and turned towards the midnight marshes and forests.

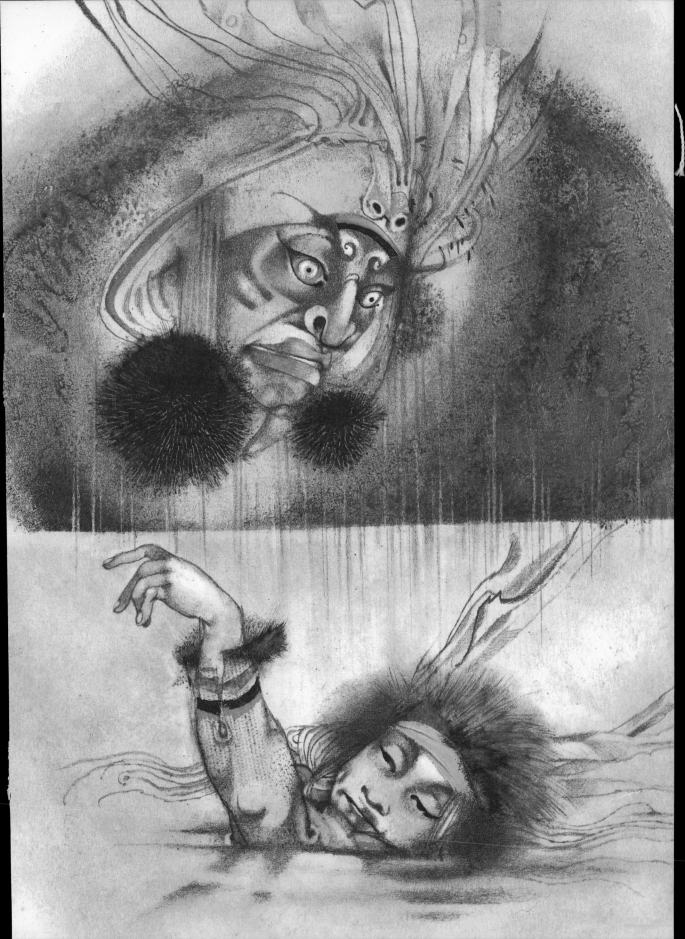

The insult burnt, like a red-hot cinder in Hoof's heart. He would have his revenge on the chief. The witch-doctor was sure to be in league with his chief anyway. Perhaps the Great Spirit had agreed with the marriage and the witch-doctor had twisted the message to the chief's order.

That night Hoof and his warriors crept back to the Chakto camp. They slit the guard dogs' throats, so they could not give them away, then slipped into the chief's tent and kidnapped his daughter.

They managed to inch their way through the sleeping camp,

without anyone hearing or seeing them. Then they sped back towards the midnight forests and marshes.

They reached their tribe without any difficulty.

The entire village was happy to see Hoof at last with a bride. Long into the night drums echoed through the forest, singing merged with camp-fire smoke, and dancing feet tore the earth.

All at once thunder roared threateningly over the forest. The earth rumbled and trembled. Fierce gales screamed through the valley, uprooting trees and breaking them like frail twigs. Tents were blown to the ground. The Indians, confused and terrified, cowered, pressing themselves against the earth.

The heavens opened and the Great Spirit called out in a hair-raising voice,

'Chief Hoof! I warned you. You disobeyed. Your tribe will not escape punishment.'

At that moment the mighty father of all rivers roared with a tremulous voice, his waters rose, carrying revenge on their waves.

Muddy waters flooded the whole valley, spilling far into the distance; whirlpools swirled in the spot where once stood the village of the Chikaso tribe. And the lake that covered that once noble tribe was known from that day onwards as Hoof Lake.

THE CROOKED-MOUTHED FAMILY

A family for sore eyes!

Father with a chin thrust forward, his lower lip so thick it hid the upper lip.

Mother blessed with such an enormous upper lip, that it folded right over her mouth down to the chin.

Daughter's mouth slanted crookedly to the left, whereas her elder brother was endowed with a mouth pointing strictly to the right.

The youngest son Johnnie was the only member of the family to have a normal mouth like normal people.

Father made and mended shoes, stooping over his work bench each day well into the night.

'I'd like better fate for you, my children,' he often remarked.

When they grew up, father brought out the savings he and his wife had put away for many long years, and said,

'Children, this is all we possess. Take the money and get yourselves schooled, so you won't have to spend all your life chasing poverty and want out of your house.'

The daughter and the eldest son were lazy. They did not fancy learning and books and chose to stay in the cottage—they would get by somehow!

Only Johnnie, the youngest son, prepared to leave. He put the money into his pocket, thanked his parents and bade them goodbye, then left for the town.

As soon as he was gone, winds began to blow from the stubble fields, leaves turned yellow, summer was on its way out. The days grew shorter and shorter and the evenings were long, unbearably long.

Inside the cottage fire crackled in the hearth, while outside sleigh bells rang, and sledges swished everywhere down snowy slopes from farm to farm, from town to town.

On such a day Johnnie came home for Christmas on a fast sleigh.

Everyone in the cottage burned with excitement at all he would tell them.

Mother baked an apple pie and father brought out of the attic a fine oil lamp, so they could see Johnnie properly while he talked.

The daughter sliced the apple pie and piled everyone's plate high.

Father lifted his portion right up to his nose, so he would not have far to reach. Mother's plate was held by her chin, the daughter's near the left corner of her mouth, the elder brother's near his right.

For they all had very crooked mouths.

That is all except Johnnie, whose own mouth was just like other people's and who could eat his apple pie in comfort.

After supper, father cleaned the smokey cylinder with crumbled newspapers, poured oil into the lamp, and cut off the old blackened wick with scissors.

When the lamp was alight, the family spread round the hearth to listen to Johnnie.

It was pleasantly warm in the room.

Mother was the first to doze off, next father's head began to droop then, a few minutes later, the elder brother's eyes closed and, after that, the daughter dropped off, too.

Last to nod off was Johnnie, tired after his long sleigh ride.

The fire in the hearth died down and father awoke, shivering with cold. He shook mother and cried,

'Get up! We're wasting the light. Lets all go to bed, then at least we'll keep warm.'

'Put the lamp out then,' said mother.

Father breathed in deeply and breathed out with all his might in the flame's direction. But the breath from his crooked mouth went up his nose instead of hitting the flame.

'You clumsy oaf,' mother muttered, pushing him aside, to have a go herself.

She bent over the lamp and blew very hard, but instead of putting out the flame, the breath from her crooked mouth scattered bread crumbs from the table all over the floor.

'You push your way into everything, then mess things up,' grumbled father.

'I'll put that light out,' the daughter offered.

Bending over the glowing lamp she blew with all her strength, but the breath aimed at the flame went from her crooked mouth up into her left ear.

'I can't bear to watch this circus any longer,' cried the elder brother, 'let me have a go at that lamp, I know what to do.'

'You think you'll succeed?' wondered mother.

'Why shouldn't I? It's child's play.'

The young man, his legs astride, drew in his breath for all he was worth, then let go—but instead of the flame, the breath hit his right ear.

Johnnie stood by the hearth, waiting to see what would happen next.

'Let Johnnie put out the lamp,' mother suggested.

Father laughed. 'Our Johnnie? Why, he's all dried up with all that learning. He wouldn't have enough puff to blow out a candle.'

'I may be lucky,' said Johnnie.

He bent over the lamp and blew—and the flame was gone.

Mother was surprised, the sister astounded, the brother dumbfounded.

Father thoughtfully nodded his head.

'Now you see, children, what one can learn at school . . .'

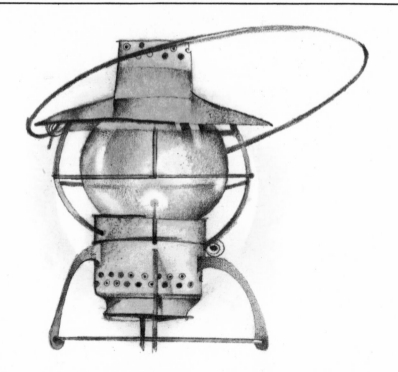

THE BIG SHAGGY DOG

'What if we called on your brother today?' Mr Kelly said to his wife.

It was a hot Sunday in June, and above the mountain valley the toll of bells echoed far and wide.

'We could do just that,' the wife agreed.

Little Tylda begged her mother to let her come, too, but Mrs Kelly refused.

'It is too far, my sweet. Your little legs would ache. Stay comfortably at home and play with your dolls. We'll be back before it is dark.'

Mother cooked lunch and cleared up, and soon after noon they left.

They did not notice that little Tylda crept out unseen after them.

She hid behind bushes and trees, and among the corn. Her parents had no inkling Tylda was following further back.

Tylda picked daisies along the way. She admired the metalic blue of a passing beetle and then turned her eyes to the blueness above, searching for the lark who made the sky vibrate with his song. Next she found a coloured pebble on the path, and another and another, till she had quite a collection in her apron pocket. When her pocket was full to the brim, she squatted by the edge of a wheat field and played with the coloured stones.

Her parents soon disappeared from sight.

Tylda did not really mind. She was not afraid to be on her own in the fields, or in the forest, she often came here alone to pick berries and nuts.

When she grew tired of playing with the gay pebbles, she walked to the nearby forest, where there was some shade; there she stretched out under an old bushy oak in the moss and fell asleep.

Back home her brother and sister did not worry about the little one. They knew she would not get lost in the fields or in the forest, and that she would soon reappear when she was hungry.

At dusk the parents returned home.

'Where is little Tylda?' asked the mother.

'She followed you, of course,' her sister answered.

'That is very strange,' the father remarked worriedly. Walking up a little hillock behind the homestead, he called out towards the forest, 'Tylda, Tilly! Where are you? Come on home!'

Darkness was descending upon the countryside, but there still was no sign of the little girl.

'If she wandered off the path and went deep into the forest, she will get lost!' sobbed the mother.

The father rounded up the neighbours and armed with lanterns,

they all went into the forest. They called and searched, but they did not find little Tylda. Night wrapped her starry cloak round the forest and fields, the owls set off on their night hunt, spreading their silky wings, but of Tylda there was not a sign.

The father and the neighbours returned home and the mother burst into tears.

They did not sleep the whole night long.

Even the next day Tylda did not return.

On Tuesday night the skinner knocked on Kelly's window. Apparently he had travelled along the forest path, and had seen two sets of footprints. One belonged to a child, the other to a bear.

'Both sets of footprints, the child's and the bear's, keep going along the path next to each other—it seems very strange,' said the skinner.

The following morning a neighbour called.

'Last night I dreamt I found your Tylda. She was fast asleep under an old oak, warmed by a huge brown bear.'

People smirked, but the neighbour paid them no heed. Alone he set off to the forest. And Mr Kelly went too.

They agreed, that if either of them found the little girl, he would fire his gun three times.

At noon three gun shots echoed from the depth of the forest, and Mr Kelly rushed towards the sound.

The neighbour carried little Tylda in his arms.

She was weak with hunger, but alive and well.

She told of unbelievable things!

Night after night a huge, funny, shaggy dog came to her and kept her warm. She cuddled close to his furry coat and felt safe and warm.

And, ever since that day, people have called her Tylda Bear.

THE HEAD DEVIL IN TEXAS

Devils in hell were piling logs on the fire, till thick smoke curled upwards.

'Don't be stingy with the wood,' shouted Sakumpak, the ruler of hell himself. 'Let's make sure our three new-comers won't complain of cold.'

The devils kept on adding pitchy pine logs, while Sakumpak, dressed in his very best cloak, waited for the new additions. The manager of hell's head office had examined the lists the previous day and had discovered that a barber, a student and a banker were on their way.

Now someone was hammering on hell's gates.

'Have a look who it is,' Sakumpak ordered the gate-keeper.

The gates opened wide to three penitent earth-dwellers; the barber, the student and the banker. They trembled with fear, their teeth chattering with horror.

Someone else slipped into hell through the gates behind them, a man like an oak.

No one could say he looked scared. He wore a cowboy hat with a very wide rim, a checked shirt and a belt, blue jeans and high boots with jiggling spurs. In his hand he had a lasso which was circling over his head.

He made straight for the heap of logs.

He pushed aside the sweating devil who was toiling with a shovel by the smouldering ashes, spat into his hands, and in a jiffy long flames were shooting up again, and thick steam was rising from the red-hot water drums on the fire.

The head devil, Sakumpak, was frowning. What a way to behave!

Who does that worm of a fellow think he is! He doesn't even introduce himself, no one knows him, he's not on the list, he doesn't shake with fear, or even show surprise. He makes straight for the shovel and behaves as if he had lived in hell from the day he was born.

Sakumpak hissed with temper, banged his fork against the floor, rattled the chain, but in spite of all that din the fellow in the wide-rimmed hat carried on as if he did not see or hear.

That really was too much for Sakumpak.

He jumped off his hell-throne and tripped helter-skelter, his cloak entangled in the fork, towards the strange chap in his strange hat. He stormed at him.

'Put that shovel down, you idiot. Don't you know you have to introduce yourself to me—the ruler of hell? Or do you expect me to send a special messenger to earth to find out who you are? These certainly are strange manners.'

The fellow in the wide-rimmed hat did not even look up, but

shovelled on, throwing away the ash and putting back fresh logs, till the water drums moaned with the heat.

'Have it your own way,' Sakumpak gave in with a wave of the hand. 'Have it your own way, if you insist and stay with the shovel and with the axe, tend the fire, you certainly have ample strength for it. But tell me at least who you are and where you come from. I am dying with curiosity.'

'Why should I keep it a secret,' the man in the hat at last spared a few words. 'I don't have to be ashamed of my name, or of the work I do. They call me Billy Filly. That's 'cause I used to deal in horses. I had plenty of dollars to pocket with no trouble at all, but I lost the lot at cards and had to go about begging round farms. But nobody wants to employ me. They say I am a lazy fellow. Me — lazy. So here at this fire I aim to show you what a worker I am.'

Sakumpak was shaking his head in astonishment, he'd never had such a fellow in hell before, and he pried further. 'Where are you from, Billy Filly, that you don't seem to mind this hellish heat?'

Billy Filly replied,

'Where from? Why, from Texas, of course. From the most beautiful land under the sun. Have you ever been there? I am sure you'd love it.'

The head devil shook his head, for he never had the pleasure of visiting Texas, and immediately pummelled the chap with questions. How could he get there? Where does that land lie? What does it look like?

'Listen then,' the fellow in the wide hat agreed, 'and I will explain the lot to you.'

Sakumpak filled his fiery pipe, his servant Thundersack poured him a glass of chopped nails with pepper and paprika, and then he was ready to listen to all Billy Filly had to relate about Texas.

Sakumpak listened, puffed, sipped, while Billy talked and then ended with,

'It might well interest you, that the Texas folk are very hard working. They are real demons for work, always on their toes and they never let the grass grow under their feet.'

When the head devil heard this, he came to life. That would really be something — to have in hell several such workers from Texas, some such as Billy Filly. Then his subjects would not need to work, would have more time to spare and so could lead a greater number of people astray to commit sin and injustice, and lead them towards hell, along the path paved with such intentions.

'Just one thing, Billy Filly,' Sakumpak remarked, scratching behind his ear. 'You mentioned that all over Texas cows graze in pastures. I can't imagine what such a cow looks like, I've never seen one.'

'You'd recognize a cow easily enough,' Billy Filly pacified Sakumpak. 'Actually it resembles you quite a lot, it has horns, long like yours, and also a tail. Don't worry, you'll soon make friends with the cows.'

During the night Sakumpak tossed and turned on his bed of red-hot cinders, he simply could not sleep, he was so excited.

The following day, long before the hell alarm clock sounded, Sakumpak, the ruler of hell, was already opening the fiery gate and rushing to Texas.

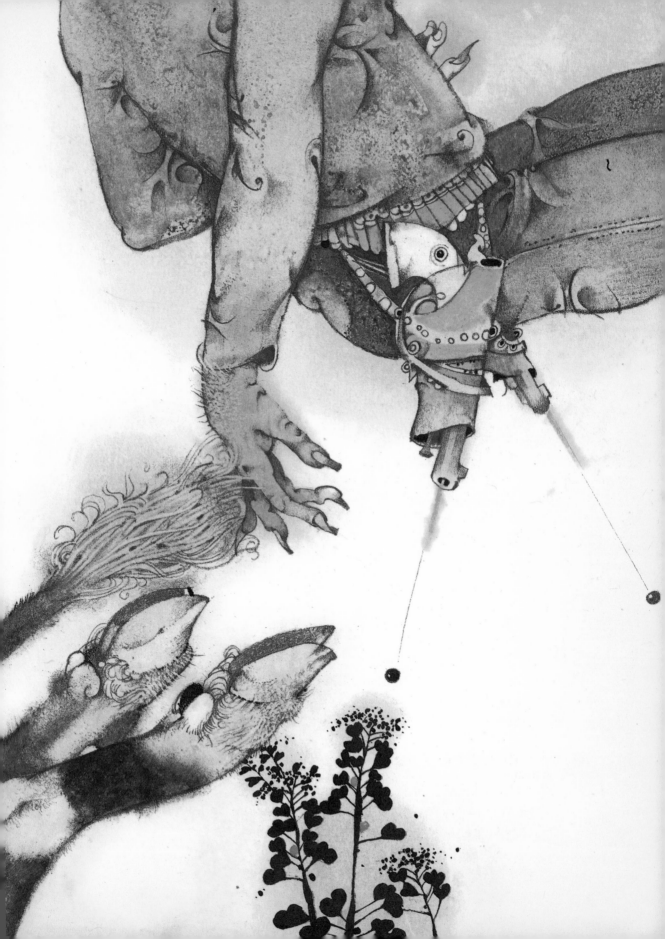

It was a hot summer's day and Sakumpak reached a great pasture surrounded by a river. By then he was so thirsty, that his tongue stuck to the roof of his mouth; there wasn't a tree, even a bush in sight under which he could hide his head which was burning from the hot sun. Fine dust, flying in circles over the earth, was getting into his ears and eyes, choking his throat. Fat flies squatted upon his perspiring back-side, biting it hard; mosquitoes buzzed and nipped, and Sakumpak snorted and sneezed, coughed and wheezed, sizzled and seethed, sweating like mad, his hands and tail whizzing to left and right. But it was no good, the sun mercilessly poured its boiling flood upon the earth, the dust hung like a thick curtain over the pasture, the hot wind breathed upon Sakumpak like an open stove, and those flies were as painful as fiery stabbing arrows.

Suddenly Sakumpak glimpsed a muddy brook which slithered through the pasture between low bushes. And those bushes were full of red berries.

I am sure they must be raspberries, that Billy Filly talked about, the head devil thought joyfully. He made a dash for the bushes, and soon had his cap filled with the beautiful fruit.

He did not think twice, but stuffed them into his mouth and swallowed them quick, so not a single berry would drop out.

Thunder and lightning!

What is a mere mouthful of hellish cognac made of powdered nails in a pepper and paprika solution against this!

His lips, his tongue, the roof of his mouth and his gullet were aflame and Sakumpak was writhing as if he were on fire.

He had swallowed a handful of hot, red peppers.

He rushed to the brook, immersed his whole head into the water, swallowing it mud and all, plus the water spiders and other insects, but he could not put out the terrible fire in his mouth.

Towards the evening Sakumpak had somewhat recovered. By then, there was nothing but mud left in the brook and Sakumpak walked on.

From a distance he heard the barking of dogs but he went on and on, till he came to a ranch.

There he found some four-legged, horned animals. He knew immediately these must be cows. A cowboy approached one of the creatures, and before she knew what was what, she was flat on the ground.

The ruler of hell was quite astonished. I must find out how this is done. Such a feat might come in quite handy in hell, thought he.

He came to the cowboy and asked,

'Could you tell me, friend, how you managed to down that cow?'

The cowboy raised his head and saw this smartly dressed, polished gentleman. He smirked slightly and explained.

'It's quite simple really, sir, all you have to do is to twist the cow's tail and she lies down flat straightaway.'

'Could I have a go?'

'Help yourself by all means.'

Sakumpak stepped to the cow from behind, grasped her tail and twisted it hard.

The pain made the cow's eyes bulge. She bent her hind leg and whop! she kicked dear Sakumpak in his tummy.

He yelled and crawled into the bushes.

He stayed there for some time, sighing, moaning and fuming.

In the night, when the dew freshened him up slightly, he managed to stagger to his feet and to slink back to hell.

By the time he got there, the barber had chopped off all the devils' hair, the student had taught them to read five letters and the banker how to count up to ten.

Only Billy Filly was still by the fire, piling on the logs and shovelling away the ashes.

'Why didn't you tell me,' Sakumpak complained, 'that those cows kick so hard?'

'Be glad you didn't get kicked by a horse. You would enjoy a horse's hoof so much, that you wouldn't even be able to find your way back to hell from Texas,' Billy laughed at Sakumpak, tossing such a beautifully pitchy log on to the fire, that the whole of hell turned into a scented pine forest.

THE MYSTERIOUS MUSIC FROM THE DEEP

In the region where the mighty river spills into the sea, there once lived an Indian tribe. Its ancestors—so the aged men say—emerged long, long ago from the sea in which they were born, and then settled on the cliffs by the river mouth.

Their skin was white and they were fine, noble people, living on fish and oysters, loving to sing and to dance.

On top of the cliff they built an impressive temple and on moonlit nights they flocked to the temple to kneel before the mermaid, carved from the white rock.

Their strange string instruments gave out haunting, soft sounds, like wind playing with aspen leaves, like rain drops humming in the forest.

One day huge ships sailed to the banks from far away lands on the other side of the ocean, and lines of soldiers hurried ashore. They occupied the coast and followed the rivers into the green prairie. It was then that a mysterious stranger with a long white beard and a flowing cloak appeared suddenly in the Indian village.

On his fine string instrument he called together the entire tribe. Under the light of the moon he played and sang far into the night strange songs of the tribe's bygone glory, of ancestors, who lived in the sea, of streams of blood, with which the white conquerors would flood the prairie.

The scarlet moon rolled on above the cliffs and nature paused in uncanny silence. The white-haired old man's slender fingers strummed the strings as he slowly descended down the cliff into the valley.

Behind him followed the men carrying the statue of the mermaid. The old man went to the shore, stepped on to the water's surface, walking along it safely and easily, as if he were on ice.

The river then burst into song with a mysterious, magic voice. From shore to shore it trembled with strange sweet murmurs and haunting melodies, as if awakening from a long sleep, as if recalling a happy dream whilst combing its locks into long tresses.

All the members of the Indian tribe heard the magic music from the deep.

The old man parted the water with his hand and slowly and majestically disappeared under the surface.

And the river sang of the tremulous melody of the awakened waters.

The Indians gazed at the disappearing old man with awe. Then, one after the other, they climbed down from the cliff to the river, and one after the other they too disappeared in this river which sang to them in its haunting, sweet voice.

When the last member of the tribe had gone below the surface of the singing river, a light breeze started to blow above — just as if a window had opened into a flowering garden, and then the river flowed as of old peacefully into the sea.

The white conquerors found the village empty.

The entire tribe was gone — gone into the river.

Since then to this very day strange music flows from the deep in that place. Particularly on clear moonlit nights.

Tremulous melodies, silky and soft like the murmur of reeds, rise above the water, echoing in the rocks; from shore to shore, from cliff to cliff flows the song of the river, mysterious as the tribe which disappeared into the deep forever, because it had no desire to bow its head before the conqueror.

A NOSEFUL OF GOLD

As news spread far and wide that gold had been found beyond the mountains and deserts, hopeful adventurers streamed to the West. They were all shaking with excitement, impatient to pluck from the earth a nugget of gold as big at least as a horse's head.

But the gold had a habbit of playing hide-and-seek in the earth with the gold-diggers, just like a crafty red fox plays with them in the bushes. A frustrated prospector often turned tons and tons of stone and sand over, without even a whiff of gold.

There were, of course, luckier creatures. Someone's horse tripped over a boulder, for instance, knocked it over and where it stood, a gold vein appeared.

Such is life. Some have too little, others too much.

One night in a small western town, prospectors were drinking in a bar; they played cards, talked of their failures and successes in prospecting, whilst a brass band gratingly played a Turkish march. Suddenly, into the saloon stepped a bearded chap in a checked shirt, a hat flat on his head, a red scarf round his neck. He made straight for the bar and ordered a whisky.

His fingers played with the filled glass, whilst he gazed round him, muttering under his breath, as if talking to himself.

'I sure am surprised to see these fellows lolling about here, when a pile of gold is a mere few steps away. All one has to do is to uncover it.'

The gamblers dropped their cards, the drinkers forgot to drink. Everything stopped with the mention of the magic word; gold.

They crowded round the blackbeard. Only when they were standing themselves did they notice that he was only a scrap of a chap and they bombarded him with questions.

'Gold? Where's the gold? You've found gold? Is there any left for us?'

Blackbeard in the checked shirt hummed and hawed and dilly

dallied—you needed a pair of horses to drag every word out of him—he just shrugged his shoulders and shuffled his feet, coughed, snuffled and grunted.

The more he dithered and dothered, avoiding a decent reply, the more he was pestered by the gold-diggers.

Blackbeard allowed them to treat him to an excellent supper, graciously permitted the bar-keeper to place a bottle of his best whisky in front of him, with someone else footing the bill and only then, the words crawled out of him at a snail's pace.

'Gold. That stream is so stuffed with gold, the water can't flow properly.'

The fellows' eyes were almost popping out of their sockets.

'And that's not all,' blackbeard's voice trickled on. 'When there's a puff of wind, the gold rises and gets into your nose and throat. Gentlemen, you could choke with that gold.'

'Can such a thing be possible, can it be true?' muttered some cautious fellows, shaking their heads mistrustfully. But others shouted them down. 'Why shouldn't it be true. In this world anything is possible.'

Blackbeard downed the whisky and continued.

'Worst off are those luckless fellows who have a cold or a cough. You sneeze, and so much gold flies out of your nose, that you could have bought a house with it and a carriage and a pair of horses thrown in. You cough, and riches evaporate in the air. If any of you

206

chaps have a cold or a cough, I suggest you sweat it out first, before going after that gold in the stream.'

The saloon was like a bee-hive.

The men were talking one over the other, running around, bunching up, planning for the next day.

The slip of a chap in his checked shirt ate up his food in peace, finished off the whisky and walked out of the bar.

The next day it all started.

Still before daybreak, a crowd of gold-diggers poured through the silent streets towards the mountains to the gold-yielding stream. The sun rolled over the horizon just as they arrived. The men rolled up their sleeves, dug the spades into the stony stream bed and were

soon busily sifting stones and sand. Nothing—only some transparent scales of mica glittered in the sunlight.

They tried their luck again. Again, and again.

A waste of time. The stream gurgled laughingly at them, crows sneered and sniggered from willows above. Then one of the gold-diggers turned round and noticed a piece of paper attached to a twig on the bank. He climbed out of the water and read:

> Thanks for the friendly welcome. The supper was excellent, the whisky wasn't bad. Unfortunately I have a very large nose and all the gold dust has settled in it. You will just have to wait till I sneeze, then there will be some for you, too.

THE HAWK AND THE RATTLESNAKE

It was a sunny autumn day when the prince went deer-hunting into the forest.

On a mountain track he came across a rattlesnake fighting a hawk.

The hawk was by then utterly exhausted by the duel, and was weakening by the minute, with the rattlesnake more and more on the attack, preparing to deliver the deadly bite and eat the bird.

The prince unsheathed his hunting knife and chopped off the rattlesnake's head.

'Thank you, prince, you have saved my life,' said the hawk.

'Sit on my back, I will show you how lovely it is high up under the clouds.'

The prince climbed on the hawk's back and the bird spread his wings and carried the prince higher and higher, till they had climbed to a great height in the sky.

Underneath, seven snow-capped mountains glistened blue, like seven bells; the hawk was flying round them all.

As they were circling over the last mountain, the sun dropped behind the forests and darkness fell at once.

'Do you know what?' said the hawk to the prince. 'Night is coming fast. My eldest sister has a house just beyond these forests. I will take you there. If you tell her that you have killed the rattlesnake and saved my life, she will feed you and keep you for the night. I will come back for you in the morning.'

The bird flew down to the ground with the prince, and disappeared over the wood before the prince could bid him goodnight.

The prince rapped on the door and the hawk's eldest sister opened. When he explained all that had happened, she cooked him an excellent supper and gave him a bed as soft as forest moss to sleep the night through.

The hawk returned the following morning, and with the prince on his back soared high into the sky. Deep down underneath, seven wide rivers glistened in the sun. As they were flying over the seventh—the widest one—the sun went down, it grew dark and the hawk said to the prince, 'Night will be here any minute now, I will carry you to my second sister. Can you see her house over there by the river? When you tell her how you saved my life, she will invite you to supper and will offer you a bed for the night.'

The second sister prepared a fine meal for the prince, and made him up a bed as silky as swan's feathers.

In the morning the hawk came back, but the moment his feet touched the ground, he changed into a handsome youth.

'A wicked witch turned me into a hawk and you saved my life,' said the youth. 'By seeking shelter with both my sisters, you have

broken the power of that evil sorceress. But now I have no wings to take you to my youngest sister. There is nothing left but for you to go to her on foot. She lives in a house by a forest lake. If you tell her you saved my life, she will feed you and keep you overnight.'

The prince walked and walked all day long, and as the sun was going down, the forest lake appeared before him. A magnificent house stood by the lake, in which the hawk's youngest sister lived.

When the prince told her everything, the youngest sister cooked him a delicious dinner and made up a bed as soft as lamb's fleece for him to sleep on.

When the next morning they were saying goodbye, the sister said,

'Because you saved my brother's life, I will give you a magic pouch. But you are to open it only when you come to a place you will like more than any other.'

The prince thanked the sister and went on his way.

He walked and walked till he came into a beautiful valley.

Meadows sparkled green, the stream bubbled and gurgled and birds sang merrily in the birch wood.

'I like it here,' said the prince, 'this is where I'll stay.'

He opened the magic pouch — and in a trice a magnificent palace stood before him, surrounded by a garden scented by many rose trees.

The prince tapped on the gate, the gate opened of its own accord, and from a blossoming apple-tree a peacock screeched in greeting.

The moment the peacock screeched, there was a blast of wind, and from the forest behind the palace a one-eyed giant leapt up and roared,

'How dare you, you miserable human worm, build a palace on my estate? Can't you see that only I have the right to dwell here? Bid the world goodbye, for I am just about to eat you up.'

The prince had no intention of losing his life for such a trivial reason. He therefore said to the giant,

'Let me stay alive, mighty lord, and I will make whatever you wish come true.'

'Did I hear "whatever I wish"?' the giant roared so loudly that the rocks cracked. 'Very well then. I'll let you live, if you give me the son your wife will give birth to, when the roses have flowered seven times after the day he is born.'

The prince did not think twice, but nodded his head.

The giant laughed so loudly the rivers burst their banks, and then he disappeared into the forest.

The prince shut the magic pouch, and with that the palace disappeared into it, together with the scented rose garden, and the shrieking peacock on the flowering apple-tree.

Once again the prince was on his way.

He wandered on and on till he came to a blue river. White clouds floated above and under them high blue mountains towered into the sky, swallows flashed in their flight above ripening grain and in the meadows grasshoppers and crickets were clicking away merrily.

'I like it here,' said the prince, 'and here I'll stay.'

He opened the magic pouch, and out came the beautiful palace surrounded by scented roses, red, white and yellow. The prince knocked on the gate and the gate opened of its own accord, and at the same time the cry of the peacock in the flowering apple-tree greeted him.

A dark-haired maiden came out of the palace.

'I have been expecting you,' she smiled at the prince. 'I am the youngest sister of the hawk whose life you saved. Come in, I have prepared supper for you.'

The next day the prince married the beautiful maiden and, a year later, they had a dark-haired son.

In spring he played among trees in the palace garden; in summer he bathed in the lake and picked woodland strawberries; in autumn he gazed at the flight of wild geese; in winter he sat by the side of fire, while snow fell outside and gales moaned in the crowns of the age-old oaks.

Then it was spring again, and summer, autumn and winter came around, and it seemed in no time at all roses flowered seven times in the boy's garden.

The wind roared, the forest rocked and the one-eyed giant emerged from it. He rapped on the palace gate and thundered,

'I have come for your son, prince. The roses have flowered seven times since he was born. Do you recall your promise?'

'Wait a minute,' the prince's voice floated from the palace, 'I must prepare my son for the journey.'

The giant shuffled his feet by the gate, while the prince ordered the palace kitchen boy to be dressed in the son's clothes, who up till then was scraping potatoes in the kitchen.

The kitchen boy was presented to the one-eyed giant, who disappeared with him in the forest. When they had crossed three mountains and three rivers, the giant halted with the boy and said,

'Which rose in the palace garden smells most of all?'

'How can I know which rose in the palace garden smells most of all,' replied the boy, 'when I've never had the chance to smell any of the roses. But I can tell you that a chicken sings most of all when it is being roasted in the oven.'

The giant spat in disgust, threw the kitchen boy over his shoulder and hurried back to the palace.

He hammered at the gate and roared,

'You've cheated me, prince. You gave me your kitchen boy instead of your son.'

'I made a mistake,' the prince humoured the giant. 'It was dark inside the palace. Be patient a little longer, I'll get my son ready, he will be with you in a minute.'

The prince then ordered that the little boy who looked after the geese should be dressed in his son's clothes. They led the goose-boy out of the palace, the giant seized him by the hand and disappeared with him into the forest.

They walked on and on, across seven valleys and seven hills; the giant stopped before a rocky cave and said to the boy,

'I'd like to know which rose in the palace garden has the most thorns.'

The goose-boy laughed. 'I'd like to know that too. I've never been close enough to the roses in the palace garden to find out! But I can tell you why a goose has only two legs. Because when roasted, one leg ends up on my master's plate and the other on my mistress'. You see, the little prince doesn't care for goose legs. That's why a goose has only two.'

The giant exploded, errupted like a volcano, making the trees snap. He perched the lad on his shoulder and stormed back to the palace.

'You've cheated again, prince. You gave me a goose-boy instead of your son. If you don't bring him to me at once, I'll turn this palace to rock and everyone in it into snakes and toads.'

The prince realized all was lost, so he dressed his own son, bade him a tearful goodbye and led him to the one-eyed giant.

The giant took the little boy and they disappeared in the forest.

'Which is the most beautiful rose in the palace garden?' the giant asked the little prince.

'The most beautiful rose in our garden? Why, the rose my mother planted when I was born.'

'You truly are the prince,' the giant smiled, 'and that is your good fortune.'

He led the little prince towards the castle, past nine mountains, nine rivers and nine valleys. The giant's daughter was playing with the swans by the castle lake.

She was as lovely as a June day, and she and the little prince spent their days playing hide-and-seek and blind man's buff, picking flowers from the meadows and fields, bathing with the swans in the lake, listening to the singing birds in the forest.

Spring gave way to summer, apples ripened in the orchard, leaves turned russet and yellow, snow fell, and then again it was spring, and after spring the summer. Year followed year like wave follows wave in the river. The prince grew into a handsome youth and the giant's daughter blossomed into a beautiful maiden. And because they loved each other long and deeply and could not bear to live without one another, they decided never to part.

'So you would like my daughter for your bride?' the giant asked the youth one day. 'I have no objections, we'll hold the wedding, but first you must carry out three tasks which I will give you. Do you agree?'

The prince nodded.

'Then listen carefully,' the giant continued. 'During this night you must clean out the cow-shed. It has to be spotless by the time the sun rises.'

There were ninety-nine cows munching away in that cow-shed, and the shed had not been cleared out for ninety-nine years.

The youth picked up a fork and set to work. It was long past midnight and the cockerels in the yard were already crowing, but the cow-shed was still knee-deep in muck.

At that moment the giant's daughter came out of the castle. Quietly she sang a song and, from a distance, a river rushed through the cow-shed, taking with it all the muck and straw.

When the sun came out, the giant awoke and rushed to the cow-shed.

The cow-shed was sparkling clean, with the cows munching away contentedly. The giant growled,

'You have fulfilled the first task. Here is the second. During this night, before the sun rises, you must cover the whole of the castle roof with bird feathers. And every feather must be off a different bird. Not a single feather may resemble another one.'

The youth wasted no time, but sped to the forest with a net to catch the birds. He managed to net one, then a second and a third, but the sun was dropping behind the mountains and birds were hiding in their nests. The prince roamed the forests long into the night with only owls and bats on their nocturnal hunt laughing at him.

Just then the giant's daughter came out of the castle, quietly singing a song. There was a sudden gust of wind and a cloud of bird feathers descended from the sky. An eagle feather, a pigeon feather, a swan feather, thousands and thousands of feathers were strewn upon the castle yard.

There was another gust of wind and it lifted the bird feathers off the ground and covered the castle roof with them.

Next morning at sunrise, the giant awoke, walked out of the castle and looked up at the roof.

'You have carried out the second task,' he growled sourly. 'But you haven't won yet. The third task will be the hardest. Do you see that tall pine tree in the forest? I want you to climb to its very top, where you will find a crow's nest. Before the sun rises tomorrow, I want you to bring me the eggs from that nest.'

The youth ran into the forest and started to climb the tall pine. But the higher he climbed, the taller the pine grew. Dusk was falling, then the evening star appeared, midnight passed and the top of the pine was still towering high above the youth's head.

The giant's daughter came out of the castle, quietly singing a song. An eagle flew to the pine, picked three crow eggs with his beak from the nest and dropped them gently on to the mossy ground. The youth placed the eggs in his cap and carried them towards the castle.

But on their way back through the forest, the giant's daughter lost her ring.

At sunrise the giant awoke and immediately asked for the crow eggs.

'Here they are,' said the youth, handing over his cap with the three crow eggs inside.

Three days later there was a wedding at the giant's castle.

During the feast the bride whispered to the bridegroom, so that no one else could hear,

'I have a suspicion that my father wants to deceive you. If he casts a magic spell on me, you will recognize me easily. The ring I lost will be missing from my middle finger.'

After the feast the giant rose from the table, clapped his hands, the guests grew quiet and the giant then turned to the bridegroom.

'You say you love my daughter very dearly, so you are sure to recognize her easily among other women.'

He waved his hand, and at that moment the bride and all the maidens and women round the table looked exactly alike, they were all dark-haired, they were all dressed the same.

'Tell me now, which one of these women is my daughter, your chosen one, my son-in-law to be?' the giant laughed.

The bridegroom looked round the banqueting hall and examined one woman after the other most carefully. Each one had a glittering ring on her middle finger.

Only on one woman's middle finger a ring was missing.

'This is my bride,' said the bridegroom.

The giant frowned, and picking up a giant goblet of wine from the table, he swallowed it in one gulp, then waddled to his bedroom and fell asleep.

'This is a good moment to run away,' the bride whispered to the bridegroom. 'Before my father wakes, we shall be miles away.'

The bride took an apple from a fruit bowl and with the groom they left the banqueting hall unobserved.

In her father's bedroom the bride cut the apple into three pieces. The first piece she placed under her father's pillow, the second upon the window-sill, the third on the hearth. Then she led the giant's fastest horse out of the stable, they both mounted and the horse galloped away into the darkness.

He flew like the wind, sparks flashing from his nostrils, wind rising behind him, stones flying from under his hooves.

When the cockerel in the castle yard crowed for the first time, the giant awoke and called to his daughter.

'Are you asleep yet, daughter?'

'Not yet, father,' the first portion of the apple replied, instead of the bride, from under the giant's pillow.

The giant, quite content, went back to sleep.

The cockerel crowed the second time, the giant awoke and asked,

'Are you asleep yet, daughter?'

'Not yet, father,' answered the second piece of the apple on the window-sill.

The cockerel in the yard crowed the third time, and the giant opened his eyes.

'Daughter dear, are you asleep yet?'

'Not yet, father,' replied the last third of the apple on the hearth.

Once again the giant was about to go back to sleep, quite content. But just then a cheeky fly tickled him under his nose and he sneezed, waking up properly. He jumped off the bed and ran into his daughter's bedroom. The bed was empty, the door wide open.

The giant wasted no time, but led a fast horse out of his stable, mounted him, and the horse raced out of the yard, with the giant urging him on.

'I'll give you a tubful of oats if you catch up with my daughter and her bridegroom before the sun comes out.'

Before long the giant glimpsed the runaways in front of him.

At the same time the bride tore her wedding veil from her head and threw it behind her.

The whole area between them was immediately overgrown with a dense forest.

The giant halted his horse, turned him round and returned to the castle for his two-bladed axe.

He brought it back to the dense forest and began to cut his way through. It did not take long before he was once again hot on the runaways' heels.

The bride quickly took off one of her sandals and threw it behind her.

Immediately steep, snow-covered mountains rose from the ground to the clouds as far as the eye could see.

The giant stopped his horse and galloped at the double back to the castle for the giant hoe.

He dug and he dug, making a path through the mountains.

Before very long the giant was catching up with the runaways again.

Then the bride tore the pearl necklace from her neck and threw it behind her.

The pearls turned into a wide river, the horse with the giant had no time to stop on the shore in his mad race, he ran into the deep water and tossed the giant off his back.

Then water closed over the giant forever.

The prince and his young wife dismounted. Dawn was breaking, thrushes and mocking birds in the forest were bursting into song and, as they left the forest, they noticed a well glittering between alder trees and willows.

'We have nothing to fear now,' said the prince. 'You must rest now, my dearest. Climb into the crown of the alder tree by the well, so wolves cannot tear you apart. I shall ride on home, to our palace, so my father and mother can prepare a great feast. Then I will return for you and will take you to our palace.'

The young wife agreed a little uncertainly, climbed up the tall alder tree and called down to the prince,

'I will wait here till you come back. But remember, when you enter the palace, do not allow anyone to kiss you. Otherwise you would forget all about me in that very instant.'

The prince mounted his horse, waved goodbye to his wife and raced towards his paternal palace.

He hammered on the gate, and his mother and father ran to the gate to greet him. They embraced their long lost son, wanting to kiss him, but the prince drew away from them. He remembered well the warning of his young bride, as she bade him goodbye.

But the little dog, of whom the prince was very fond, pressed his front paws against the prince's chest and before the prince knew what was happening, he licked his face in welcome.

That instant the prince forgot all about his young bride.

Day followed day, the prince rode out hunting, he bathed in the lake, he strolled without a care in the world in the palace gardens amid the roses, forgetting everything that had happened.

His young wife sat on the alder tree, waiting, waiting endlessly.

There was a tumble-down cottage near the well and a cobbler with a very lazy wife and an even lazier daughter lived in this cottage.

He was bowed over his work day after day, mending boots and shoes, he hardly had time during the day just to stretch his aching back.

'Wife,' said the cobbler, 'I have been terribly thirsty all morning and I'd still like to nail new soles to these battered old boots before noon. Get out of bed, take the bucket and please fetch me some water from the well.'

The wife yawned and stretched awhile, still in her bed, but eventually she did get up and dress and, taking the bucket from the hall, she went to the well.

As she was leaning above the water, she saw a beautiful face mirrored in the water's surface.

'I've grown younger-looking overnight,' the cobbler's wife said excitedly to herself. 'Now I am more beautiful than all the women in the district.'

She sat in the moss by the well and thought. She reproached herself for having married a mere cobbler. As I am so young-looking and so beautiful, I could have married even a king, she muttered, self-accusingly. And she sat and pondered, rejoicing in her beauty, dreaming of the royal throne.

'What is holding that wife of mine up all this time?' wondered the cobbler, his tongue sticking to the roof of his mouth with the thirst: 'There's nothing left for it, Barbie, but for you to get out of that bed and to bring me some water.'

The daughter rubbed her eyes, yawning and having a good stretch. In the end she crawled out of bed, drank a jugful of milk and with the empty jug in her hand she waddled off to the well for the spring water.

She leaned over the surface and, what a surprise, instead of the untidy, messy girl with hair all over the place, she looked upon the face of a dark-haired beauty.

'I had no idea I was so beautiful,' marvelled the cobbler's daughter, 'but it's a long time since I've looked at myself in the mirror. Whoever heard of such a beauty as I sweeping floors, peeling potatoes and fetching water for a dirty old cobbler? That's not for me, no, no, no!'

She threw away the jug into the bushes and went to town to buy beads and a ring, for the day she was certain to be invited to the ball by the king.

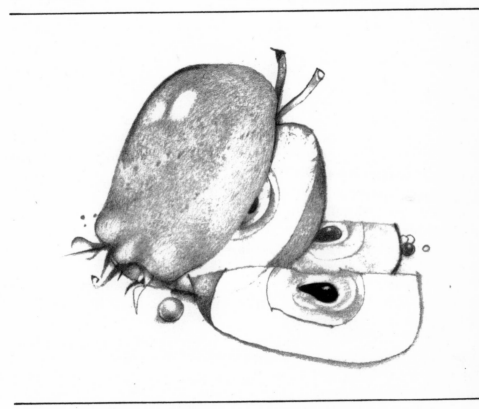

'Curse the boot and blast the sandal,' the cobbler growled. 'What a scandal that I have such womenfolk in my house. That pair of hens has forgotten all about me and about the water.'

He flung the old boot to the floor, stuck his needle into his stool and, taking a glass, he went to fetch the fresh water himself.

He came to the well, bent over the water, and the surface was painted with the portrait of a beautiful maiden.

'I hardly think I could have changed into a beautiful girl overnight,' the cobbler said to himself. And because all cobblers, while they are sewing and nailing and sticking shoes have plenty of time to think and to ponder, this thirsty cobbler had by now gained his share of wisdom. He therefore raised his head and screwed up his eyes, focusing them on the crown of the alder tree.

Through the branches he saw the lovely wife of the prince.

'Why are you sitting, my beautiful girl, up there in the alder tree? You don't have to be afraid of me, all cobblers have a kind heart. Be a good girl and climb down, mother earth is safer than a tree. And if you are hungry, come with me to our cottage, I expect I will be able to find you a bite to eat.'

The prince's young bride climbed down from the tree and went to the cottage with the cobbler.

Before the lazy wife of the cobbler finished napping in the bushes, and before the cobbler's even lazier daughter returned with the ring and beads from the town, the prince's wife had scrubbed the floor which had not been washed for more than a year, she had washed up all the saucepans and plates, unwashed for more than a month, she had fed the cow who was mooing with hunger and had let the hens out of the hen-house, and she still had time to sing whilst she worked.

She remained with the cobbler in the cottage, working ceaselessly from morn till night, there was always plenty to do.

The cobbler's wife and daughter were all blown out and unhealthy from their everlasting daily naps and yawns, but the princess, whilst she worked, grew even lovelier.

One afternoon a servant from the palace knocked on the cobbler's door. The prince was sending the cobbler thirty-three pairs of boots and shoes to be mended.

'You must work fast, cobbler,' the servant commanded. 'Our prince is just about to get married, and he wants all the boots and shoes in order within the week. Otherwise, my dear, grubby cobbler, you will be smaller by the head.'

'Confound the heels, confound the soles,' lamented the cobbler, 'how can I, a miserable soul repair thirty-three shoes and boots within one week. If I stoop over my bench non-stop night and day, on Saturday and Sunday too, I'll never mend such a heap of footwear in a single week. That is not unless our young lovely here learned the cobbler trade and helped me out.' The prince's young wife turned from the bowl filled with dirty dishes and smiled.

'Why ever not. I am willing to have a go.'

When the servant's eyes fell upon the maiden, his heart leapt for joy. He had never before seen such a lovely human being, not even in the palace. And yet the girls and the women who attend the palace balls are often as lovely as china dolls.

'Wouldn't you like to marry me, you lovely creature?' the servant without dilly dallying took the prince's wife unaware. 'You'd have a fair time of it with me in the palace. I am not one of those bowing 'yes sir, no sir,' servants. When everyone in the palace goes to sleep, I am its master.'

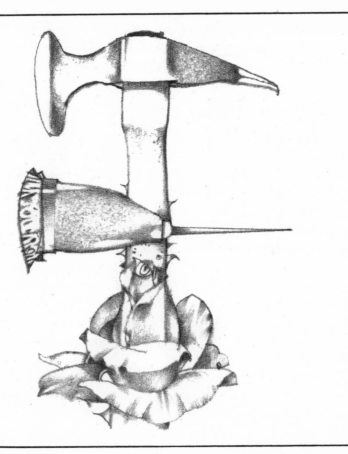

'I shall not have you for a husband,' laughed the prince's wife, 'but I will come with you to the palace. Perhaps some work can be found for me there.'

The cobbler did his best to persuade the lovely maiden to stay. He promised to make her sandals from snake skin but when the prince's young wife insisted, he relented, with a wave of his hand and a sigh.

'Very well, go then, you ungrateful creature, but if you had stayed, you'd probably have worked yourself to death. My lazy wife and even lazier daughter will be round my neck probably forever, and the work-bench too. That is life, I suppose, there'll be no one here again to hand me even a cup of water.'

Inside the palace everything was astir. Cooks were busily plucking geese, turkeys and chickens, bakers were mixing dough for cakes and pies and decorators were painting rooms, whilst gardeners were bringing baskets filled with fruit and vegetables into the kitchen.

'Make yourself useful,' said the servant to the prince's wife, 'go into the garden and water the roses, so that they are fresh and moist when the gardener cuts them for the wedding celebration.'

The prince's young wife took the green watering can, filled it in the lake with water, watered the flowers and sang:

> *I had a young husband, a prince*
> *He forgot me, was kissed by another since.*
> *Yellow roses, you must tell*
> *That he left me by the well.*

The prince was just returning from a hunt and he heard the young woman's song. His memory came back immediately, and he jumped off his horse and embraced her.

Instead of a wedding, the king and the queen held a huge feast in the palace to celebrate; the palace was scented with roses and everyone present was happy and gay.

They forgot all about the cobbler and all about the thirty-three pairs of prince's shoes and boots, so the cobbler is still mending those shoes and boots today, and still waits in vain for his lazy wife, or his even lazier daughter to bring him a glass of fresh water from the well.

If anyone feels like fetching it for him, beware, for the steps leading to the cottage are falling to bits.

HOW DONALD SOLOMON BECAME THE STATE DEPUTY

As the sun was disappearing over the prairie, several farmers sat side by side on a wooden fence, just like sparrows on a wire. They were chatting away.

The wheat and the maize were safely stacked in the dry and it was easy to relax now the harvest was over.

'It was nice listening,' said farmer Campbell, 'but I think it is time I made a move.'

With that he jumped off the fence and bade the others goodbye.

'What's the hurry?' wondered his friends.

'I want to go to town to that pre-election meeting.'

'I'll come with you then,' farmer Cramer joined in. 'I always enjoy listening to Donald Solomon.'

'What ... d'you ... mean?' wheelwright Umbach stuttered. Most people were well aware that Umbach never received his fair share of brains when they were giving them out—probably slept through the whole thing!

'I'll tell you,' Campbell now said to him teasingly. 'Donald Solomon wanted to be our State Deputy, but I believe that tonight he's just about to announce that after thinking it over, he's proposing you, wheelwright Umbach, for that office. What a hoot!'

The farmers on the fence giggled and sniggered.

'Talking of hooting reminds me of shooting,' farmer Wolfson began. 'That Donald Solomon is a fantastic shot. He brought down his first bear before he was five! They say that last autumn he shot one hundred and five bears in all!'

'Do you remember what happened that awful winter with the sun?' said Wolfson, at the same time giving Campbell a knowing wink.

Campbell, busy chewing tobacco, nodded, 'I'll tell you this, and then I'll be off. Seven years ago, as you probably recall, we had such a bad winter that the tongues of rabbits froze to their teeth. One morning, the sun came out and before it could start its run along the sky, it froze too.'

Wheelwright Umbach stammered, 'What . . . d'you . . . mean? Froze?'

'Yes, froze, froze solid I say,' farmer Campbell continued. 'But to tell the whole truth, it didn't just freeze on its own, but became firmly attached to two iced up pancakes which it was just about to have for breakfast.'

Wheelwright Umbach stared at Campbell, all agog for more.

'Donald Solomon came out of his front door, saw the frozen sun glued to the two frozen pancakes, and thought straightaway if I don't get that sun away from those pancakes, the whole world will freeze up — for there'll be no sun to warm it; that makes sense. He racked his brain how to save the world from such a terrible fate. Then he had a brainwave. Inside his barn was a fat bear he'd shot. He heated that bear over a fire, till the fat under its skin melted. Then Donald Solomon poured this sizzling melted fat over the two iced-up pancakes; this de-iced them, the sun gobbled them up and after such a nourishing breakfast new strength flowed through its veins. It swung high into the sky and the world was saved. But it was a near thing!'

'Well . . . I never . . .,' Umbach whispered, 'I can hardly . . . believe . . . my . . . ears . . .'

'There's one more thing,' farmer Campbell added, his face bright scarlet with suppressed laughter. 'That same day Donald Solomon lit his pipe off that sun and came back to his ranch, his pocket stuffed with hot sunbeams. They kept the whole household warm all winter — he didn't even have to light the stove.'

'The Solomons must have saved an awful lot of fuel,' Umbach reasoned, 'when the winter was so . . . bad.'

The farmers were still giggling as they were preparing to leave. They all decided to go with Campbell to look Solomon over at the pre-election meeting.

The Wet Jug bar was packed solid.

Farmers had gathered from all around to hear what Donald Solomon, who wished to be their State Deputy, had to say.

'We're thirsty!' someone in the bar shouted, 'what about buying a round of beer, Solomon, before you start!'

Donald Solomon turned to the licensee. 'Give everyone a beer, Joe. Put it on my account.'

The licensee in his white apron and round cap shook his head. 'Let you have it on trust? No fear, I want payment!'

The farmers stopped talking.

What would Donald Solomon do now? They had no intention of electing a fellow who didn't have all the answers up his sleeve.

Donald Solomon rose from the table, borrowed a gun from the licensee and went out. A quarter-of-an-hour later he was back with a shot weasel. He threw it across the bar counter. 'Enough?'

'Enough,' agreed the licensee and began to draw the beer.

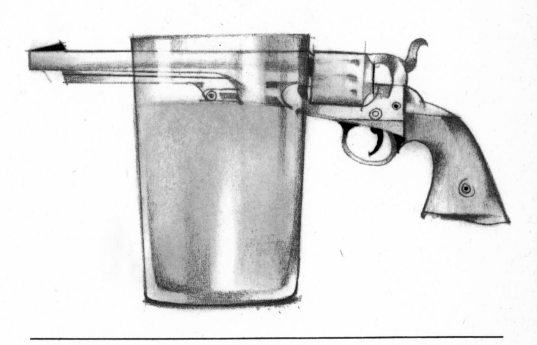

Donald Solomon started his speech. He promised the farmers a new highway, if they elected him as deputy.

When he was really warming up, someone else shouted in the bar. 'We are thirsty!'

Donald Solomon took the gun and went outside.

When in the yard, he noticed several beaver and weasel skins hanging in the barn. Making sure that no one was looking, he pulled one weasel skin off the hook, waited a moment or two, then returned to the bar.

He threw the skin across the counter. 'I've even pulled the skin off,' he stated quite truthfully — for after all, he had pulled the skin off the hook — 'to save you work.'

The licensee nodded gratefully and began to draw the beer at speed.

Donald Solomon left the tavern five times more and each time he brought the licensee back his own weasel or beaver skin to pay for the beer.

That evening, the farmers voted him in unanimously and nick-named him the Weasel State Deputy.

TOMMY THE FAITHFUL TROUT

Watchmaker Rosichan liked to go fishing in the river.

One day he caught a fine trout, beautifully speckled with red dots. He was just about to end his life, when he noticed that the trout was winking at him.

'This is most unusual,' muttered watchmaker Rosichan, 'I have never known a fish to wink.'

He took the trout home and put him in a barrel filled with rain water. He fed him on worms and flies and the trout grew big and fat.

Whenever the watchmaker leaned over the barrel and called out 'Tommy', the trout swam to the surface, stuck his head out and opened his mouth, so his master Rosichan could toss some wormy delicacy into it.

One day the watchmaker came to the barrel and found trout Tommy lying tummy-side up in the water.

Mr Rosichan was indeed an excellent fisherman who had studied many a fishing handbook, so he realized at once that the trout badly needed fresh water.

He wasted no time, but pumped the stale water out of the barrel and filled it with a fresh supply.

Trout Tommy started to swim again, darting from side to side, waiting for a tasty wormy mouthful.

But watchmaker Rosichan did not fancy the idea of having to change the barrel water each week. He decided there must be an easier way out.

He thought and he thought, till he had a brainwave.

'I shall teach trout Tommy to live out of water,' he decided and started training him immediately.

He fished the trout out of the barrel and placed him for a moment on the grass. Then he slipped him back into the water.

The second day he left the trout in the dry for five minutes, the third day the trout managed without water for a whole half hour.

Before very long, Tommy trout was able to stay in the damp grass the whole day through.

Soon afterwards the watchmaker taught Tommy more advanced tricks. He placed the fish in the sand in the sun and, just fancy! the trout stayed there, not bothered at all, waterless for three days. The following evening, when watchmaker Rosichan slipped Tommy back into the barrel, he was fit and full of energy; the long spell in the dry did him no harm.

The training was over.

After that watchmaker Rosichan started taking walks with Tommy trout. The fish slithered behind him like a snake. People were quite astonished, but Mr Rosichan explained with due modesty,

'There's nothing strange about this. If I had more time, I could, for instance, teach a worm to do the high jump.'

When at night watchmaker Rosichan went digging for Tommy's worms, the trout followed him out and used his mouth to shovel a worm or a grub out of the mud.

Such a clever trout was he.

One day the watchmaker even took the trout into town.

On the pavement the trout was at his heels like a faithful dog, though of course he did not run like a four-legged animal, for a trout has no legs. He slithered behind the watchmaker like an adder. Now and again a pretty picture book about the river caught Tommy's eye in a shop window, or a pair of shoes, whose shoe laces — so resembling worms — he stopped to admire, and then he had to do a series of half-leaps to catch up with his master. He even managed to climb with him into a tram.

A man in a top hat offered watchmaker Rosichan one hundred dollars for Tommy, but the watchmaker would not part with him. He had grown so used to the trout, he did not want to live without him.

One day, watchmaker Rosichan and Tommy were on their way to town again. The journey was quite long, but the watchmaker wanted to save money, so he went on foot.

Trout Tommy was slithering behind as usual.

They went through some meadows, where Tommy caught grass-hoppers and crickets, jumped after butterflies and forest flies, not minding in the least that the hot sun beat down upon him. By then he was completely at home out of the water.

Their path led across the river.

The watchmaker crossed the wooden bridge and walked on through the field.

All at once he noticed that Tommy trout was not at his heels.

He stopped and waited. Tommy must be dawdling somewhere, the watchmaker thought, probably nosing out a worm or two by the shore.

But the trout did not show up and the watchmaker thought it rather strange.

He turned back to look for Tommy.

As he was crossing the bridge, he noticed that one plank was missing. He did not give it much thought and carried on, till he had crossed to the other side. There he called and searched and whistled, but Tommy trout was not to be seen.

Once again the watchmaker Rosichan turned on his heels and made his way towards the opposite side.

He stopped by the missing plank, for it occurred to him that Tommy trout could have slipped through the hole into the river.

He peered down the gap between the boards and what did he see! A lifeless Tommy trout, tummy-side up, floating in the water.

'He choked to death in that water,' watchmaker Rosichan sadly said.

WINGS

In ancient times every black man had wings and was able to fly like a bird. But with the passing of years the men grew lazy, and the wings became stunted. Eventually they forgot that they could ever fly.

On a few islands scattered in a boggy river, a handful of winged black men still remained. They looked the same as a normal man, but their shirts concealed a pair of wings.

Then came the white planter, he had all the black people on the islands rounded up and dragged in irons to his cotton plantation. As there were too few of them, he paid slave traders to bring other black people by ship from across the sea to his fields.

The black slaves were forced to toil from dark to dark; they were at work in the plantation before sunrise and returned to their bunks long after the white men had retired to their beds.

Some planters allowed their slaves to rest awhile at noon, when the sun was the hottest. But this slave driver forced the black people to work even in the most scorching heat. His fields were framed by old, leafy mulberry trees, whose shade tempted the field-workers to rest. But the overseer would scream at anyone who dared to stop even for a minute under a tree. He would quickly rush at the man exhausted with the heat, driving him back to work with heavy blows of his stick.

Old men and women and children, too, had to work all day long.

One black woman had given birth to a baby, now a week old. The young mother was still weak and frail, but was forced to work. She tied a sack with the infant in it to her hip, and with the other slaves, she tended the cotton plants.

The baby was hungry and thirsty but, whenever the mother tried to feed him, the brutal overseer forced her with his abuse and his stick to work on.

The burning sun's stabbing beams dazed and dazzled the slaves mercilessly. The terrible noon heat was suffocating the plantation — like a red-hot copper plate placed upon it.

The young mother's head started to spin, she saw burning circles whirl before her eyes. She collapsed with the infant among cotton plants.

The overseer dashed to her side at once, cursing and ordering her back on her feet, or else he'd let his cane dance upon her back.

The woman turned to an aged white-haired man—the eldest Negro of all the slaves—and whispered to him.

The old man smiled at her, but shook his head.

The overseer was all ears, but he could not catch the woman's words.

Once more the young mother with the infant at her hip stooped over the cotton plants, working with the hoe, moaning with pain at the same time. Awhile later she turned ashen and fell again to the ground.

The ruthless overseer made her get up at once.

Once again she turned to the aged white-haired man with a wordless question.

'Not yet, daughter,' the white-haired old man whispered.

So she picked up her hoe and worked on, with the relentlessly scorching sun beating down on her head.

When the young mother sank to the ground the third time and the overseer was still forcing her with threats and blows to her feet, her eyes turned to the old white-haired man, her mouth framing words with difficulty.

'Is it time, father?'

The old man smiled and nodded.

'It is time, my daughter, it is time.'

All at once she was aware of the wings on her back, and that she could move them and open them. The young mother parted from the scorching earth, flying upwards to the crowns of trees. She flew like a black swan, feeling light and airy, as with ease she waved her wings slowly above the cotton plantation. The woman flew further still, across the boundary, rising higher above the forest and then disappearing with the baby at her hip in the blueish distance.

The overseer, scarlet as a turkey with fury, pounced upon the slaves, shouting that now they would have to work all the harder, to make up for the woman who had flown away.

Before long, a black man fainted on the plantation. The overseer was immediately upon him, striking him wildly with the stick. But the old man with the white hair whispered to the slave, and the slave smiled, spread his wings and rose to the sky, higher and higher, till he disappeared beyond the tall trees.

The black slaves collapsed one after the other while they worked under the burning sun in the parched plantation fields, and each time they collapsed, the old man with the white hair whispered something.

Then, one after the other the slaves spread their wings and with a smile rose to the sky, flying higher and higher, till they were lost in the clouds.

The slave owner was darting about the field like someone demented, screaming to the overseer,

'Kill that old white-haired devil!'

The overseer raised his stick and showered blow upon blow on the old man's stooping back.

'I will beat you to death,' he fumed, 'I will beat the soul out of your body and feed you to the hounds.'

But the smile never left the old man's face.

He whispered a few inaudible words to the black slaves.

He whispered to those who had been rounded up on the islands in the boggy river.

He whispered also to those who were transported in irons across the sea from the faraway Negro-land.

All the slaves suddenly remembered that once they could fly.

They remembered the strength they were endowed with.

And all the slaves crowded together, waiting for the white-haired old man's signal. He raised his hand. All at once, just like a sudden swish of wind, there was a murmur of dozens of wings.

The young, the aged, the men, the women and children—all the black people from the plantation flew into the air like a flock of black crows. They circled above the field, rising higher, crossing the boundary and passing the tall trees, turning towards the deep forest.

The white-haired old man was the last to spread his wings.

Down below on the deserted plantation stood the fuming planter and his overseer, shaking their fists and their sticks at the sky.

Their eyes never left the black cloud—the winged crowd of slaves—rising above the woods, flying over the river, merging finally with the blue sky on the never-ending horizon.

THE SORCERER FROM LOUDON HILL

One warm evening in May there was a clatter of horse's hooves outside, and someone knocked on the door of Kaler's log cabin.

Kaler was a Fin, like his mother. His parents had emigrated to America fifty years ago.

Nobody called him anything but sorcerer Kaler.

He could predict the weather, chase away illnesses, cure animals; he also sold rabbit's paws to sailors to bring them luck, to bring them safely and in good health from long voyages.

On this particular May evening, someone was knocking on the door of the smoky cabin — so Kaler went to open it.

'My name is Andrew,' the young man behind the door introduced himself, 'and this is Miss Green. We are on our way to Hallowell to be married. My bride's parents don't like me, so we wanted to elope in secret, but the cook gave us away and they are at our heels. Can you hear?'

It was true, from the distance a clatter of hooves could be heard.

'And what can I do for you?' asked the bewildered Kaler.

'Everyone says that you can turn the wind and change the weather. Here is one hundred dollars and, when we get back, you'll get another hundred for your good services.'

Kaler took the bag with the silver dollars without speaking, then took a leather bag off the shelf and handed it to the youth.

'Go back a little along the road, untie this little bag and shake what is inside over the road. Then you'll be left in peace and can go on to get married with Miss Green. No one will be after you.'

The rider and his bride-to-be mounted their horses and galloped speedily away.

A moment later they were back. The youth tapped on the window of Kaler's cabin and shouted,

'If you have cheated us, I will set your cabin alight!'

But Kaler just smiled, pointing with his hand towards the mountains and saying,

'Can you hear anything?'

Indeed, a storm was approaching fast from the mountains, lightning zig-zagged in the sky, thunder boomed, just as if barrels of beer were rolling down the hills. The run-aways rode off.

The moment they disappeared round the bend, the wind rose, trees bent their heads to the very ground and from low clouds poured torrential rain — the storm was raging in its full strength.

Kaler went inside the cabin and muttered to himself,

'It seems to me I've somewhat overdone it.'

He walked over to the shelf and, quite so, the little leather bag containing the moderate storm and short-termed rain was still there.

He had made a mistake, he gave the elopers a bag with a cloudburst!

The next morning Kaler could judge for himself what a foolish thing he had done. The brook had turned into a lake, the flooded road was impassable, the hard rain had carried away the top soil from the fields, and the gardens were strewn with uprooted trees.

Kaler waited a week for the water to go down, then set off to town.

What if he were to make yet another mistake and called forth snow in the summer, when they were gathering maize!

He really must go and buy himself a pair of glasses!

THE BOY IN THE DONKEY SKIN

Once there was a plantation king and he was terribly impatient to
have a baby. He had a beautifully carved crib made for the infant,
and a swing, which his servants put up in the garden and, in a pool
set among the cotton fields, ninety-nine little golden fishes darted
about—placed there to give the baby pleasure when it was born. The
impatient man had everything prepared for the baby, but the desired
little girl or a little boy just did not come.

His wife was most upset to see her husband so unhappy.

One day, as she sat by the pool in the cotton fields, thinking as
always about the baby, she cried out, quite subconsciously,

'I wouldn't care if the baby had the skin of a donkey, as long as it
was our baby.'

All at once an ugly old witch emerged from the pool and
screeched,

'I'll make your wish come true!'

That evening, when the plantation king returned from a hunt
and looked for his wife, he could not find her anywhere. He looked
in one room, then the next and the next, he searched the whole big
house through and through. Not until he came to the very last—the
thirty-third chamber, did he see her.

His wife sat all huddled in the dark in an armchair, holding in
her arms some object wrapped in a brocade shawl.

'Why do you sit here in the dark?' he asked.

'I would rather you did not ask,' the wife replied sadly. 'I dare not
tell you. Our baby has been born, but I cannot show him to you.
I am so horrified, I am trembling all over.'

The husband stepped inside the room, leaned over his wife and
with the torchlight in one hand, drew aside the brocade shawl with
the other—and froze with shock.

It was true—the wife really did hold a baby in her arms. But the
baby looked just like a little donkey.

The plantation king loved his wife dearly and would never

dream of hurting her—not even with words. He did not want to add to her sorrow, so he said,

'This is indeed a lovely baby.'

'I know you only want to cheer me up,' sobbed the mother, bursting into tears; 'the best thing would be for me to drown our child in the pool.'

But her husband would not hear of it.

'What will our slaves and our friends say when they learn that their future master looks like a donkey? They will sneer at him and make fun of him in song,' the wife remarked bitterly.

'They will get used to him,' her husband spoke convincingly. 'And if anyone dares to spread rumours about our son resembling a donkey, he will be hanged without mercy.'

The following day the plantation king assembled all his slaves, stepped on the balcony of his palatial house, lifted the babe in his arms for all to see, and cried,

'Here is your future master! If anyone dares to imply that he does not look like a human being, I will have him hanged, or his head chopped off. As you all can see, our son is a beautiful boy, and those of you who think he looks like a donkey, are asses themselves. Remember this well.'

'He truly is a lovely boy,' the slaves cried joyfully. 'We are so glad we shall have such a handsome master, when he takes the plantation over from you!'

The little boy grew fast. Soon he was running about the garden, bathing in the pool among the cotton fields, playing on his swing, and then riding out to hunt at his father's side.

The plantation king allowed him every pleasure but his son was forbidden to look in a mirror. The house servants had to destroy every mirror in every room.

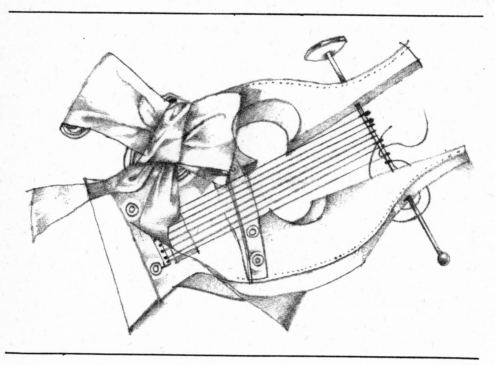

Above all the boy loved music. He loved to listen to the song of birds in the wood, music flowed to him even from the brook as it gurgled and danced over the stones in the grounds. The trees hummed too, as if their branches were made of musical strings.

Most of all he liked to play the harp. By the time he was a young man he could play so well, that far and wide there was not a single harp player to match him.

One day the youth went with his harp to the pool and sat among the thyme plants on the bank. As he touched the harp strings, he leaned over the water and saw the reflection of a donkey.

He turned around, wondering where the donkey had suddenly come from. But there was no donkey. Now he knew. He realized then it was he who had the form of a donkey.

Filled with horror he ran away with his harp into the forest, never to return to his parents' house.

He walked on and on until he came to another plantation.

He slumped into the grass by the entrance to the big house, and as he was feeling very sad, he started to pluck his harp.

The daughter of the plantation owner happened to be looking out of the window and she shouted to her father.

'Father, father, a donkey is sitting by our house playing the harp.'

The father thought his daughter was making fun of him, but as she refused to drop the subject, he sent his valet to bring the harp player inside.

The doors of the big house opened and the valet pushed the donkey into the hall.

The youth with the form of a donkey greeted everyone, and everyone was astonished that he spoke in a human tongue.

They were even more astonished when the youth in the donkey skin sat on a chair and played his harp.

He played and played and everyone enjoyed what he played very much.

The young maiden most of all.

When the youth in the donkey skin stopped playing, the plantation owner said,

'You must be hungry after all that effort. Go to the kitchen, my house servants are just having dinner, and you may eat with them.'

But the youth in the donkey skin shook his head.

'I am not accustomed to eat with servants. I am no servant and therefore I will not eat with your butlers and lackeys and valets.'

So the plantation owner sat the youth in the donkey skin at his own table and, from then on, the boy dined with him and his family.

Evening after evening the youth in the donkey skin played to the daughter of the house on his harp. She always wanted to hear more and more.

One day the plantation owner found the youth in the donkey skin sitting sadly by the window.

He was gazing into the garden, where apple and pear trees were in blossom, where bees were buzzing and birds were singing.

'It is May and yet you are sad,' wondered his host. 'Does not the beauty of the flowers and the song of the birds gladden your heart? Or do you perhaps want to be paid to play?'

'I don't want money,' replied the lad.

'Then you must be homesick.'

'I am not homesick,' said the youth, shaking his head.

'Or do you perhaps want my daughter for your wife?' the man asked jokingly.

'I do,' sighed the youth in the donkey skin.

The plantation owner liked to joke, so he went on,

'I will let you have my daughter for a wife, if she wants you.'

He called her to him and laughingly said,

'Just imagine. This harp player of ours in the donkey skin wants you for his wife! What do you say to that?'

'What do I say? That I will marry him gladly!'

Her father was flabbergasted at such words, but what could he do? He had to keep his word.

After the wedding the youth in the donkey skin went for a stroll by a stream with his young bride.

It was a hot summer's day and his new wife had an idea.

'Let us bathe in the stream, I have not swum here for quite some time.'

'I have never swum in a stream before,' said the bridegroom doubtfully. 'For some reason or other I am afraid of water.'

'There is nothing to fear,' the girl assured him. 'When I am with you, nothing bad can happen to you.'

The youth gave in and paddled in. The minute his feet were wet, the donkey skin fell away from him — and before the bride now stood a handsome, dark-haired youth.

The gardener happened to be watering roses in the grounds, and saw everything.

He ran to the big house, shouting,

'Master, master, the husband of your daughter is not a donkey! As soon as he stepped into the stream, he shed the donkey skin. I saw it with my very eyes.'

'You liar,' the master scolded him; 'such a joke is not in good taste.'

But when the gardener was gone, the father started thinking. Anger left him and he remembered how the youth first came to the plantation, how beautifully he played his harp and spoke the human tongue. He left the big house and crept unseen through the bushes to the stream.

And what did he see!

A dark-haired youth bathing with his daughter in the water.

The donkey skin lay in a heap on the bank.

The plantation owner tiptoed to the stream, picked up the donkey skin and threw it on the bonfire, on which the gardener was burning dry twigs.

All at once an ugly old witch emerged from the stream and croaked,

'If you had thrown that donkey skin into the water, master, you, your wife, your daughter and all your slaves would have turned into donkeys. But you burned my magic powers in the fire. I am lost, alas, three times alas, forever!'

No sooner had she spoken than the ugly old witch turned into a green frog and slid into the deep through the long reeds.

Everyone rejoiced. For three days they sang and danced and voiced their thanks to their clever master.

And forever after, the youth lived happily with his young wife in the big house.

And when his father-in-law grew old and died, the plantation had a new master. The donkey skin he lost for ever, but his harp he wouldn't give up — never!

Night after night the slaves gathered by the big house to hear their young master play to them and sing songs merry and sad.

> *As his fingers touched the string*
> *He sang about a plantation king*
> *Who had a son in a donkey skin.*
> *Now this son was a plantation king*
> *And this son, who'd shed his donkey skin*
> *Played sweet, heady music on his harp*
> *Which, like roses, warmed every heart.*

LOCOMOTIVE BILL

A noisy Negro sauntered through the woods towards the town. He was whistling happily, a gun under his arm. He was on the look-out for a rabbit or two.

As he was leaving the forest, he met the sheriff. The man with the star first walked past him, then turned. 'One moment, friend, don't you know that a gun can be carried only on your shoulder? Put it there right now, or I'll confiscate it!'

The Negro did nothing, so the sheriff pounced on him, trying to wrench the gun away. For awhile they wrestled, then the gun went off and the bullet shot straight through the sheriff's heart.

The Negro ran on across the railway track. From the direction of the town a goods train was just approaching. He crouched behind a bush, then ran out and alongside the train, which at that particular point slowed down in order to climb a steep hill. Still running he tore open the wagon door and climbed inside.

It was then that Negro Morris Slater lost his name.

People started to call him Locomotive Bill.

When the goods train was travelling through a large, desolate forest, Bill jumped off. The green fur coat of the forest hid him well, there he could lose himself as if he were an inconspicuous fly.

The forest fed him, too. It was abundant with rabbits and deer.

One day Bill came upon a log-cabin.

A blind Indian witch-doctor lived in it.

Bill supplied him with game, cooked for him and slept on the mossy bed by his side. In return, the Indian witch-doctor revealed the secret of how to avoid gun shots and how to escape from pursuers.

Locomotive Bill feared nothing now. Hidden by bushes, he would lie in wait by the railway lines, and when a goods train chugged past, he would force open a wagon door and jump inside.

Then, when the train was making its way through the forest, he would throw a crate, or a sack of goods from the wagon, and jump out too. So he became a train robber.

Law officers searched for him and tried to track him down in vain. They had dogs to help, but Bill was always laughing at them. Whenever it appeared he was within their grasp, he slipped through their fingers.

Once they surrounded Bill from all sides.

'Now we've got you,' said the police sergeant. 'Men, he is hiding behind that boulder!'

The circle of men crept towards the boulder, but instead of Bill

they found a horny ram grazing in the glade.

It raised its head and bleated.

The officers halted, gazed all round them, whilst the sergeant shook his head in disbelief: 'This I cannot understand. I saw quite clearly how that scoundrel ran behind this very boulder!'

They discussed it for awhile, then went away.

The moment they disappeared in the forest, the ram turned into Bill and Bill sauntered away happily in the opposite direction.

Another time Bill was pursued by trained dogs.

When they had just about caught him up, Bill turned into a fox, who made a face at the hounds, then zig-zagged through the whole pack and disappeared in the bushes.

He knew how to turn into a scarecrow, or a general, into a sheaf of wheat, even a bog. Then the policemen sank in up to their waist and Bill sneered at their efforts to fight their way back to dry land.

So Bill carried on robbing the wagons. Best of all he liked canned food. What he could not eat, he sold cheaply or gave it free to poor folk.

The merchants put up notices all over that region. 'Whoever helps to catch Locomotive Bill will receive one thousand dollars.'
any more. We can buy much cheaper off Locomotive Bill!'

The merchants put up notices all over that region. Whoever helps to catch Locomotive Bill will receive one thousand dollars.

It was then that a certain farmer betrayed Bill.

That is the way of the world.

He lured him to his farm, and whilst his wife was purchasing a scarf from Bill, the farmer fetched the sheriff and his men. Bill did not have time to change even into a sparrow and to escape through the open window.

The bullet found its target. The officer's aim was good.

But the folk in their homesteads believe to this day that Locomotive Bill wriggled out of that trap even then. For Bill to them was indestructible.

JAGUAR PETRONIUS —
A FRIEND OF THE FAMILY

An old farmer walked into the workshop of an animal-stuffer.

Over his shoulder he carried a dead mountain lion, a jaguar.

The animal stuffer asked, 'Would you like him to be made into a bedroom mat, or perhaps into a fur coat for your wife?'

'Wrong on both counts,' growled the farmer. 'I want him stuffed, so he looks real and alive. I'll put him right by the fireplace.'

'Of course, of course,' nodded the obliging animal-stuffer, 'such a magnificent piece will truly stand out in your house!'

'A piece? A piece did you say? This jaguar of mine is a family tomb, dear sir!'

The animal stuffer looked wonderingly at the farmer.

The latter sat down, lit his pipe and began.

'I found him near a rock, when he was only a small kitten. I took this kitten home. It soon made friends with our dog Pluto. Who wouldn't make friends with a friendly soul like him!

The kitten grew and then was a kitten no more, but a large agile cat to be sure.

One morning Pluto, that kind-hearted old dog, disappeared.

And Petronius turned up his nose at his supper that night.

You beast, I said to myself, no wonder you don't want your supper, when poor Pluto lies in your belly!

A week later our billy-goat Brutus disappeared.

Then came the turn of my hens and ducks.

And when the last chicken was gone and that scoundrel Petronius was making up to me, a chicken wing still sticking out of his mouth, I hit the table with my fist and shouted, 'That is enough, you rascal!'

One shouldn't waste words on thieves, isn't that so!

I took my old gun from the corner, ready to finish him off.

But that artful dodger Petronius kept rubbing himself against my legs, and my anger soon melted away.

I said to myself, Pluto was old, the billy-goat most unpleasantly smelly, and the chickens and ducks would have ended up in the roasting tin come what may, so what!

I put away the gun right behind the cupboard and went to pick melons.

Dorothy is, or rather was, my wife.

For nearly forty years we've walked side by side through life. A good wife is better than an empty barn, don't you agree!

One evening I came back home from the fields and my wife was gone. In the kitchen I found just one of her slippers.

And Petronius did not enjoy his supper.

In my sorrow I leapt towards the cupboard, grabbed the gun and

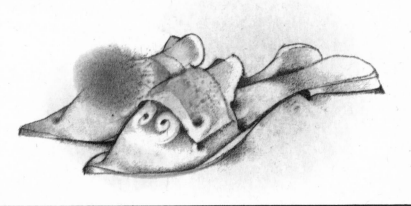

pierced Petronius with my eyes. That scoundrel, that creep, purred round me with the innocence of an Easter newborn lamb.

I fell into a chair and thought. My wife had been ill for quite some time, so at least she won't have to suffer more.

Once again I hid that old gun behind the cupboard and went to cook potatoes for my supper.

Solitude might be a kind sister for a day, but after a month it becomes an evil step-mother, don't you think!'

A lump came to the farmer's throat, and he coughed, relighting his pipe.

'Yesterday evening, just imagine, mister, that good-for-nothing

Petronius hid behind an oak tree. I was on my way back from the fields, and before I noticed him, he jumped on me and bit off half of my back-side. Now that was too much!

Who plots evil, should fear evil, don't you agree!

Here he is. Take the greatest care of him. All my family is hidden inside.'

THE HITCHHIKER

It was a chilly November night, it drizzled persistently and the bare branch of a maple tree knocked monotonously against the ranch window.

David climbed into his sports car and drove off quickly along the country lane which zig-zagged through the naked fields towards the motorway. His college was holding a dance for the students, the ranch was a long way from town and David did not want to be late.

A girl hitchhiker waved to him at the crossroads.

He stopped and she slipped inside.

'Are you also going to the dance?' David asked.

The girl nodded silently.

David liked her at first glance. The whole evening he danced only with her — with Magdalena.

Before midnight, when the entertainment was at its height, the girl whispered to him.

'Could you take me home? I must go now.'

David did not feel like leaving when he was enjoying himself so much, but as by now he had eyes for none but Magdalena, he nodded and led her to the car.

The girl curled up in the seat, shivering with cold in her thin dress.

David took off his coat and put it over her shoulders.

It was still drizzling and swirling balls of fog were rolling along the road. David had to drive slowly, so as not to go off the highway.

'Faster, please, can you go faster?' Magdalena whispered.

When they drove up to the white house surrounded by trees, the time signal in the car radio was just announcing midnight.

The girl got out, looked at David, thanking him with just a nod of her head for the lift and opened her front door.

'When shall I see you again, Magdalena?' David called into the fog.

'In a year's time,' the girl whispered and disappeared.

Driving slowly, David returned to his ranch through the mist. But his thoughts were all the time with Magdalena, he could not understand why he would have to wait a whole year to see her.

The following day was a Sunday, so David had his breakfast and prepared to go out. He always played basketball in the student club.

But all he could think of was the mysterious Magdalena.

As he was driving into town, past the white house in the trees, he could not resist and stopped. It was a lovely sunny day, and a blue sky shone above the house.

David rang the door-bell. The door opened and a sad-looking woman asked, 'What do you want?'

'May I see Magdalena?'

'Magdalena?' asked the grey-haired lady, 'so you have come to see Magdalena! Come in!'

She led David into the hall.

'Here is our Magdalena,' the lady whispered, pointing to the wall. A photograph of Magdalena was hanging there, with a fresh rose underneath.

'But I'd like to talk to her,' David insisted.

The woman sighed: 'I cannot grant you that wish. Magdalena has been dead for five years now. It is exactly five years since we lost her. She was killed in a car accident by the crossroads, where the country lane leads on to the motorway.'

'But that is impossible! We spent the whole evening yesterday dancing together, she stopped me at the crossroads and later that night I drove her back here! I saw her enter this house!'

The lady shook her head doubtfully and said,

'If you don't believe me, come and see for yourself!'

And she led David to the cemetery.

They came to a grave, over which stood a beautiful maple tree and the woman silently pointed to the grave-stone. David read:

> 'Here rests our beloved Magdalena.
> Sleep sweetly, dear daughter.'

'That is my coat,' said the bewildered David, pointing to the grave-stone. The coat which he had put round Magdalena when she was cold in his car, was hanging on it.

The lady nodded, placing a bunch of winter flowers on the grave. She prayed silently and David tiptoed from the grave to the cemetery gate.

Since that day no young man from the town of New Haven will stop at night to give a lift even to the prettiest hitchhiker!

THE PARTING SONG

Old Mark realized that his last hour was approaching. He was gazing across the vast prairie interwoven here and there with low shrubs. His eyes travelled over the huge herd of cattle, numbering more than a thousand head and rested on the bunch of tired drovers sitting by the camp fire after their heavy day's labour, waiting for supper. He watched the white smoke rise to the evening sky tinged with gold, then walked slowly over to the boss herdsman.

'Pat,' Mark asked, 'would you do something for me?'

The boss looked at the old man searchingly but, as Mark was not one to ask favours, he nodded willingly, without questions.

'In that case, Pat,' old Mark continued in a whisper, 'please round up the whole herd. I'd like to see it all together just once more.'

Pat bit his lip, for he knew this would be no small task. But he did not intend to go back on his word. He summoned the drovers and gave his orders.

All night long the drovers chased the huge herd scattered over the prairie.

It was nearly four in the morning, just before sunrise, when the drovers' working day begins. Pat came to Mark, who was shivering with inner fever and announced that the whole herd was rounded up.

Bulls and cows were bellowing loudly, calves were bleating plaintively, heifers mooed proudly that they too were present.

The drovers circled the herd, so it would not scatter again, their horses neighed and snorted, the dogs barked.

'I know,' Mark whispered in a faint voice, 'I can hear everything very clearly.'

'Tell me, Mark, why did we have to round up the herd? What do you want to do now?'

'Nothing, nothing at all, boss. Just leave the cows, bulls and calves together. I feel there are not many hours left of my life. And before I depart, I want to listen to my favourite song for the last time.'

THE WHITE STALLION

The wild white stallion, a mustang, is galloping across the prairie.

The green grass opens before him, the white stallion flies through the green grassy sea.

By the clear mountain river the white stallion lowers his head and drinks, drinks long and deep the cool water.

Wild yellow sunflowers bow their heads in the light prairie breeze refreshed with the breath of mountains and forests, thousands of little suns in the grass, their flowers reflecting the mighty sun which wanders day after day across the sky above the green vastness.

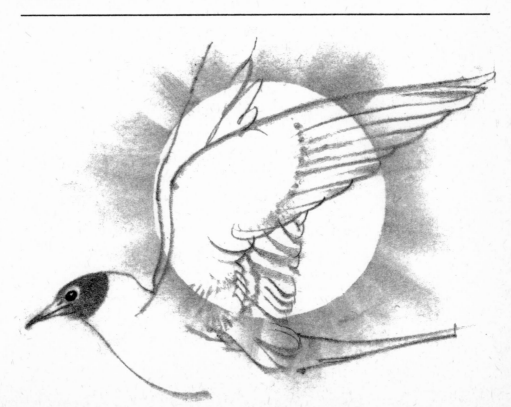

Drifts of prairie wormwood perfume the air with heady scent as the white stallion wades across the mountain river and races towards the distant horizon across the endless sea of the green prairie.

Above an eagle spreads his wings under the sparkling sun. High, high above the columns of snow-capped mountains, circles the eagle, and the white stallion flies tirelessly over the prairie, like a fairy tale without an end and without a beginning.

Across the prairie gallops the white stallion.

No one will catch him.

He is like a legend from ancient times, like smoke from an Indian fire, like a sad song of black slaves on a cotton plantation, like the singing of new settlers as their wagons trudge along the green prairie from east to west.

If a hunter were to hear the galloping wild horse, the white mustang would turn into a white gull.

The gull flutters his wings, soars high into the sky and turns towards the sea.

The green prairie grass is a mass of green waves, heady with wormwood perfume and the white gull glides on his wings to the west, to the sea.

Above the sea the gull changes into a white cloud and the sea breeze carries him further, across the richly blue waves and further still, into the world, into the far away, wide wide world.

Across the prairie gallops the wild stallion, white as a gull, airy as a beautiful summer cloud.

White horse, white bird, white cloud.

And in the blue boundless sky flames the scarlet sun. The mane of the wild white stallion is bleached golden with constant sun.

The sun is reflected on the wings of the white gull, the white cloud is taking into the world the glow of the warmth-giving sun.

Across the prairie gallops the white mustang.

He is like a fairy tale, which has no beginning and no end, he is like the boundless blue of the sky, which spreads its mighty wings above the green grassy seas.

Across the prairie gallops the stallion.